A Dance to the Music of Time

At Lady Molly's

ANTHONY POWELL was born in London in 1905. His father was a soldier, of a family mostly soldiers or sailors which moved from Wales about a hundred and fifty years ago. He was educated at Eton and Balliol College, Oxford, of which he is now an Honorary Fellow.

From 1926 he worked for about nine years at Duckworths, the publishers, then as scriptwriter for Warner Brothers in England. During the Second World War he served in the Welch Regiment and Intelligence Corps, acting as liaison officer with the Polish, Belgian, Czechoslovak, Free French and Luxembourg forces, and was promoted major.

Before and after the war he wrote reviews and literary columns for various newspapers, including the *Daily Telegraph* and the *Spectator*. From 1948–52 he worked on the *Times Literary Supplement*, and was literary editor of *Punch*, 1952–8.

Between 1931 and 1949, Anthony Powell published five novels, a biography, *John Aubrey and His Friends*, and a selection from Aubrey's works. The first volume of his twelve-volume novel, *A Dance to the Music of Time*, was published in 1951, and the concluding volume, *Hearing Secret Harmonies*, appeared in 1975. In 1976 he published the first volume of his memoirs, *To Keep the Ball Rolling*, under the title *Infants of the Spring*.

In 1934 he married Lady Violet Pakenham, daughter of the fifth Earl of Longford. They have two sons, and live in Somerset.

Books by Anthony Powell

Novels
Afternoon Men
Venusberg
From a View to a Death
Agents and Patients
What's Become of Waring

A Dance to the Music of Time
A Question of Upbringing
A Buyer's Market
The Acceptance World
At Lady Molly's
Casanova's Chinese Restaurant
The Kindly Ones
The Valley of Bones
The Soldier's Art
The Military Philosophers
Books Do Furnish a Room
Temporary Kings
Hearing Secret Harmonies

To Keep the Ball Rolling (Memoirs)
Volume I: Infants of the Spring

General
John Aubrey and His Friends

Plays
The Garden God *and* The Rest I'll Whistle

Anthony Powell

At Lady Molly's

A Novel

FLAMINGO

Published by Fontana Paperbacks
by agreement with Heinemann

For J.M.A.P.

First published by
William Heinemann Ltd 1957
First issued in Fontana Paperbacks 1969
Eighth impression March 1983

This Flamingo edition first published
in 1984 by Fontana Paperbacks,
8 Grafton Street, London W1X 3LA

Printed and bound in Great Britain by
Richard Clay (The Chaucer Press) Ltd,
Bungay, Suffolk

ONE

We had known General Conyers immemorially not because my father had ever served under him but through some long-forgotten connexion with my mother's parents, to one or other of whom he may even have been distantly related. In any case, he was on record as having frequented their house in an era so remote and legendary that, if commission was no longer by purchase, regiments of the line were still designated by a number instead of the name of a county. In spite of belonging to this dim, archaic period, traces of which were sometimes revealed in his dress and speech— he was, for example, one of the last to my knowledge to speak of the Household Cavalry as "the Plungers"—his place in family myth was established not only as a soldier with interests beyond his profession, but even as a man of the world always "abreast of the times". This taste for being in the fashion and giving his opinion on every subject was held against him by some people, notably Uncle Giles, no friend of up-to-date thought, and on principle suspicious of worldly success, however mild.

"Aylmer Conyers had a flair for getting on," he used to say. "No harm in that, I suppose. Somebody has got to give the orders. Personally I never cared for the limelight. Plenty of others to push themselves forward. Inclined to think a good deal of himself, Conyers was. Fine figure of a man, people used to say, a bit too fond of dressing himself up to the nines. Not entirely friendless in high places either. Quite the contrary. Peacetime or war, Conyers always knew the right people."

I had once inquired about the General's campaigns.

"Afghanistan, Burma—as a subaltern. I've heard him talk big about Zululand. In the Soudan for a bit when the Khalifa was making trouble there. Went in for jobs abroad. Supposed to have saved the life of some native ruler in a local rumpus. Armed the palace eunuchs with rook rifles. Fellow gave him a jewelled scimitar—semi-precious stones, of course."

"I've seen the scimitar. I never knew the story."

Ignoring interruptions, Uncle Giles began to explain how South Africa, grave of so much military reputation, had been by Aylmer Conyers turned to good account. Having himself, as a result of his own indiscretions, retired from the army shortly before outbreak of war in the Transvaal, and possessing in addition those "pro-Boer" sentiments appropriate to "a bit of a radical", my uncle spoke always with severity, no doubt largely justified, of the manner in which the operations of the campaign had been conducted.

"After French moved over the Modder River, the whole Cavalry Division was ordered to charge. Unheard of thing. Like a gymkhana."

"Yes?"

For a minute or two he lost the thread, contemplating the dusty squadrons wheeling from column into line across the veldt, or more probably assailed by memories of his own, less dramatic, if more bitter.

"What happened?"

"What?"

"What happened when they charged?"

"Cronje made an error of judgment for once. Only sent out detachments. Went through to Kimberley, more by luck than looking to."

"But what about General Conyers?"

"Got himself into the charge somehow. Hadn't any business with the cavalry brigades. Put up some excuse.

6

Then, day or two later, went back to where he ought to have been in the first place. Made himself most officious among the transport wagons. Line of march was like Hyde Park at the height of the Season, so a fellow who was in the advance told me—carriages end to end in Albert Gate—and Conyers running about cursing and swearing as if he owned the place."

"Didn't Lord Roberts say something about his staff work?"

"Bobs?"

"Yes."

"Who said that, your father?"

"I think so."

Uncle Giles shook his head.

"Bobs may have said something. Wouldn't be the first time a general got hold of the wrong end of the stick. They say Conyers used to chase the women a bit, too. Some people thought he was going to propose to your Great-aunt Harriet."

Other memories, on the whole more reliable, gainsay any such surmise regarding this last matter. In fact, Conyers remained a bachelor until he was approaching fifty. He was by then a brigadier-general, expected to go much further, when—to the surprise of his friends—he married a woman nearly twenty years younger than himself; sending in his papers about eighteen months later. Perhaps he was tired of waiting for the war with Germany he had so often prophesied, in which, had it come sooner, he would certainly have been offered high command. Possibly his wife did not enjoy following the drum, even as a general's lady. She is unlikely to have had much taste for army life. The General, for his own part, may have felt at last tired of military routine. Like many soldiers of ability he possessed his eccentric side. Although no great performer, he had always loved playing the 'cello, and on retirement occupied much of his time with music; also experimenting with a favourite theory that poodles, owing to their keen natural intelligence, could profitably be trained as gun dogs. He began to live rather a social life, too, and was appointed a member of the Body Guard; the role in which, from early association of ideas, I always think of him.

"Funny that a fellow should want to be a kind of court flunkey," Uncle Giles used to say. "Can't imagine myself rigged out in a lot of scarlet and gold, hanging about royal palaces and herding in and out of a crowd of young ladies in ostrich feathers. Did it to please his wife, I suppose."

Mrs. Conyers, it is true, might have played some indirect part in this appointment. Eldest daughter of King Edward VII's friend, Lord Vowchurch, she had passed her thirtieth birthday at the time of marriage. Endless stories, not always edifying, are—or used to be—told of her father, one of those men oddly prevalent in Victorian times who sought personal power through buffoonery. His most enduring memorial (to be found, with other notabilities of the 'seventies, hanging in the damp, deserted billiard-room at Thrubworth) is Spy's caricature in the *Vanity Fair* series, depicting this high-spirited peer in frock-coat and top hat, both grey: the bad temper for which he was as notorious at home as for his sparkle in Society, neatly suggested under the side whiskers by the lines of the mouth. In later years Lord Vowchurch grew quieter, particularly after a rather serious accident as a pioneer in the early days of motoring. This mishap left him with a limp and injuries which seem to have stimulated that habitual banter, rarely good-natured, for which he had often been in trouble with King Edward, when Prince of Wales; and, equally often, forgiven. His daughters had lived their early life in permanent disgrace for having, none of them, been born a boy.

My parents never saw much of the General and his wife.

8

They knew them about as well as they knew the Walpole-Wilsons; though the Conyers relationship, with its foundations laid in a distant, fabled past, if never more intimate, was in some way deeper and more satisfying.

Like all marriages, the Conyers union presented elements of mystery. It was widely assumed that the General had remained a bachelor so long through conviction that a career is best made alone. He may have believed (like de Gaulle, whom he lived to see leading the Free French) in a celibate corps of officers dedicated like priests to their military calling. He wrote something of the sort in the *United Service Magazine*. This theory rested upon no objection to the opposite sex as such. On the contrary, as a young officer in India and elsewhere he was judged, as Uncle Giles had indicated, to have enjoyed a considerable degree of quiet womanising. Some thought that ambition of rather a different sort—a feeling that he had never fully experienced some of the good things of life—had finally persuaded him to marry and retire. A few of the incurably romantic even supposed him simply to have "fallen in love" for the first time on the brink of fifty.

General and Mrs. Conyers seemed to "get on" as well, if not better, than many married couples of a similar sort united at an earlier age. They moved, on the whole, in a circle connected, it might be said unpretentiously (because nothing could have been less "smart", for example in Chips Lovell's use of the term, than the Conyers *ménage*) with the Court: families like the Budds and Udneys. In the limited but intense—and at times ornamental—preoccupations of these professional courtiers, the General seems to have found an adequate alternative to a life of command. They had an only daughter called Charlotte, a rather colourless girl, who married a lieutenant-commander in the Navy. I used sometimes to have tea with her when we were both children.

9

In 1916, towards Christmas, at a time when Mrs. Conyers was assembling "comforts" for troops overseas (still at this period in more amateur hands than the organisation that employed Uncle Giles after America came into the war) I was taken—passing through London on the way home from school—to her flat near Sloane Square. My mother paid the call either to add some knitted contribution to the pile of socks, scarves and Balaclava helmets lying about on chairs and sofas, or to help in some matter of their distribution. In the corner of the room in which all these bundles were stacked stood the 'cello in a case. Beside it, I at once noticed a large photograph of the General, carrying a halberd and wearing the plumed helmet, swallow-tailed coat and heavy gold epaulettes of a Gentleman-at-Arms. That is why I always think of him as a statuesque figure at levées and court balls, rather than the man of action he must for the greater part of his life have been. Retired from the army too long for any re-employment of the first importance, he had acquired soon after the outbreak of war some job, far from momentous, though respectably graded in the rank of major-general.

We had finished tea, and I was being shown the jewelled scimitar to which Uncle Giles had referred, which was kept for some reason in the London flat instead of the small house in Hampshire where the poodles were trained. This display was made by Mrs. Conyers as some amends for the fact that Charlotte was in the country; although no apology was necessary as it seemed to me more amusing without her. I was admiring the velvet-covered scabbard, wondering whether to draw the steel from its sheath would be permissible, when the maid showed someone into the room. This new arrival was a young woman wearing V.A.D. uniform, who strode in like a grenadier. She turned out to be Mildred Blaides, youngest sister to Mrs. Conyers.

Difference of age between the two of them must have

been at least that of Mrs. Conyers and her husband. This Miss Blaides, indeed, represented her parents' final, unsuccessful effort to achieve an heir, before Lord Vowchurch's motor accident and total resignation to the title passing to a cousin. She was tall, with a long nose, no more handsome than her sister, but in my eyes infinitely more dashing than Mrs. Conyers. Her face was lively, not unlike the mask of a fox. Almost immediately she took from her pocket an ornamental cigarette-case made of some lacquer-like substance and lit a cigarette. Such an act, especially in one so young, was still in those days a sign of conscious female emancipation. I suppose she was then about twenty.

"Mildred is at Dogdene now," explained Mrs. Conyers. "You know the Sleafords offered their house as an officers' hospital when the war broke out. They themselves live in the east wing. There are huts all over the park too."

"It's absolutely hell having all those blighters in huts," said Miss Blaides. "Some of the tommies got tight the other night and pushed one of the stone urns off the Italian bridge into the lake. It was too bad of them. They are a putrid unit anyway. All the officers wear 'gorblimeys'."

"What on earth are those, Mildred?" asked Mrs. Conyers, nervously.

I think she feared, after asking the question, that they might be something unsuitable to mention in front of a small boy, because she raised her hand as if to prevent the exposure of any too fearful revelation.

"Oh, those floppy army caps," said Miss Blaides, carelessly. "They take the stiffening out, you know. Of course they have to do that when they are up at the Front, to prevent bits of wire getting blown into their coconuts, but they might try and look properly turned out when they are over here."

She puffed away at her cigarette.

"I really must check all these gaspers," she said, flicking

ash on to the carpet. "But now it's got up to about thirty a day. It just won't do. By the way, Molly Sleaford wants to come and see you, Bertha. Something about the distribution of 'comforts'. I told her to look you up on Wednesday, when she is next going to be in London."

For some reason this announcement threw Mrs. Conyers into a state of great discomposure.

"But I can't possibly see Lady Sleaford on Wednesday," she said, "I've got three committee meetings on that day and Aylmer wants me to have five Serbian officers to tea. Besides, dear, Lady Sleaford is Red Cross, like you—and you remember how I am rather wedded, through Lady Bridgnorth, to St. John's. You see I really hardly know Lady Sleaford, who always keeps very much to herself, and I don't want to seem disloyal to Mary Bridgnorth. I——"

Her sister cut her short.

"Oh, I say, what a bally nuisance," she remarked. "I quite forgot about beastly old St. John's. They are always cropping up, aren't they? I really think they do more than the Germans to hold up winning the war."

After voicing this alarming conjecture, she paced up and down the room, emitting from each nostril a long eddy of smoke like the trail of a ship briskly cutting the horizon. Throughout the room I was increasingly aware of the hardening of disapproval, just perceptible at first even on the immediate arrival of Miss Blaides: now not by any means to be denied. In fact a sense of positive disquiet swept through the small drawing-room so powerfully that mute condemnation seemed to rise in a thick cloud above the "comforts", until its disturbing odour reached the ceiling and hung about the whole flat in vexed, compelling waves. This disapproval was on the part not only of Mrs. Conyers, but also—I felt sure—of my mother as well, who now began to make preparations to leave.

"A blinking bore," said Miss Blaides, casting away her

cigarette-end into the grate, where it lay smouldering on the tiles. "That's what it is. So I suppose I shall have to tell Molly it's a wash-out. Give me another cup of tea, Bertha. I mustn't stay too long. I've got plans to scramble into some glad rags and beetle off to a show tonight."

After that, we said good-bye; on my own part with deep regret. Later, when we were in the train, my mother said: "I think it a pity for a girl like Miss Blaides to put on such a lot of make-up and talk so much slang. I was rather interested to see her, though. I had heard so much about her from different people."

I did not mention the fact in reply, but, to tell the truth, Miss Blaides had seemed to me a figure of decided romance, combining with her nursing capacity of a young Florence Nightingale, something far more exciting and perhaps also a shade sinister. Nor did I realise at that time the implications contained in the phrase to "hear a lot about" someone of Miss Blaides's age and kind. However, the episode as a whole—the Conyers' flat, the General's photograph, the jewelled scimitar, the "comforts" stacked round the room, Miss Blaides in her V.A.D. uniform—all made a vivid impression on my mind; although, naturally enough, these things became soon stored away, apparently forgotten, in the distant background of memory. Only subsequent events revived them in strong colours.

That afternoon was also the first time I ever heard Dogdene mentioned. Later, of course, I knew it as the name of a "great house" about which people talked. It came into volumes of memoirs like those of Lady Amesbury, which I read (with some disappointment) at an early age after hearing some grown-up person describe the book as "scurrilous". I also knew Constable's picture in the National Gallery, which shows the mansion itself lying away in the middle distance, a faery place set among giant trees, beyond the misty water-meadows of the foreground in which the impastoed cattle browse: quite unlike any imaginable military hospital. I knew this picture well before learning that the house was Dogdene. By then the place was no longer consciously associated in my mind with Miss Blaides. I was aware only vaguely that the owners were called Sleaford.

Then one day, years and years later, a chance reference to Dogdene made me think again of Miss Blaides in her original incarnation as a V.A.D., a status become, as it were, concealed and forgotten, like relics of an early civilisation covered by an ever-increasing pile of later architectural accretion. This was in spite of the fact that the name of Mildred Blaides would sometimes crop up in conversation after the occasional meetings between my parents and General or Mrs. Conyers. When she figured in such talk I always pictured a person somehow different from the girl chattering war-time slang on that winter afternoon. In fact the original memory of Miss Blaides returned to me one morning when I was sitting in my cream-distempered, strip-lighted, bare, sanitary, glaring, forlorn little cell at the Studio. In that place it was possible to know deep despondency. Work, sometimes organised at artificially high pressure, would alternate with stretches of time in which a chaotic nothingness reigned: periods when, surrounded by the inanities and misconceptions of the film world, a book conceived in terms of comparative reality would to some extent alleviate despair.

During one of these interims of leisure, reading a volume of his Diary, I found Pepys had visited Dogdene. A note explained that his patron, Lord Sandwich, was connected by marriage with the then Countess of Sleaford: the marquisate dating only from the coronation of William IV.

"So about noon we came to Dogdene, and I was fain to see the house, and that part newly builded whereof Dr. Wren did formerly hold converse with me, telling me here was one of the first mansion houses of England contrived as a nobleman's seat rather than a keep moated for warfare. My Lord Sleaford is yet in town, where 'tis said he doth pay court to my Lady Castlemaine, at which the King is not a little displeased, 'tho 'twas thought she had long since lost her place. The Housekeeper was mighty civil, and showed us the Great Hall and stately Galleries, and the picture by P. Veronese that my Lord's grandfather did bring with him out of Italy, a most rare and noble thing. Then to the Gardens and Green Houses, where I did marvel to see the quickening of the Sensitive Plant. And so to the Still Room, where a great black maid offered a brave glass of metheglin, and I did have some merry talk with her begging her to show me a painted closet whereof the Housekeeper had spoken, yet had we not seen. Thither the bold wench took me readily enough, where I did kiss her twice or thrice and toyed wantonly with her. I perceive that she would not have denied me *qui je voudray*, yet was I afeared and time was lacking. At which afterwards I was troubled, lest she should speak of what I had done, and her fellows make game of me when we were gone on our road."

Everyone knows the manner in which some specific name will recur several times in quick succession from different quarters; part of that inexplicable magic throughout life that makes us suddenly think of someone before turning a street corner and meeting him, or her, face to face. In the same way, you may be struck, reading a book, by some obscure passage or lines of verse, quoted again, quite unexpectedly, twenty-four hours later. It so happens that soon after I read Pepys's account of Dogdene, I found myself teamed up as a fellow script-writer with Chips Lovell. The question arose of some country house to appear in a scenario.

"Do you mean a place like Dogdene?" I asked.

"That sort of thing," said Lovell.

He went on to explain, not without some justifiable satisfaction, that his mother, the current Lord Sleaford's sister, had been brought up there.

I was then at the time of life when one has written a couple of novels, and moved from a firm that published art books to a company that produced second-feature films. To be "an author" was, of course, a recognised path of approach to this means of livelihood; so much so, indeed, at that period, that to serve a term as a script-writer was almost a routine stage in literary life. On the other hand, Lovell's arrival in the Studio had been more devious. His chief stock in trade, after an excellent personal appearance and plenty of cheek, was expert manipulation of a vast horde of relations. Much more interested in daily journalism than in writing scenarios, he coveted employment on the gossip column of a newspaper. I knew Sheldon slightly, one of the editorial staff of the evening paper at which Lovell aimed, and had promised to arrange, if possible, a meeting between them.

Lovell delighted in talking about his relations. His parents had eloped on account of family opposition to their marriage. There had not been enough money. The elder Lovell, who was what Uncle Giles used to call "not entirely friendless in high places", was a painter. His insipid, Barbizonish little landscapes, not wholly devoid of merit, never sold beyond his own circle of friends. The elopement was in due course forgiven, but the younger Lovell was determined that no such grass should grow under his own feet. He was going to get on in life, he said, and in a few years make a "good marriage". Meanwhile, he was looking round, enjoying himself as much as business permitted. Since there were few enough jobs about for young men at that time, his energies, which were considerable, had brought him temporarily into the film business; for which every one, including himself, agreed he had no particular vocation. Something better would turn up. The mystery remained how, in the first place, he had been accepted into an overcrowded profession. Our colleague, Feingold, hinted that the American bosses of the company dreamed of some intoxicating social advantage to be reaped by themselves, personally, through employing an eligible young man of that sort. Feingold may have been right; on the other hand, he was not wholly free from a strain of Jewish romanticism. Certainly it would have been hard to think of any fantasy too extraordinary for the thoughts of these higher executives to indulge.

One night, not long after we had talked of Dogdene, I had, together with Lovell, Feingold and Hegarty, unwillingly remained later than usual at the Studio in an effort to complete one of those "treatments" of a film story, the tedium of which is known only to those who have experienced their concoction. On that particular evening, Feingold, in his mauve suit and crimson tie, was suffering from an unaccustomed bout of depression. He had graduated fairly recently from the cutting-room, at first full of enthusiasm for this new aspect of his craft. The pink skin of his plump, round face had begun to sag, making pockets around his bluish chin, as he lay back in a chair with an enormous pile of foolscap scribblings in front of him. He looked like a highly-coloured poster designed to excite compassion for the sufferings of his race. Hegarty was also in poor form that day. He had been a script-writer most of his grown-up life—burdened by then with three, if not four, wives, to all of whom he was paying alimony—and he possessed, when reasonably sober, an extraordinary facility for constructing film scenarios. That day, he could not have been described as reasonably sober. Groaning, he had sat all the afternoon in the corner of the room facing the wall. We were working on a stage play that had enjoyed a three-weeks West End run twenty or thirty years before, the banality of which had persuaded some director that it would "make a picture". This was the ninth treatment we had produced between us. At last, for the third time in an hour, Hegarty broke out in a cold sweat. He began taking aspirins by the handful. It was agreed to abandon work for the day.

Lovell and I used to alternate in which of us brought a car (both vehicles of modest appearance) to the Studio. That night it was Lovell's turn to give me a lift. We said good night to Feingold, who was moving Hegarty off to the pub at the end of the road. Lovell had paid twelve pounds ten for his machine; he started it up, though not without effort. I climbed in beside him. We drove towards London through the mist, blue-grey pockets of cloud drifting up ominously from the river.

"Shall we dine together?"

"All right. Let it be somewhere cheap."

"Of that I am strongly in favour," said Lovell. "Do you know a place called Foppa's?"

"Yes—but don't let's go there."

Although things had been "over" with Jean for some time by then, Foppa's was still for some reason too reminiscent of her to be altogether comfortable; and I was firmly of the opinion that even the smallest trace of nostalgia for the immediate past was better avoided. A bracing future was required, rather than vain regrets. I congratulated myself on being able to consider the matter in such brisk terms. Lovell and I settled on some restaurant, and returned to the question whether Sheldon would be able to arrange for the job to be offered at just the right moment: the moment when Lovell's contract with the film company terminated, not before, nor too long after.

"I'm going to look in on an aunt of mine after making a meal," Lovell said, tired at last of discussing his own prospects. "Why not come too? There are always people there. At worst, it's a free drink. If some lovely girls are in evidence, we can dance to the gramophone."

"What makes you think there will be lovely girls?"

"You may find anything at Aunt Molly's—even lovely girls. Are you coming?"

"I'd like to very much."

"It's in South Kensington, I'm afraid."

"Never mind. Tell me about your aunt."

"She is called Molly Jeavons. She used to be called Molly Sleaford, you know."

"I didn't know."

Confident that Lovell would enjoy giving further information, I questioned him. He had that deep appreciation of family relationships and their ramifications that is a gift of its own, like being musical, or having an instinct for the value of horses or jewels. In Lovell's own case, he made good practical use of this grasp, although such a talent not uncommonly falls to individuals more than usually free from any desire for personal advancement: while equally often lacking in persons rightly regarded by the world as snobbish. Lovell, almost as interested in everyone else's family as his own, could describe how the most various people were in fact quite closely related.

"When my first Sleaford uncle died," said Lovell, "his widow, Molly, married a fellow called Jeavons. Not a bad chap at all, though of rather unglamorous background. He couldn't be described as particularly bright either, in spite of playing quite a good game of snooker. No live wire, in fact. Molly, on the other hand, is full of go.'

"What about her?"

"She was an Ardglass."

"Any relation of Bijou Ardglass?"

"Sister-in-law, before Jumbo Ardglass divorced Bijou— who was his second wife, of course. Do you know her—

probably slept with her? Most of one's friends have."

"I've only seen her about the place. No other privileges."

"Of course, you wouldn't be rich enough for Bijou," said Lovell, not unkindly. "But, as I was saying, Bijou got through what remained of the Ardglass money, which wasn't much, and left Jumbo, who'd really had enough himself by that time. Since then, she has been keeping company with a whole string of people—Prince Theodoric—God knows who. However, I believe she still comes to see Molly. Molly is like that. She will put up with anyone."

"But why do you call him your 'first' Sleaford uncle?"

"Because he died, and I still have an uncle of that name—the present one is Geoffrey—the first, John. Uncle Geoffrey was too poor to marry until he succeeded. He could only just rub along in one of the cheaper cavalry regiments. There were two other brothers between him and the title. One was killed in the war, and the other knocked down by a bus."

"They don't seem much good at staying alive."

"The thing about the Sleafords," said Lovell, "is that they've always been absolutely mad on primogeniture. That's all very well in a way, but they've been so bloody mean to their widows and younger children that they are going to die out. They are a splendid example of upper-class stinginess. Geoffrey got married at once, as people do when they come into a peerage, however dim. Of course, in this case—with Dogdene thrown in—it was something worth having. Unfortunately they've never managed to knock up an heir."

Lovell went on to describe his "first Sleaford uncle", who seems to have been a chilly, serious-minded, competent peer, a great organiser of charitable institutions, who would have done well for himself in any walk of life. For a time he had been taken up with politics and held office under

Campbell-Bannerman and Asquith.

"He resigned at the time of the Marconi scandal," said Lovell. "He hadn't been making anything on the side himself, but he thought some of his Liberal colleagues had been a bit too liberal in the ethics of their own financial dealings. He was a selfish old man, but had what is called an exaggerated sense of honour."

"I think I've seen Isbister's portrait of him."

"Wearing the robes of the Garter. He took himself pretty seriously. Molly married him from the ballroom. She was only eighteen. Never seen a man before."

"When did he die?"

"Spanish 'flu in 1919," said Lovell. "Molly first met Jeavons when Dogdene was a military hospital in the war. He was rather badly wounded, you know. The extraordinary thing was they didn't start a love affair or anything. If Uncle John hadn't died, she would still be—in the words of an Edwardian song my father hums whenever her name is mentioned—'Molly the Marchioness'."

"Where did she re-meet her second husband?"

"At the Motor Show. Went to Olympia in her widow's weeds and saw Jeavons again. He was acting as a polisher on one of the stalls. I can't remember which make, but not a car anyone would be proud to own. That represented just about the height of what he could rise to in civil life. They were married about six months later."

"How does it go?"

"Very well. Molly never seems to regret the Dogdene days in the least. I can't think what they use for money, because, if I know the Sleafords, she didn't get much in the way of a jointure—and I doubt if she has a hundred a year of her own. The Ardglass family have been hopelessly insolvent since the Land Act. However, she manages to support herself—and Jeavons—somehow. And also get some fun out of life."

"Doesn't Jeavons bring in anything?"

"Not a cent. I think he feels pretty ill most of the time. He often looks like death itself. Besides, he is quite unemployable. As a matter of fact, it isn't true to say he does nothing. Once in a way he has some appliance he is marketing—an automatic bootjack or new cure for the common cold. Something he gets a commission on, or perhaps some firm is paying him a trifle to recommend the thing."

The description made an impression on me. The picture of Jeavons took on a more positive shape: not a particularly attractive one. "Realism goes with good birth," Lovell used to say, and he himself certainly showed this quality where his own relations were concerned. The statement might be hard to substantiate universally, but, by recognising laws of behaviour operating within the microcosm of a large, consanguineous network of families, however loosely connected, individuals born into such a world often gain an unsentimental grasp of human conduct: a grasp sometimes superior to that of apparently more perceptive persons whose minds are unattuned by early association to the constant give and take of an ancient and tenacious social organism. Of course, it does not always work that way, but Lovell, with his many limitations, was himself a good example of the principle.

"The chief reason I want to visit Aunt Molly," he said, "is to take another look at Priscilla Tollard, who is quite often there."

"A sister of Blanche Tolland?"

"Yes. Do you know Blanche?"

"Only by sight, and years ago. She is rather dotty, isn't she?"

"Quite dotty," said Lovell. "Lives in a complete world of her own. Fairly happy about it though, I think."

"Then there is one called Norah, isn't there, who set up house with a rather strange girl I used to know called

Eleanor Walpole-Wilson."

"That's it. She is rather dotty too, but in a different way. That couple are said to be a *ménage*. Then there is Isobel. She is rather different. Priscilla is the youngest. She isn't really 'out' yet."

I was about twenty-eight or twenty-nine at that period, to Lovell's twenty-three or twenty-four, and through him had become aware for the first time that a younger generation was close on my heels. I told him I felt much too old and passé to take an interest in such small fry as young ladies who were not yet "out".

"Oh, I quite realise that," said Lovell indulgently. "There will certainly be elder persons there too for chaps like you who prefer serious conversation. You might like Isobel. I believe she is a bit of a highbrow when she isn't going to night clubs."

We drove precariously down Gloucester Road, the car emitting a series of frightening crepitations and an evil fume, while Lovell artlessly outlined his long-term plans for the seduction of Priscilla Tolland. We turned off somewhere by the Underground station. I liked the idea of going to this unknown place for an hour or so, surroundings where the cheerless Studio atmosphere might be purged away. Lovell stopped in front of a fairly large house of dark red brick, the architecture of which sounded a distant, not particularly encouraging, echo of the High Renaissance. After waiting on the doorstep for some time, the door was opened by a man of indeterminate age in shirt-sleeves and carpet slippers. He might have passed for a butler. Pale and unhealthy looking, he had the air of having lived for months at a time underground in unventilated, overheated rooms. He brought with him odours of beer and cheese. Closer examination of this unkempt, moody fellow revealed him as older than he had appeared at first sight.

"Good evening, Smith," said Lovell, rather grandly.

" 'Evening," said Smith, speaking without the smallest suggestion of warmth.

"How are you, Smith?"

Smith looked Lovell up and down as if he considered the inquiry not merely silly, but downright insulting. He did not answer.

"Is her Ladyship upstairs?"

"Where do you think she'd be—in the basement?"

The tone of Smith's voice made no concession whatever towards alleviating the asperity of this answer. Lovell showed no sign of surprise at being received so caustically, passing off the retort with a hearty laugh. Smith shambled off down the stairs, muttering to himself. He seemed thoroughly fed up, not only with Lovell, but also with his own job.

"Smith is wonderful, isn't he?" said Lovell, as we mounted the staircase. "Aunt Molly sometimes borrows him from Erridge, when, for one reason or another, Thrubworth is closed down. I should warn you there is never an electric light bulb in the downstairs lavatory here and sometimes no bromo."

I followed him to the first floor; and into a double drawing-room in which eight or nine persons were standing or sitting. A general though never precisely defined suggestion of chinoiserie, sustained by a profusion of Oriental bowls and jars, pervaded the decoration. Some of the furniture was obviously rather valuable: the rest, gimcrack to a degree. Pictures showed a similar variation of standard, a Richard Wilson and a Greuze (these I noted later) hanging among pastels of Moroccan native types. A dark, handsome woman, now getting a trifle plump by the emaciated standards of the period, came towards us.

"Why, Chips," she said. "Here you are at last. We thought you would be earlier."

"Couldn't get away, Aunt Molly," said Lovell. "This is

24

Mr. Jenkins. He and I slave away writing films together."

"What will you drink?" she asked. "Teddy, get them something to drink quickly. They must be in dire need."

She smiled at me as if she were rather proud of that last phrase. Jeavons now appeared before us and began to make some rather hopeless gestures in the direction of several bottles and decanters standing on a table at the far end of the room. It was at once apparent that he was something left over from the war. I found it almost impossible to believe that he would so much resemble the mental picture conjured up by Lovell's earlier description of him. Like one of those mammoths—or, in Jeavons's case, somewhat less gigantic form of primeval life—caught in a glacier and physically preserved into an age when his very kind was known only from fossilised bones, or drawings on the walls of subterranean caves, he somehow managed to look just as he must have looked in 1917: hardly a day older. Perhaps a better simile to indicate the effect of remoteness he gave, standing there with a vacant expression and both hands in his pockets, would be that of some rare insect enclosed in amber. He wore a minute Charlie Chaplin moustache, his dark, shiny hair, in which there was a touch of red, rolling away from his forehead like the stone locks of a sculpted head of Caracalla.

At this point I became suddenly aware that at least one of the guests present was already well known to me. This was my family's old friend, Mrs. Conyers. Although I had not seen her at all recently, we had met from time to time—usually at intervals of several years—since the distant day when I had been taken to her flat and shown the scimitar. The last occasion had been the wedding of her daughter, Charlotte, to the lieutenant-commander. Evidently Mrs. Conyers had been dining with the Jeavonses. However, it appeared that she did not know them well, and, perhaps not greatly at ease in their society, she was clearly much relieved at finding, in myself, someone she knew of old. I was not sure that I myself was equally pleased, for, although I liked Mrs. Conyers well enough, I thought it preferable to explore new ground like the Jeavons house unobserved by old friends of my parents. However, nothing could have been less admonitory than Mrs. Conyers's manner towards myself; if admonition properly defines the attitude threatened, when one is young, by the presence of old family friends.

In appearance Mrs. Conyers retained, no doubt from her childhood, the harassed, uncertain expression of those who have for many years had to endure close association with persons addicted to practical joking. Like the rest of her sisters, she must have suffered in no small degree from her father's love of horse-play. One of six daughters, she had been regarded as, "on the shelf" by her parents when the General proposed to her. She herself had probably abandoned thought of marriage, because she was by then devoting most of her time to attending an elderly, intractable relation, Sybil, Lady Amesbury, whose memoirs I mentioned earlier. One of her father's exploits had been recorded in this book, the occasion when Lord Vowchurch, in his younger days, had loosed half a dozen monkeys wearing tail-coats and white ties at an ambassadorial ball: a casual relic of innumerable similar anecdotes that have passed into oblivion.

Although never exactly handsome, Mrs. Conyers was not without a look of sad distinction. In public she deferred to her husband, but she was known to possess a will of her own, displayed in that foxy, almost rodent-like cast of feature, which, resembling her sister's in its keenness, was not disagreeable. It was said that she had entirely reorganised the General's life after he had left the army; and much for the better. When I went across the room to speak with her, she raised her eyebrows slightly to indicate, if not precise disapproval, at least a secret signal that she felt herself not altogether at home. The message read that she required any support she could get.

Lovell had made for a red-faced, grey-moustached, elderly man, who seemed, like Mrs. Conyers, to have been a member of the dinner-party. This person possessed a curiously old-world air, suggesting an epoch considerably more remote than the war-time span conveyed by his host's outward appearance. Although not so old, he seemed to belong more, at least in spirit, to the vintage of General Conyers. I caught the words "Uncle Alfred". Lovell called so many men uncle that one could not be sure how closely related to him, if at all, any of them might be. This uncle acknowledged Lovell's greeting fairly curtly. There was something familiar about that red face, white moustache and muffled, uneasy manner. Then I realised that he was Tolland, that lonely, derelict character accustomed to frequent the annual Old Boy dinner of Le Bas's house. In fact, I had myself once sat next to Tolland at one of those functions: an occasion when I had made up my mind never to attend another.

It was a surprise to find Mrs. Conyers and Tolland here, but there was no reason why they should not both be friends of Lady Molly Jeavons. Mrs. Conyers was now engaged by her hostess, and led up to a swarthy young man, also wearing a dinner-jacket, who was standing by the gramophone turning over the pages of a book of records. They all began to talk French together. At that moment my eye caught Tolland's. He stared back, not without a certain apprehension in his look. Then he cleared his throat and advanced towards me.

"I didn't see you at the Le Bas dinner this year," he said.

He spoke with reproach, as if to mention such a breach of faith was an embarrassing duty his conscience laid upon him. In these surroundings, evidently his own ground, I felt

27

less ability to cope with his peculiarities than at the Le Bas dinners. It seemed better to conceal the decision never to attend another one.

"I didn't manage to get there."

"It went off all right," said Tolland slowly, as if ghastly failure had been a matter of touch and go. "I always accept when the card comes round. It makes a pleasant evening. Got to keep in touch. Of course Le Bas always says that in his speech."

Molly Jeavons, after talking for a minute or two with Mrs. Conyers and the young man with the black moustache, now rejoined Tolland and myself.

"I couldn't keep it up any longer," she said. "French is too exhausting. My governess said I was the worst pupil she'd ever had at the irregular verbs. All the same, I wanted to hear if there was anything new about Theodoric."

She pointed her finger at me.

"Is he another of your relations, Alfred?" she asked.

Her tone suggested that potential relationship with Tolland might explain everything: why I had come to the house: why I looked as I did: why we were talking together. I attempted to reduce my appearance to something as negative as possible, so that no one might be unduly committed by the inquiry, which had thrown Tolland into an appalling access of embarrassment.

"Really, I believe you have more relations than I have myself," she went on. "My grandfather had ninety-seven first cousins, and he was only three up on my grandmother on my mother's side."

"No—no—no," said Tolland, hurriedly. "At least I don't think we are, are we? Never know—perhaps I oughtn't to have been so definite—quite on the cards, I suppose, as a matter of fact. Shouldn't speak hastily about such things. Certainly got a lot of 'em. Some people might think too many, as you say, Molly. No—no—no. Perhaps you can tell better than me. Are we related? No? Thought not. Always try to keep track of 'em. Hard to manage sometimes. Go abroad and get married and get divorced and into debt, glad to see the back of 'em sometimes. But where you and I meet is at the Le Bas dinner. That's where *we* meet."

He gasped a bit after all this, as if not only breathless from speaking at such length, but also overcome with confusion at the predicament into which he had been thrown by the question. Yet, even in spite of this floundering, he seemed to feel himself on much surer ground in this house than at our previous meetings. He might be temporarily at a disadvantage here with his hostess, even on guard against attack from her (a minute or two later I found he had good reason to fear that), but at least his credentials were known and freely accepted in the Jeavons drawing-room. I was by no means sure that I felt myself equally at ease. The atmosphere of the house was not exactly restful. The other persons who made up the party were nondescript enough, but there was also the feeling that one had penetrated the outskirts of a secret society. Mrs. Conyers had seemed as subject as myself to this sense of disquiet. Perhaps it was merely that she had passed on to me her own agitation; for I was sure she was agitated about something. Lovell had certainly tried to prepare me for an unusual household, but to absorb such antecedent descriptions is never easy. Molly Jeavons's noisy, absolutely unrestrained directness of manner was of a kind that suggested both simplicity of nature and certainty of her own position: both characteristics that can stimulate that streak of social cruelty that few lack. There could be no doubt that Tolland was showing signs of preparing himself for some onslaught. The reason for his fears soon became apparent.

"I didn't know you ever met anyone but your own relations, Alfred," she said, evidently determined to pursue that subject. "You always pretend to me that you never go anywhere. I only got you here tonight because you wanted to hear from her own lips Mrs. Conyers's story about the Empress Frederick. I believe your quiet evenings at home are all make-believe and that you live a disgracefully fast life—the gayest of gay bachelors."

Tolland denied this imputation emphatically. He did not seem in the least flattered at the suggestion that he might be, so far as social life was concerned, a dark horse. He was patently without the smallest personal vanity, open or secret, on the matter of cutting a dash in life. He came at last to the end of his protests.

"Alfred was talking about his family all through dinner," said Molly Jeavons, turning once more to me. "You know they are all in trouble—every blessed one of them."

"It's too bad of you to say that, Molly. I only asked for your advice about some of my nephews and nieces."

Now he sounded thoroughly aggrieved, although at the same time unwilling to withdraw voluntarily from a conversation devoted to his relations.

"What's the matter with the Tollands this time, Aunt Molly?" asked Lovell.

He had been making a tour of the room, ending with our group.

"Oh, it's Erridge again," she said.

She spoke as if the question were hardly worth asking.

"What's Erridge's latest?"

Lovell, for his part, spoke as one expecting to hear an enjoyable piece of gossip about a character always to be relied upon to provide a good story.

"Living as a tramp," said Molly Jeavons. "So I'm told at least. Somewhere in the Midlands. Grew a beard. He has still got it, they say. I don't think he actually slept in casual wards. The other tramps must have had an awful time if he did. As a child he used to talk in his sleep and bawl the house down with night terrors."

"Is he doing that now?" asked Lovell. "Being a tramp, I mean, not bawling the house down—though I shouldn't wonder if he doesn't have night terrors still."

"He is back at Thrubworth. Getting cleaned up after his adventures—as much as Erry ever gets cleaned up. Smith goes back tomorrow. I am more and more coming to think that Smith is more trouble that he is worth. It's convenient to have a manservant in the house, but I found this morning we were completely out of gin, and I know at least two inches remained in the bottle left when we went to bed last night."

Lovell was obviously disappointed that nothing more sensational about Erridge was to be revealed.

"Feingold had some story about 'a lord' who was doing 'social research'," he said. "I thought it might be Erridge. I don't expect the dumps he stopped at were any more uncomfortable than he has made Thrubworth by now. The whole place has been under dust-sheets since he succeeded, hasn't it? Do you know Erridge, Nick? He must be about a contemporary of yours."

"He is a year or two older. I used to know him by sight. His brother, George Tolland, was nearer my age, though I didn't know him either. But he isn't 'Erridge' any longer, is he?"

"No, no, he is 'Warminster' now, of course," said Molly Jeavons, impatiently. "But Alfred's family always call their eldest son by the second title. I don't even know what Erry's Christian name is. Perhaps he hasn't got one."

"Nonsense, of course he has," said Tolland, quite angrily. "His name is Alfred, like my own. You know that perfectly well, Molly. Besides, to call him 'Erridge' is perfectly usual, isn't it? In fact, off-hand, I can't think of a single family that does differently."

"We always used to think it rather pompous," said Molly Jeavons. "I can't imagine myself ever addressing Jumbo as

'Kilkeel' when he was alive. It would sound like a race-horse."

"Well, 'Jumbo' sounds like an elephant to me," said Tolland.

This retort must have struck him as one of unusual subtlety, since he looked round at Lovell and myself in an appeal for applause; or at least for sympathy.

"That's just it," said Molly Jeavons, now speaking almost at the top of her voice. "My poor brother did look like an elephant. Nobody denied that, not even himself. But he did not look like a race-horse. Not one I would have put my money on, anyway."

"Bijou put her shirt on him," said Lovell.

"Rubbish, she didn't," said Molly Jeavons, beginning to laugh. "He put his shirt on her, you idiot—and lost it, too."

I remembered, then, that Tolland had spoken of "my nephew, Warminster", at the Le Bas dinner where we had met; at the same time mentioning that this young man had succeeded his father some years before. Tolland had added that his nephew was "a funny boy". Erridge (as it seems simplest—like his parents—to continue to call him, anyway for the time being) remained in my mind as a gloomy, cadaverous schoolboy, trudging along the road close to the wall, his hands in his pockets and a pile of books slipping from under his arm. Angular, sallow and spotty, he was usually frowning angrily to himself, weighed down with anxiety, as if all the troubles of the world rested on his shoulders. The only time I could recall seeing him in later life was, years before, at a dance given by the Hunter-combes. On that occasion, Erridge had looked so hot, cross and untidy that only the fact that he was wearing a tail-coat and white tie—neither in their first freshness—prevented him from resembling, even then, a harrassed young tramp. His appearance that night had certainly borne out this recent account of him. The ball at the Huntercombes' remained always with peculiar clarity in my mind as the night Barbara Goring had poured sugar over Widmerpool's head.

"Does Erridge often do this sort of thing?" I asked. "Go off on 'social research', I mean?"

"Oh yes," said Molly Jeavons. "He has the oddest ideas. All your family have, haven't they, Alfred? The whole blessed lot of them."

Tolland made a nervous movement with his head, as if attempting to deny the principle of the accusation while at the same time regretfully having to admit, anyway in part, some of its immediate justice.

"Warminster was not like that," he said. "I'm not like that. Not in the least. Nor are Frederica and George. And I trust the younger ones will turn out different from Erridge. They all seemed all right when they were children. Ran about and made a lot of noise. Just can't tell, I suppose. Just—can't—tell."

If he expected this exhibition of philosophic resignation in some manner to appease Molly Jeavons, he was mistaken.

"Certainly Frederica is not strange," she said, laughing uproariously at the idea. "Frederica is ordinary enough for anyone. Got to be in her job. Frederica is as ordinary as you like."

This agreement with his conclusion—the complete, the absolute ordinariness of his niece, Frederica—seemed to bring some temporary alleviation to Tolland's feelings. He nodded several times with satisfaction. I had some vague idea as to Frederica's identity. She had married one of the Budds, brother or cousin of a "beauty" called Margaret Budd, and her husband had been killed in a hunting accident only a few years later. People had talked about his death in the days when I used to dine with the Walpole-

33

Wilsons. I remembered Anne Stepney talking about the accident.

As I was by then committed to this conversation about a lot of people regarding whom I knew little or nothing, I decided to take an active part by seeking further information. I asked what Frederica Budd's job might be that required such extreme correctness of behaviour.

"She is Lady-in-Waiting," said Molly Jeavons. "Or she may be an Extra Woman of the Bedchamber. Something like that. Anyway, she has to behave herself jolly well. I'm surprised you haven't met her, if you are an old friend of Mrs. Conyers. She and Frederica are great cronies."

At that period, as I have said, I knew little of the Tollands, although increasingly during the past few years I had been hearing scraps of information about one or other of them, as happens when a large family, close to each other in age, begin in quick succession to appear in the world. Lovell had given some account of them at dinner. Molly Jeavons's sister, Katherine, a childless widow, had married the late Lord Warminster as his second wife. "As a result," Lovell had said, "she possesses a dozen step-children." It turned out, in fact, that Erridge had only nine brothers and sisters. Even that number seemed preposterously large to an only child like myself. There is something overpowering, even a trifle sinister about very large families, the individual members of which often possess in excess the characteristics commonly attributed to "only" children: misanthropy: neurasthenia: an inability to adapt themselves: all the traits held to be the result of a lonely upbringing. The corporate life of large families can be lived with severity, even barbarity, of a kind unknown in smaller related communities: these savageries and distillations of egoism often rendered even less tolerable if sentimentalised outside the family circle. The Tollands, from what Lovell reported of them, sounded no exception to this prejudiced judgment.

"Of course it was hard for them losing their mother—being left orphans, in fact," said Tolland. "Though of course Katherine has always done her best—been splendid, really."

By introducing the name of the second Lady Warminster into the conversation, he may have hoped to carry the war into the enemy's country. By then his face was more flushed than ever. His hostess was determined to let him off nothing. I had the impression that she was teasing him, not precisely for my especial benefit, but, at the same time, that my presence as a newcomer to the house afforded a particularly favourable opportunity for the application of torments of this sort. I found later that she was indeed what is called "a tease", perhaps the only outward indication that her inner life was not altogether happy; since there is no greater sign of innate misery than a love of teasing. Later, too, I understood how much that night Alfred Tolland must have been torn between a pride that made him hesitate to discuss his relations in front of a stranger, and a taste for talking about his family, too rarely satisfied in his lonely life. It was a treat to visit someone who understood the niceties of family gossip, even if Molly Jeavons required her pound of flesh by ragging him. His face, completely masculine in cast, had at the same time that air of being quite untouched by sexual passion: a look noticeable sometimes among men of his generation. Lovell explained to me later that Tolland had always had a taste for good works and had been much used by the late Lord Sleaford in connexion with his charities. He was a fine example of my friend Barnby's observation that "melancholy is the curse of the upper classes".

"And what about Norah?" said Molly Jeavons.

She had to repeat the question twice, for the first time Tolland made no attempt to reply. He seemed completely knocked out. The challenge was apparently unanswerable.

He could only nod his head. There was no spirit left in him. To bridge the silence, I asked if it were not true that Norah Tolland shared a flat with Eleanor Walpole-Wilson.

"She does, she does," cried Molly Jeavons, laughing loudly again at my question, as if I had shown myself to have missed the whole point of what was being said. "Do you know them? I didn't think they ever saw any young men. I'm jolly glad to hear they do. Tell me about them. Is it true that Eleanor has been seen in a green pork-pie hat and a bow tie?"

Mrs. Conyers, escaped from the man to whom French must be talked, now joining our group, nodded her head and pursed her lips, as if to emphasise the depths to which Eleanor had fallen.

"As a matter of fact, I haven't seen Eleanor for years," I said. "I used to dine with them once in a way. I saw Sir Gavin Walpole-Wilson at the Isbister Retrospective Exhibition when it was on, and he said something about Norah Tolland. I've never met her."

"They look like a couple of stable-boys," said Molly Jeavons. "And talk like stable-boys, too. I hear they swear like troopers."

From the way she spoke, I suspected she knew very little about these two young women, and was, in fact, anxious to learn more. Finding me unable to offer a closely observed report on their activities, she abandoned the subject and renewed her general attack on Tolland.

"And then Hugo," she said. "What about Hugo?"

She spoke as if Hugo clinched every other argument. If the name of Norah had knocked Tolland out, that of Hugo reduced him to the position of an army not only defeated in the field, but also forced to join as an ally its victorious adversary.

"I hear his clothes are—well, awful," he muttered, almost inaudibly.

So far as Hugo was concerned, he seemed to agree absolutely with Molly Jeavons in thinking the situation could scarcely be worse.

"But all undergraduates are like that," said Mrs. Conyers, unexpectedly. "I mean they all wear extraordinary clothes, don't they? They always have—and say things to try and shock people. My father used to say they were like that even in his day. I know he himself, just after he had been sent down from Oxford, said some terrible thing to Mr. Gladstone when he was introduced to him at Holland House. My father had to write and apologise, or I don't know what would have happened. I am not sure the Ministry might not have fallen."

"Well," said Molly Jeavons, "I've known some undergraduates in my time—Jumbo, for instance, you should have seen him in his young days—but I've never met one who dressed like Hugo. I was talking to the Bridgnorths' boy, John Mountfichet, when he was here the other day. He is at the same college as Hugo. He told us some things that would make your hair stand on end. They made Teddy laugh, and you know how difficult that is."

"Even Sillery says Hugo goes too far," said Lovell. "He drives all the other dons quite mad, of course, but I should have thought Sillery would have stuck up for him. The other undergraduates are very disapproving too. Apart from anything else, aesthetes have gone completely out of fashion at both universities these days. I told Hugo when I saw him the other day that he was hopelessly out of date."

"What did he say?"

" 'My dear, I love being *dated*. I hate all this bickering that goes on about politics. I wish I'd lived in the *Twenties* when people were *amusing*.' "

Lovell spoke the words with the mannerism he judged appropriate to such an impersonation.

"He'll grow out of it," said Mrs. Conyers, surprising me

with this repeated display of toleration. "Lots of nice young men go through a stage of being rather silly."

"Let's hope so," said Alfred Tolland, with a sigh.

He did not sound very confident.

"At any rate, George is all right," he added a moment later.

I had the impression he was playing his last card, but that this card was a trump.

"What is George Tolland doing now?" I asked. "He was the one of the family who was my contemporary, though I never really knew him."

"In the Coldstream for some years," said Alfred Tolland. "Then he thought he ought to try and make some money, so he went into the City. He has done fairly well, so they say. Never know what people mean by that—but they say pretty well."

"Oh, yes," said Molly Jeavons. "I am sure that George has done well. But what a correct young man—*what a correct young man*! I don't think I ever met a young man who was so correct. I can't see how we are ever going to get him married, he is so correct—and even if we found a correct wife for him, I am sure they would both be much too correct to have any children. And even if they did, what frightfully correct children they would have to be."

"You can't have it both ways, Molly," grumbled Tolland. "You blame some of them for misbehaving themselves. Perhaps you are right. But then you don't approve of George because he is what you call 'correct'. Can't understand it. There is no pleasing you. It isn't reasonable."

"Well, now I'll tell you about the rest of them," said Molly Jeavons, turning to me. "Of course I really adore them all, and just say these things to make Alfred cross. There is Susan, who is showing every sign of getting engaged to a nice young man, then there is Blanche——"

"I've seen Blanche, though I don't know her."

"Blanche is dotty. You must know that much, if you've seen her. But she's not a bad old thing."

"Of course not."

Alfred Tolland showed no disposition to deny the "dottiness" of his niece, Blanche.

"Robert is a bit of a mystery. He is in some business, but I don't know whether he will stay there. Isobel—well, she is a bit different too. I'm not sure she isn't going to get engaged soon herself. Then there is Priscilla, who is on the point of coming out, and was to have been here tonight, but she doesn't seem to have turned up yet."

I made an effort to take in this bird's-eye view of the Tollands, who now seemed to surround me on all sides after this vivid exposition of their several characters. Instinctively, I felt the greatest interest in Isobel, who was "different"; and also an odd feeling of regret that she might be about to become engaged in the near future. While I was brooding on this, Jeavons joined us. He stood there, scanning everyone's face closely, as if hoping for some explanation of the matter in hand; perhaps even of life itself, so intense was his concentration: some resonable interpretation couched in terms simple enough for a plain man to understand without undue effort. He also gave the impression of an old dog waiting to have a ball thrown to retrieve, more because that was the custom in the past than because sport or exercise was urgently required. However, no one enlightened him as to the subject under discussion, so he merely filled up my glass, and then his own. His wife and Alfred Tolland had now embarked on some detailed aspect of Tolland life, too esoteric for an outsider to follow.

"In the film business like Chips?" Jeavons asked, in a low husky voice, as if he had a cold coming on, or had drunk too much whisky the night before.

"Yes."

"Ever met any of the stars?"

"Not so you'd notice. I'm on the scenario side. The studio only makes English pictures for the quota. They wouldn't be likely to employ anyone very grand in the way of an actor or actress."

Jeavons seemed disappointed at this answer.

"Still," he urged, "you must see some beauties sometimes, don't you?"

"I've sat next to Adolphe Menjou," said his wife, suddenly abandoning the subject of the Tollands, and breaking in with her accustomed violence, though not, I think, with any idea of preventing him from pursuing the question of film actresses and their looks. "He had such nice manners. Of course Garbo is the one I should really like to meet. I suppose everyone would. Wouldn't you like to meet Garbo, Alfred?"

"Never heard of him," said Tolland.

Inevitably there was some laughter at this.

"It's a *she*," said Molly Jeavons. "It's a *she*, Alfred."

"An actress, I suppose," said Tolland, "or you wouldn't be using that tone of voice. I don't think I particularly want to meet Miss Garbo—or perhaps it is Mrs. Garbo."

There was more laughter at that. I was not sure—I am not sure to this day—whether he was feigning ignorance of the famous film star, whose name at that moment, the zenith of her fame, was a synonym for mysterious, elusive, feminine beauty; or whether he had, in truth, never heard of her.

"I once met Mrs. Patrick Campbell when I was a young man," he said, speaking as if the statement was an afterthought. "Heard her read aloud *High Tide on the Coast of Lincolnshire*. Wonderful experience. Felt different all the evening. Couldn't sleep after it. Lay awake—well—till the morning, nearly."

Possibly Molly Jeavons felt that for a brief second the tables had been turned on her, because she now returned to the charge in the game of baiting him about his family, probably feeling in that activity on safer ground.

"Tell us more about the stained-glass window, Alfred," she said.

This request galvanised him once again to the point of anger. She seemed to have touched some specially sensitive nerve.

"I've told you already, Molly," he said, "the window has never been put up as it should have been. Erridge isn't interested."

"Surely somebody in the family can tell him to do it," she said. "Why can't you tell him to get on with the job yourself? He must do it, that's all."

She spoke as if her own decision made the matter final. Alfred Tolland shook his head gloomily.

"As well ask him to lead the glass himself," he said. "Better, in fact. He might have a try at that. Dignity of labour or something. But as for taking an interest in his own grandfather's memorial——"

Tolland shook his head, finding metaphor, as applied to Erridge, impotent.

"Can't George take it on?" insisted Molly Jeavons. "You think so highly of George."

Tolland shook his head again.

"Difficult for George," he said. "Delicate, with Erridge the eldest son. George doesn't want to be snubbed."

"Oh, goodness," said Molly Jeavons, throwing up her hands, "you Tollands drive me mad."

Some new guests came into the room at that moment, so that her own plan for solving the problem of the stained-glass window was never revealed. In the reshuffle of places, I found myself *tête-à-tête* with Mrs. Conyers. After a few preliminary inquiries about my parents, she explained that the General was indisposed, though not seriously, having fallen headlong from the stable loft where the poodles' food was stored. He must at that time have been a few years short of eighty.

"But I did not remember you knew Lady Molly," said Mrs. Conyers in a low voice.

"I did not, until tonight."

"Rather a happy-go-lucky household. That very extraordinary butler. One does not know what is going to be said next."

"So I should think."

"Too much so for me. I am old-fashioned, I'm afraid. I do not at all mind admitting it."

I was reminded of Hugo Tolland, said to like being "dated", but thought it wiser not to remind Mrs. Conyers of the parallel. I wondered why she had agreed to dine with the Jeavonses if she felt so inimical to them.

"But you yourself must have known Lady Molly for a long time?"

"Of course we have known her for years and years. But never well. When she was Lady Sleaford my youngest sister, Mildred, knew her, and we used to meet sometimes. I have hardly seen her since her second marriage. We know the present Sleafords, but I don't think Lady Molly ever sees anything of them. That is to be expected, perhaps."

"You dined here?"

"It was really on account of my sister. I can't remember whether you have ever met Mildred."

"Only when I was a child. When you showed me the sword the sultan gave the General."

Mrs. Conyers smiled.

"That was a long time ago," she said. "Then you really do not know her."

Some of the subsequent history of Mildred Blaides was, in fact, familiar to me from occasional talk on the part of my parents. Considered rather "fast" in her early days—as might be expected from my memory of her—she had married a Flying Corps officer called M'Cracken, who had been killed not long after the wedding in a raid over Germany. Then there had been a period of widowhood, when her behaviour had been thought "flighty". From the manner in which this interlude in her career used to be discussed, I imagine that my parents' generation supposed her to be about to go to the bad in a spectacular manner. However, this very generally prophesied débâcle never took place. Mildred Blaides married again: the second time to an Australian business-man, a Mr. Haycock, retired, fairly rich, who owned a villa in the South of France and spent a good deal of his time travelling round the world. Mr. Haycock, who was said to possess sterling virtues in addition to his comfortable income, was also agreed to be "rather rough". The marriage, so far as I knew, had been quite a success. There were children, but I did not know how many.

"As a matter of fact, my sister Mildred is a very old friend of our hostess," said Mrs. Conyers, as if the matter was weighing on her mind. "As I say, she knows Lady Molly far better than I do. Mildred nursed at Dogdene during the war."

"I remember her in nurse's uniform."

"She is coming here tonight. She was to have dined, but at the last moment she was unable to be at dinner. She is—more or less engaged to a friend of Lady Molly's. As I expect you know, Mildred's husband died about a year ago. Unfortunately a business engagement prevented her—I suppose I should say—fiancé from dining. He is a very busy man. He just could not get away tonight in time. Then Mildred herself is always changing her plans. Goodness knows why she herself could not come here without him. However, she couldn't, so there it was. They are both looking in later."

There could be no doubt now that the matter which

worried, or at least unusually preoccupied, Mrs. Conyers was connected with her sister's arrival. I could not at first decide exactly what had upset her.

"This is not the first time you have met him—the fiancé?"

"As a matter of fact, I haven't seen him yet," she said, almost apologetically, as if that was the least I could expect of her. "You see, it only happened yesterday. That was why Lady Molly arranged the dinner. She didn't seem to mind their not turning up in the least. Of course, she is much more used to people changing their arrangements than I am."

It seemed probable that she was merely suffering some anxiety regarding the potentialities of the man who was to be her sister's third husband. I knew enough about the reputation of Mildred Blaidés to realise that anxiety was reasonable enough.

"He is a good deal younger than Mildred," she said.

After announcing this fact, Mrs. Conyers decided to abandon the subject, perhaps fearing that in her own over-wrought state she might say too much. She gave a sigh.

"If I must talk French," she went on, with rather forced gaiety, "I do so much prefer not to have to talk the language to a Frenchman. They are so terribly severe. I always tell them that they will never admit that any other Frenchman speaks correct French, so how can they possibly expect me to do so. That young man over there actually complimented me on my French accent."

"Who is he?"

"From one of the Balkan Legations. I think his father was Minister over here, and used to stop at Dogdene. He was invited about rather more than you might expect because he was an unusually good shot. In the end the poor fellow was shot himself by an anarchist in his own country. The son had news of Prince Theodoric. In fact, I think he

44

has just ceased to be a member of the Prince's personal household. As you probably know, Theodoric was rather a special friend of the divorced wife of Lady Molly's brother, Lord Ardglass, who died some years ago. Our hostess always likes to hear about him on that account. Between you and me, I am afraid she is a tiny bit of a gossip, but don't say I said so."

Mrs. Conyers smiled a little slyly.

"Who are the two girls who have just come in and are talking to Chips Lovell?"

"He is the young man you arrived with, isn't he? The nearest is one of the Tolland girls, Priscilla, I think. She was going to see a film with a former school friend of hers whose name I was not told."

Priscilla Tolland looked more than seventeen: even so, she had not entirely lost a long-legged, childish awkwardness in the manner in which she stood with her legs crossed. I could see she bore a strong likeness to the "dotty" Blanche, though certainly free herself from any such disability. The girl with her, prototype of all school friends, was small and dark with horn-rimmed spectacles and an air of bossing everyone about. I thought I would have a word with them in a minute or two; when Mrs. Conyers had finished speaking of the misty past, into which she was now making a deep excursion. However, opportunity to approach the girls never came, because a second later, just as Mrs. Conyers had invited me to tea with herself and the General the following Sunday, two more persons, a man and woman, entered the room.

"Ah, there is Mildred at last," said Mrs. Conyers, fumbling with her lorgnette, her thin hands, almost pale mauve in colour, shaking with excitement and anxiety.

I myself was curious to see what Mildred Blaides—or rather Mildred Haycock—might look like after all these years, half expecting her to be wearing her V.A.D. outfit and smoking a cigarette. But when my eyes fell on the two of them, it was the man, not the woman, who held my attention. Life is full of internal dreams, instantaneous and sensational, played to an audience of one. This was just such a performance. The fiancé was Widmerpool. Scarlet in the face, grinning agitatedly through the thick lenses of his spectacles, he advanced into the room, his hand on Mrs. Haycock's arm. He was wearing a new dark suit. Like a huge fish swimming into a hitherto unexplored, unexpectedly exciting aquarium, he sailed resolutely forward: yet not a real fish, a fish made of rubber or some artificial substance. There was something a little frightening about him. That could not be denied. Molly Jeavons, this time supported by her husband, closed in on these new arrivals immediately.

"Well, he is no beauty," said Mrs. Conyers.

She spoke with such deep relief at her discovery of the unpleasingness of Widmerpool's features that she must have feared the worst of her sister's choice on account of the reported difference of age. Probably she had pictured some golden-haired gigolo of altogether unacceptable personal appearance. The truth was a great consolation to her. Certainly, to look at them, they seemed on the score of age to be a couple very reasonably to be associated together. Mrs. Haycock was in the neighbourhood of forty, and looked no younger, but Widmerpool, although only a year or so over thirty, had always appeared comfortably middle-aged even as a boy.

"I know him."

"Who is he?"

"He is called Kenneth Widmerpool. I was at school with him as a matter of fact. He is in the City."

"I know his name of course. And that he is in the City. But what is he like?"

Mrs. Conyers did not attempt to conceal her own impatience. The reason of her anxiety was now made plain. She had no confidence in her sister's choice of husband. She wanted to know the worst as soon as possible. Her first, and most serious, fears were passed; she wished to move on to a later stage of inquiry. Widmerpool, although giving her reason to be thankful that the outlook was not more threatening, had evidently made no very captivating impression.

"Is he nice?"

"I've known him a long time——"

By then we were both involved in general introductions taking place round the room, so that I was not forced to answer the question. Afterwards, when I got home, I pondered what I should most properly have said in reply. The fact was that Widmerpool could hardly be described as "nice". Energetic: able: successful: all kinds of things that had never been expected of him in the past; but "nice" he had never been, and showed little sign of becoming. Yet, for some reason, I was quite glad to see him again. His reappearance, especially in that place, helped to prove somehow rather consolingly, that life continued its mysterious, patterned way. Widmerpool was a recurring milestone on the road; perhaps it would be more apt to say that his course, as one jogged round the track, was run from time to time, however different the pace, in common with my own. As an aspect of my past he was an element to be treated with interest, if not affection, like some unattractive building or natural feature of the landscape which brought back the irrational nostalgia of childhood. A minute later I found myself talking to him.

"No, I haven't seen you for a long time," he said, breathing heavily as usual. "I've been trying to get hold of you, as a matter of fact, to tell you I was getting married."

"Many congratulations."

"Time to settle down," he said.

This remark was fatuous, since he had never been anything but "settled down", at least in my eyes. I could not imagine why he should specially wish to tell me about his marriage, although there could be no doubt from his manner that he was in a great state of excitement at the thought of being engaged. His nose and lips, beneath the huge headlamps of his now rimless spectacles, were twitching slightly. Lunging out towards Mrs. Haycock, who stood not far from him, he seized her arm and drew her in our direction.

"This is Nicholas Jenkins, my dear. An old friend of mine. He was somewhat my junior at school."

Mrs. Haycock, who had been talking to her sister, now turned and faced me, so that for the first time since she had entered the room I had an opportunity of observing closely the woman he hoped to make his wife. I could at once appreciate the strong impression she might have made on him the moment she showed herself prepared to accept him as an admirer. Tall, elegant, brassy, she was markedly of the same generation as Molly Jeavons, without personally at all resembling her. Mrs. Haycock's moral separateness from Widmerpool, immediately noticeable, was not on account of any difference of age, as such, for—as I have said—Widmerpool had never looked young. It was a separateness imposed upon her by the war. Like Jeavons, that was the epoch to which she belonged by some natural right. Life on the Riviera had no doubt left its mark too: a society in which Widmerpool was unlikely hitherto to have participated. She retained some of her sunburn from the previous summer, and, although dressed quite normally—indeed, rather well—her clothes seemed in some indefinable manner more adapted to a *plage* or casino than the Jeavons drawing-room.

I had always felt an interest in what might be called the theoretical side of Widmerpool's life: the reaction of his own emotions to the severe rule of ambition that he had

48

from the beginning imposed upon himself: the determination that existence must be governed by the will. However, the interest one takes in the lives of other people is, at best, feeble enough, so that, knowing little of his affairs in recent years, I had in truth largely forgotten about him. Now, for the second time that evening, I recalled the night when that noisy little girl, Barbara Goring, had poured sugar over his head at the Huntercombes' dance. He had been in love with her; and I, too, for that matter, or had thought so at the time. Then there had been his brief, painful association with Gypsy Jones, the grubby Left Wing nymph, whose "operation" he had defrayed unrewarded. After the Gypsy Jones business, he had told me he would never again have anything to do with a woman who "took his mind off his work". I wondered whether Mrs. Haycock would satisfy that condition: whether he had proposed to her under stress of violent emotion, or had decided such a marriage would help his career. Perhaps there was an element of both motives; in any case, to attempt to disengage motives in marriage is a fruitless task. Mrs. Haycock took my hand, smiling absently, and gave it a good squeeze; the clutch of a woman pretty familiar with men and their ways.

"One always has to meet such crowds of people when one gets married," she said. "It is really too, too exhausting. Did you say we had met before? Was it at Cannes? I seem to know your face."

She spoke breathlessly, almost asthmatically, in which she resembled Widmerpool, but using that faint hint of cockney, an accent in part bequeathed by the overtones of the Prince of Wales to the world to which she belonged. I tried, quite unsuccessfully and perhaps not very tactfully, to explain the circumstances of our infinitely distant former meeting. It was plainly years since she had listened to any remarks addressed to her, either serious or trivial, so that perhaps deservedly—for the exposition was a formidable

49

rigmarole upon which to embark at that moment—she swiftly disengaged herself from its demands.

"I'm absolutely longing for a drink, Molly," she said. "Oh, thank you so much, Mr. Jeavons, what an angel you are. I have been having the most awful time tonight. You know I abominate making plans. Never make them, as a matter of fact. I just won't. Well, this evening I got caught up by one of the most awful bores you ever met."

She drank deeply of the glass brought by Jeavons, and began telling him the story. Widmerpool took me aside.

"Did I hear you say you had met Mildred before?"

He spoke anxiously.

"When I was about nine or ten."

"What on earth do you mean?"

He sounded quite angry at this statement of mine, intended to set his mind at rest. He supposed I wanted to tease him.

"Just what I said. It was years ago—with her sister, Mrs. Conyers, to whom you were introduced a second ago. My family have always known General Conyers."

I hardly knew why I added this last piece of information which sounded somehow a trifle absurd and unnecessary, emphasising the fact that Widmerpool and the General would become brothers-in-law. However, Widmerpool was appeased by this amplification.

"Quite so," he said. "Quite so."

All at once he became abstracted in manner.

"Look here," he said. "Come and have luncheon with me. We haven't had a talk for a long time. What about next Sunday—at my club?"

"All right. Thanks very much."

The name of the club surprised me a little. There was no reason at all why he should not belong there, yet its mild suggestion of cosmopolitan life and high card stakes evoked an environment seemingly unsuited to his nature. When employed at Donners-Brebners, Widmerpool must have spent a fair amount of his time with foreign business-men. Indeed, his professional background at that time might well have been described as international. There was nothing against him on that count. Equally, if he ever played cards, he might, for all I knew, venture high stakes. He could presumably afford such a risk. Neither of these aspects of the scene altered the sense of incongruity. To eyes that had known him as a boy, even the smallest pretension to swagger appeared, for Widmerpool, out of place. That was the point. The verdict was inescapable. Only an atmosphere of quiet hard work and dull, serious conversation were appropriate to him. Such a demand on my part, even though unvoiced, was, of course, absurd. Widmerpool's conduct was, in any case, no concern of mine. Besides, these sentiments were utterly at variance with Widmerpool's own view of himself; a view that would obviously play the chief part in his choice of club—or, for that matter, of wife. If such a club was inappropriate to him, how much more incongruous would be a wife like Mrs. Haycock. I could not help thinking that. We talked for a time of general matters. Later on Lovell came across the room.

"I am giving Priscilla Tolland and her friend a lift home," he said. "Do you want to be taken as far as your flat?"

I had no difficulty in perceiving the reason for this offer and resigned myself to sitting in the back with the friend.

"Come and see us again," said Molly Jeavons, when saying good-bye. "Make Chips bring you, or just drop in."

"So long, old man, come again," said Jeavons.

He had been standing for a long time by the drink tray, plunged in deep thought, perhaps still contemplating the subject of film stars and their varied, disturbing charms. Now he took me by the hand, as if his thoughts were far away. I followed Lovell and the girls downstairs to the car. Outside there was a hint of fog in the air. The river mist seemed to have pursued us from the Studio. Nothing of note happened on the way home. The school friend talked incessantly of the visit she was going to pay to Florence. We dropped her at an address in Wimpole Street, after disposing of Priscilla Tolland at her stepmother's house in Hyde Park Gardens.

TWO

"We might go straight in to lunch," said Widmerpool, when we met a day or two later. "If you so wish, you can drink a glass of pale sherry at the table. We are sometimes crowded at the luncheon hour. Incidentally, you will probably see the Permanent Under-Secretary of the Home Office at one table. He honours us with his presence most days—but I forgot. It is Sunday today, so that he may not be with us. I am afraid, now I come to think of it, that it is a long time since I went to church. I shall attend a service next week when I stay with my mother in the country."

"How is your mother?"

"Better than ever. You know she literally grows younger. A wonderful woman."

"Does she still have the cottage near Hinton?"

"It is a little small, but it suits us both. We could well afford something larger nowadays, but she loves it. Her roses are the admiration of the neighbourhood."

"You still see something of the Walpole-Wilsons and Sir Magnus Donners?"

"The Walpole-Wilsons I have lost all touch with," said Widmerpool. "Sir Magnus is, of course, an old friend. Whatever his faults—some of which it would be foolish to disregard—he has rendered me in the past inestimable service. As it happens, he has not asked me over to Stourwater recently. I must ring him up. But come along. To lunch, to lunch."

He spoke with that air of bustle that infected all his dealings. During the few seconds in which we talked he had managed to convey the sensation that we were physically too close together. More than once I edged away. He seemed all the time pressing at one's elbow, like a waiter who breathes heavily over you as he irritably proffers a dish awkward to handle. Widmerpool, too, gave the impression of irritation, chronic irritation, as if he felt all the time that the remedy to alleviate his own annoyances lay in the hands of the people round him, who would yet at the same time take no step to relieve his mounting discomfort; for his manner conveyed always a suspicion that he knew only too well that things were almost as bad for those who were with him as for himself.

He swept me forward into the dining-room. The club steward, no doubt familiar with Widmerpool's predispositions, indicated a table by the window, flanked on one side by two yellow-faced men conversing in stilted, sing-song French: on the other, by an enormously fat old fellow who was opening his luncheon with dressed crab and half a bottle of hock. One of the men talking French I thought I recognised as the Balkan diplomatist seen at the Jeavonses and said to be of Prince Theodoric's entourage.

"Have anything you like to eat or drink," said Widmerpool. "Consult the menu here. Personally I am on a diet—a little gastric trouble—and shall restrict myself to cold tongue and a glass of water."

He handed me the card, and I ordered all I decently could in the face of this frugality.

"You are still—publishing—advertising——?" he asked. "Was it not something of the sort?"

His manner of asking personal questions was of that kind not uncommonly to be found which is completely divorced from any interest in the answer. He was always prepared to embark on a lengthy cross-examination of almost anyone he might meet, at the termination of which—apart from such details as might chance to concern himself—he had absorbed no more about the person interrogated than he knew at the outset of the conversation. At the same time this process seemed somehow to gratify his own egotism.

"I was in publishing. Art books. Now it is the film business."

"Indeed? What unusual ways you choose to earn a living. Not acting, surely?"

"Hardly. I am on what is called the 'scenario side'. I help to write that part of the programme known as the 'second feature'. For every foot of American film shown in this country, a proportionate length of British film must appear. The Quota, in fact."

"Ah, yes, the Quota, the Quota," said Widmerpool, cutting short any further explanation, which would certainly have been tedious enough. "Well, I never expected to sit at the same table as host of a man who wrote films for the Quota. Do you like the work?"

"Not greatly."

"It may lead to something better. If you are industrious, you get on. That is true of all professions, even the humblest. You will probably end up in Hollywood, or somewhere like that. But tell me, do you still see those friends of yours, Stringham and Templer?"

"Stringham I haven't seen since the night he got so tight, and you and I helped to put him to bed. I rang up a day or two later and found he had gone abroad. From what I hear, he is drinking enough to float a battleship. There was even a question of taking a cure."

"And Templer?"

"I see him occasionally. Not for rather a long time, as it happens. You know his marriage broke up?"

"Like Stringham's," said Widmerpool. "Your friends do not seem very fortunate in their matrimonial ventures. I run across Templer sometimes in the City. We have even done a little business together. I was able to fix up a job for Bob Duport, that rather disreputable brother-in-law of his."

"So I heard."

"Oh, he told you, did he?" said Widmerpool, gratified at this action of his being so widely known. "I believe there were various repercussions from that good turn I was able to do him. For instance, Duport was living apart from his wife. He had behaved rather badly, so people say. When he got this job, the two of them patched things up again, and she went back to him. I was glad to have been the cause of that. We all three had dinner together. Rather an odd woman. Moody, I should think. She didn't seem particularly pleased at the reunion. Not at all grateful to me, at least."

"Why not?"

"I couldn't say. She hardly spoke a word throughout the course of an extremely good dinner at the Savoy. I may say it cost me quite a lot of money. Not that I grudge it. They are in South America now, I believe. Did you ever meet either of them?"

"Met him once with Templer when I was an undergraduate."

"And her?"

"I knew her a bit. In fact I first met her ages ago when I stayed with the Templers. Peter's father was still alive then."

"Not unattractive."

"No."

"Quite elegant in her way too."

"Yes."

"Too good for Duport, I should have thought."

"Possibly."

Widmerpool could not have had the smallest notion of

anything that had taken place between Jean Duport and myself; but people are aware of things like this within themselves without knowing of their own awareness. In any case, conscious or unconscious, Widmerpool had the knack of treading on the corns of others. His next question seemed to show the extraordinary telepathic connexion of ideas that so often takes place in the mind when anything in the nature of being in love is concerned.

"You are not married yourself, are you, Nicholas?"

"No."

"Not—like me—about to take the plunge?"

"I haven't properly congratulated you yet."

Widmerpool bowed his head in acknowledgment. The movement could almost have been called gracious. He beamed across the table. At that moment the prospect of marriage seemed all he could desire.

"I do not mind informing you that my lady mother thinks well of my choice," he said.

There was no answer to that beyond agreeing that Mrs. Widmerpool's approval was gratifying. If Mrs. Haycock could face such a mother-in-law, one hurdle at least—and no minor one, so it seemed to me—had been cleared.

"There are, of course, a few small matters my mother will expect to be satisfactorily arranged."

"I expect so."

"But Mildred will fall in with these, I am sure."

I thought the two of them, Mrs. Widmerpool and Mrs. Haycock, were probably worthy of the other's steel. Perhaps Widmerpool, in his heart, thought so too, for his face clouded over slightly, after the first look of deep satisfaction. He fell into silence. When pondering a matter of importance to himself, his jaws would move up and down as if consuming some immaterial substance. Although he had finished his slices of tongue, this movement now began. I guessed that he intended to pose some question, the precise form of which he could not yet decide. The men with yellow faces at the next table were talking international politics.

"*C'est incontestable, cher ami, Hitler a renoncé à son intention d'engouffrer l'Autriche par une agression directe.*"

"*A mon avis—et d'ailleurs je l'ai toujours dit—la France avait tort de s'opposer à l'union douanière en '31.*"

The fat man had moved on to steak-and-kidney pudding, leeks and mashed potato, with a green salad. Widmerpool cleared his throat. Something was on his mind. He began in a sudden burst of words.

"I had a special reason for inviting you to lunch today, Nicholas. I wanted to speak of my engagement. But it is not easy for me to explain in so many words what I desire to say."

He spoke sententiously, breaking off abruptly. I had an uneasy feeling, unlikely as this would be, that he might be about to ask me to act as best man at his wedding. I began to think of excuses to avoid such a duty. However, it turned out he had no such intention. It seemed likely, on second thoughts, that he wanted to discuss seriously some matter regarding himself which he feared might, on ventilation, cause amusement. Certainly I found it difficult to take his engagement seriously. There is, for some reason, scarcely any subject more difficult to treat with gravity if you are not yourself involved. Obviously two people were contemplating a step which would affect their future lives in the most powerful manner; and yet the outward appearance of the two of them, and Widmerpool's own self-sufficiency, made it impossible to consider the matter without inner amusement.

"Years ago I told you I was in love with Barbara Goring," said Widmerpool slowly.

"I remember."

"Barbara is a thing of the past. I want her entirely forgotten."

"Why not? I shan't stand up at your wedding and say: 'This ceremony cannot continue—the bridegroom once loved another!'"

"Quite so, quite so," said Widmerpool, grunting out a laugh. "You are absolutely right to make a joke of it. At the same time, I thought I should mention my feelings on that subject. One cannot be too careful."

"And I presume you want Gypsy Jones forgotten too?"

Widmerpool flushed.

"Yes," he said. "She too, of course."

His complacency seemed to me at that time intolerable. Now, I can see he required only to discuss his own situation with someone he had known for a long period, who was at the same time not too closely associated with his current life. For that rôle I was peculiarly eligible. More than once before, he had told me of his emotional upheavals—it was only because of that I knew so much about Barbara Goring and Gypsy Jones—and, when a confessor has been chosen, the habit is hard to break. At the same time, his innate suspicion of everyone inhibited even his taste for talking about himself.

"Mildred is, of course, rather older than I," he said.

I felt in some manner imprisoned by his own self-preoccupation. He positively forced one to agree that his own affairs were intensely important: indeed, the only existing question of any real interest. At the same time his intense egotism somehow dried up all sympathy for him. Clearly there was much about his present circumstances that made him nervous. That was, after all, natural enough for anyone contemplating marriage. Yet there seemed more here than the traditionally highly-strung state of a man who has only lately proposed and been accepted. I remembered that he had never asked Barbara Goring to marry him, because in those days he was not rich enough to marry. He read my thoughts, as people do when their intuition is sharpened by intensity of interest excited by discussing themselves.

"She was left with a bit of money by Haycock," he said. "Though her financial affairs are in an appalling mess."

"I see."

"How long have you known Lady Molly?"

"That was the first night I had been there."

"I wish I had known her in the great days," he said. "I cannot say that I greatly care for the atmosphere of her present home."

"You would prefer Dogdene?"

"I believe that in many ways Dogdene was far from ideally run either," said Widmerpool curtly. "But at least it provided a suitable background for a *grande dame*. Mildred is a friend of the present Lady Sleaford, so that I dare say in due course I shall be able to judge how Lady Molly must have looked there."

This manner of describing Molly Jeavons somehow affronted me, not so much from disagreement, or on account of its pretentious sound, but because I had not myself given Widmerpool credit for thus estimating her qualities, even in his own crude terms. I was, indeed, surprised that he did not dismiss her as a failure, noting at the same time his certainty of invitation to Dogdene. From what Chips Lovell used to say on that subject, I was not sure that Widmerpool might not be counting his chickens before they were hatched.

"It is because of Dogdene, as you know yourself, that Mildred is such an old friend of Lady Molly's. Perhaps not a very close friend, but they have known each other a long time."

"Yes?"

I could not guess what he was getting at.

"In fact we first met at Lady Molly's."

"I see."

"Mildred is—how shall I put it—a woman of the world like Lady Molly—but—well—hardly with Lady Molly's easy-going manner of looking at things—I don't mean that exactly—in some ways Mildred is very easy-going—but she likes her own way—and—in her own manner—takes life rather seriously——"

He suddenly began to look wretched, much as I had often seen him look as a schoolboy: lonely: awkward: unpopular: odd; no longer the self-confident business-man into which he had grown. His face now brought back the days when one used to watch him plodding off through the drizzle to undertake the long, solitary runs across the dismal fields beyond the sewage farms: runs which were to train him for teams in which he was never included. His jaws ceased to move up and down. He drank off a second glass of water.

"Anyway, you know General and Mrs. Conyers," he said.

He added this rather lamely, as if he lacked strength of mind to pursue the subject upon which he hoped to embark.

"I am going to tea with them this afternoon as it happens."

"Why on earth are you doing that?"

"I haven't seen them for a long time. We've known them for ages, as I told you."

"Oh, well, yes, I see."

He seemed disturbed by the information. I wondered whether Mrs. Conyers had already shown herself "against" the marriage. Certainly she had been worried about her sister at the Jeavons house. I had supposed the sight of Widmerpool himself to have set her fears at rest. Even if prepared on the whole to accept him, she may have let fall some remark that evening unintentionally wounding to his self-esteem. He was immensely touchy. However, his present uneasiness appeared to be chiefly vested in his own ignorance of how much I already knew about his future wife. Evidently he could not make up his mind upon this last matter. The uncertainty irked him.

"Then you must have heard all about Mildred?" he persisted.

"No, not much. I only know about Mrs. Conyers, so to speak. And I have often been told stories about their father, of course. I know hardly anything about the other sisters. Mrs. Haycock was married to an Australian, wasn't she? I knew she had two husbands, both dead."

"Only that?"

Widmerpool paused, disappointed by my ignorance, or additionally suspicious; perhaps both. He may have decided that for his purposes I knew at once too much and too little.

"You realise," he said slowly, "that Mildred has been used to a lot of her own way—her own way of life, that is. Haycock left her—in fact even encouraged her—so it seems to me—to lead—well—a rather—rather independent sort of life. They were—as one might say—a very modern married couple."

"Beyond the fact that they lived on the Riviera, I know scarcely anything about them."

"Haycock had worked very hard all his life. He wanted some relaxation in his later days. That was understandable. They got on quite well so far as I can see."

I began to apprehend a little of what Widmerpool was hinting. Mrs. Haycock's outline became clearer. No doubt she had graduated from an earlier emancipation of slang and cigarettes, to a habit of life with threatening aspects for a future husband.

"Did they have any children?"

"Yes," said Widmerpool. "They did. Mildred has two

children. That does not worry me. Not at all. Glad to start with a family."

He said all this so aggressively that I suspected a touch of bravado. Then he paused. I was about to ask the age and sex of the children, when he began to speak hurriedly again, the words tumbling out as if he wanted to finish with this speech as quickly as possible.

"I should not wish to appear backward in display of affection," he said, developing an increased speed with every phrase, "and, in addition to that, I don't see why we should delay unduly the state in which we shall spend the rest of our life merely because certain legal and religious formalities take time to arrange. In short, Nicholas, you will, I am sure, agree—more especially as you seem to spend a good deal of your time with artists and film-writers and people of that sort, whose morals are proverbial—that it would be permissible on my part to suppose—once the day of the wedding has been fixed—that we might—occasionally enjoy each other's company—say, over a week-end——"

He came to a sudden stop, looking at me rather wildly.

"I don't see why not."

It was impossible to guess what he was going to say next. This was all far from anything for which I had been prepared.

"In fact my fiancée—Mildred, that is—might even expect such a suggestion?"

"Well, yes, from what you say."

"Might even regard it as *usage du monde*?"

"Quite possible."

Then Widmerpool sniggered. For some reason I was conscious of embarrassment, even of annoyance. The problem could be treated, as it were, clinically, or humorously; a combination of the two approaches was distasteful. I had the impression that the question of how he should behave worried him more on account of the figure he cut in the eyes of Mrs. Haycock than because his passion could not be curbed. However, to have released from his mind these observations had clearly been a great relief to him. Now he cheered up a little.

"There is a further point," he said. "As my name is an uncommon one, I take it I should be called upon to provide myself with a sobriquet."

"I suppose so."

"In your own case, the difficulty would scarcely arise—so many people being called 'Jenkins'."

"It may surprise you to hear that when I embark on clandestine week-ends, I call myself 'Widmerpool'."

Widmerpool laughed with reasonable heartiness at that fancy. All the same, the question of what name should cover the identity of Mrs. Haycock and himself when first appearing as husband and wife still worried him.

"But what surname *do* you think should be employed?" he asked in a reflective tone, speaking almost to himself.

" 'Mr. and Mrs. Smith' would have the merit of such absolute banality that it would almost draw attention to yourselves. Besides, you might be mistaken for the Jeavonses' borrowed butler."

Widmerpool, still pondering, ignored this facetiousness, regarding me with unseeing eyes.

" 'Mr. and the Honourable Mrs. Smith?' You might feel that more in keeping with your future wife's rank and station. That, in any case, would strike a certain note of originality in the circumstances."

At this suggestion, Widmerpool laughed outright. The pleasantry undoubtedly pleased him. It reminded him of the facts of his engagement, showing that I had not missed the point that, whatever her shortcomings, Mildred was the daughter of a peer. His face lighted up again.

"I suppose it should really be quite simple," he said.

"After all, the booking clerk at an hotel does not actually ask every couple if they are married."

"In any case, you are both going to get married."

"Yes, of course," he said.

"So there does not seem much to worry about."

'No, I suppose not. All the same, I do not like doing irregular things. But this time, I think I should be behaving rightly in allowing a lapse of this kind. It is expected of me."

Gloom again descended upon him. There could be no doubt that the thought of the projected week-end worried him a great deal. I could see that he regarded its achievement, perhaps rightly, as a crisis in his life.

"And then, where to go?" he remarked peevishly.

"Had you thought at all?"

"Of course it must be a place where neither of us is recognised—I don't want any——"

His words died away.

"Any what?"

"Any jokes," he said irritably.

"Of course not."

"The seaside, do you think?"

"Do you play any games still? Golf? You used to play golf, didn't you? Some golfing resort?"

"I gave up golf. No time."

Again he looked despairing. He had devoted so much energy to achieving his present position in the world that even golf had been discarded. There was something impressive in this admission. We sat for a time in silence. The fat man was now enjoying the first taste of some apple-pie liberally covered with cream and brown sugar. The yellow-faced couple were still occupied with the situation in Central Europe.

"La position de Dollfuss envers le parti national-socialiste autrichien serait insoutenable s'il comptait sur une gou-

vernement soi-disant parlementaire: il faut bien l'avouer."

"Heureusement le chancelier autrichien n'est pas accablé d'un tel handicap administratif."

Widmerpool may have caught some of their words. In any case, he must have decided that the question of his own immediate problems had been sufficiently ventilated. He, too, began to speak of international politics; and with less pessimism than might have been expected.

"As you probably know," he said, "my opinions have moved steadily to the left of late years. I quite see that there are aspects of Hitler's programme to which objection may most legitimately be taken. For example, I myself possess a number of Jewish friends, some of them very able men— Jimmy Klein, for example—and I should therefore much prefer that item of the National Socialist policy to be dropped. I am, in fact, not at all sure that it will *not* be dropped when matters get straightened out a bit. After all, it is sometimes forgotten that the National Socialists are not only 'national', they are also 'socialist'. So far as that goes, I am with them. They believe in planning. Everyone will agree that there was a great deal of the old Germany that it was right to sweep away—the Kaisers and Krupps, Hindenburgs and mediatised princes, stuff of that sort—we want to hear no more about them. Certainly not. People talk of rearming. I am glad to say the Labour Party is against it to a man – and the more enlightened Tories, too. There is far too much disregard, as it is, of the equilibrium to be maintained between the rate of production and consumption in the aggregate, without the additional interference of a crushing armaments programme. We do not want an obstacle like that in the way of the organised movement towards progressive planning in the economic world of today. People talk of non-aggression pacts between France, Belgium and ourselves. The plain consequences of any such scatter-brained military commitments would be merely to augment existing German fears of complete encirclement. No, no, none of that, please. What is much more likely to be productive is to settle things round a table. Business-men of the right sort. Prominent trade unionists. Sir Magnus Donners could probably play his part. If Germany wants her former colonies, hand them back to her. What is the objection? They are no use to anyone else. Take a man like Goering. Now, it seems pretty plain to me from looking at photographs of him in the papers that he only likes swaggering about in uniforms and decorations. I expect he is a bit of a snob—most of us are at heart—well, ask him to Buckingham Palace. Show him round. What is there against giving him the Garter? After all, it is what such things are for, isn't it? Coffee?"

"Yes, black."

"You can have it downstairs. I never take coffee."

"Talking of uniforms, are you still a Territorial?"

"I *am* still a Territorial," said Widmerpool, smiling with some satisfaction. "I hold the rank of captain. I can perfectly follow your train of thought. You suppose that because I am opposed to sabre-rattling in the direction of our Teutonic neighbours, that therefore I must be the sort of man incapable of holding his own in an officers' mess. Let me assure you that such is not the case. Between you and me, I am by no means averse from issuing orders. An army —even an amateur army—is no bad school in which to learn to command—and you must know how to command in business, my dear Nicholas, as much as in any army. Besides that, one has in a battalion opportunity for giving expression to one's own point of view—a point of view often new to the persons I find myself among. These young bank clerks, accountants and so on, excellent Territorial officers, are naturally quite unfamiliar with the less limited world inhabited by someone like myself. I make it my business to instruct them. However, I dare say I may have to give up my Territorials when I get married. I do not know about that yet."

At last it was time for me to go on my way.

"So you are off to have tea with some of my future in-laws, are you?" said Widmerpool, at the door of the club. "Well, you mustn't repeat to them some of the things we have talked about. I am sure the General would be greatly shocked."

He sniggered once again, making one of his awkward gestures of farewell that looked as if he were shaking his fist. I went down the steps feeling strangely dejected. It was a sunny afternoon and there was time to kill before the Conyers visit. I tried to persuade myself that the gloom that had descended upon me was induced by Widmerpool's prolonged political dissertations, but in my heart I knew that it's true cause was all this talk of marriage. With the age of thirty in sight a sense of guilt in relation to that subject makes itself increasingly felt. It was all very well mentally to prepare ribald jokes about Widmerpool's honeymoon for such friends who knew him, and certainly nothing could be more grotesque than his approach to the matter in hand. That was undeniable. Yet one day, I knew, life would catch up with me too; like Widmerpool, I should be making uneasy preparations to "settle down". Should I, when the time came to "take the plunge", as he had called it, feel inwardly less nervous about the future than he? Should I cut a better figure? This oppression of the heart was intensified by a peculiar awareness that the time was not far distant; even though I could think of no one whose shadow fell across such a speculation.

Dismissing my own preoccupations and trying to consider Widmerpool's position objectively, I found it of interest. For example, he was about to become brother-in-law of General Conyers, now little short of an octogenarian. I did not know whom the remaining Blaides sisters had married—one, at least, had remained single—but their husbands must all have been years senior to Widmerpool, even though they might be younger than the General. I attempted to find some parallel, however far-fetched, to link Widmerpool with General Conyers; thereby hoping to construct one of those formal designs in human behaviour which for some reason afforded an obscure satisfaction to the mind: making the more apparent inconsistencies of life easier to bear. A list could be compiled. Both were accustomed to live by the will: both had decided for a time to carve out a career unburdened by a wife: both were, in very different ways, fairly successful men. There the comparison seemed to break down.

However, the family connexions of Mrs. Conyers had been thought by some to have played a part in bringing her husband to the altar; similar considerations might well be operating in the mind of Widmerpool where her sister was concerned. That would not be running contrary to his character. Alternatively, any such estimate of his motives—or the General's—might be completely at fault. In either case, love rather than convenience might dominate action. Indeed, such evidence as I possessed of Widmerpool's former behaviour towards women indicated a decided lack of restraint, even when passion was unsatisfied.

Then there was Mrs. Haycock herself. Why on earth—so her circumstances presented themselves to me—should she wish to marry Widmerpool? Such an inability to assess physical attraction or community of interest is, of course, common enough. Where the opposite sex is concerned, especially in relation to marriage, the workings of the imagination, or knowledge of the individuals themselves, are overwhelmed by the subjective approach. Only by admitting complete ignorance from the start can some explanation sometimes slowly be built up. I wondered, for example, whether she saw in Widmerpool the solid humdrum qualities formerly apparent in her Australian husband: although no evidence whatever justified the assumption that her Australian husband had been either solid or humdrum. For all I knew, he might have been a good-for-nothing of the first water. Once again, it was possible that Mrs. Haycock herself was in love. The fact that Widmerpool seemed a grotesque figure to some who knew him provided no reason why he should not inspire love in others. I record these speculations not for their subtlety, certainly not for their generosity of feeling, but to emphasise the difficulty in understanding, even remotely, why people behave as they do.

The question of love was still apt to be associated in my own mind with thoughts of Jean; additionally so since Widmerpool had spoken of her brother, Peter Templer, and her husband, Bob Duport: even making inquiries about Jean herself. Evidently she had impressed him in some way. Could I safely assure myself that I was no longer in love with her? I had recently decided, at last with some sense of security, that life could proceed on that assumption. All the same, it was not uniformly easy to state this decision to myself with a feeling of absolute confidence; even though I found myself dwelling less than formerly on the question of whether we could have "made a success of it". For a moment the thought of her reunited to Duport had brought to the heart a touch of the red-hot pincers: a reminder of her voice saying "that was rather a wet kiss".

Some people dramatise their love affairs—as I was doing at that moment—by emphasis on sentiment and sensuality; others prefer the centre of the stage to be occupied by those aspects of action and power that must also play so prominent a part in love. Adepts of the latter school try to exclude, or at least considerably to reduce, the former emotions. Barnby would rarely admit himself "in love" with the women he pursued: Baby Wentworth was believed never to speak another civil word to a man after taking him as a lover. The exhibitionism of publicity is necessary to one, just as to another is a physical beauty that must be universally acknowledged. Peter Templer liked to be seen about with "obvious beauties": Bijou Ardglass, to be photographed in the papers with her lover of the moment. Most individual approaches to love, however unexpected, possess a logic of their own; for only by attempting to find some rationalisation of love in the mind can its burdens easily be borne. Sentiment and power, each in their way, supply something to feed the mind, if not the heart. They are therefore elements operated often to excess by persons in temperament unable to love at all, yet at the same time unwilling to be left out of the fun, or to bear the social stigma of living emotionally uninteresting lives.

I thought of some of these things as I made my way, later that afternoon, towards Sloane Square, the neighbourhood where General and Mrs. Conyers still inhabited the flat which I had visited as a small boy. I felt, to tell the truth, rather out of practice for paying a call of this sort. I was usually away from London on Sunday, certainly unaccustomed to spend the afternoon at tea with an elderly general and his wife. Even tea at the Ufford with Uncle Giles would take place only a couple of times within a period of about three years. However, this seemed one of several hints of change that had become noticeable lately, suggesting those times when the ice-floes of life's river are breaking up—as in that scene in *Resurrection*—to float down-stream, before the torrent freezes again in due course into new and deceptively durable shape.

Although I used to see the General or Mrs. Conyers once in a way when I was younger, usually with my parents at the Grand Military (the General himself had formerly done some steeplechasing) or at some point-to-point at Hawthorn Hill, the last of these meetings between us had taken place years before. The Conyers's flat, when I arrived there, appeared considerably smaller than I remembered. Otherwise the place was unchanged. There on the bookcase was the photograph of the General with his halberd. The 'cello I could not immediately locate. The reason for this became apparent a moment or two after I had been greeted by Mrs. Conyers, when a low melancholy wailing began all at once to echo from somewhere not far off, persistent, though muffled by several doors: notes of a hidden orchestra, mysterious, even a shade unearthly, as if somewhere in the vicinity gnomes were thumbing strange instruments in a cave. Then the music swelled in volume like a street band coming level with the window, so that one felt instinctively for a coin to throw down.

"Aylmer will be with us in a minute," said Mrs. Conyers. "He always practises until five o'clock when we are in London. As you were coming this afternoon he agreed to finish a little earlier. He is never satisfied with his execution."

"The piece seems familiar."

"*Ave Maria.*"

"But, of course."

"When it isn't Gounod, it is Marcello's sonatas."

The thought of the General at his 'cello conjured up one of those Dutch genre pictures, sentimental yet at the same time impressive, not only on account of their adroit recession and delicate colour tones, but also from the deep social conviction of the painter. For some reason I could not help imagining him scraping away in the uniform of the Bodyguard, helmet resting on a carved oak chest and halberd leaning against the wall. Mrs. Conyers dismissed her husband's cadences, no doubt only too familiar.

"What a strange household that is of Lady Molly's," she said. "I don't mind telling you that I find *him* rather difficult. He seems to have nothing whatever to talk about.

72

He once told me of a wonderfully cheap place to buy white cotton shirts for men. Of course, Aylmer was glad to know of the shop, only you don't want to go on discussing it for ever. So tedious for his wife, it must be, but she doesn't seem to mind it. All the Ardglass family are very odd. I believe you come across all kinds of people at the Jeavonses —some of them decidedly what my father used to call 'rum'. Of course that was where my sister first met Mr. Widmerpool. How funny you should know him already."

She spoke with some show of indifference, but there could be no doubt that her unconcern was simulated and that she longed to discuss the engagement exhaustively: probably hoping to hear special revelations about Widmerpool before her husband joined us.

"I know him quite well. In fact, I have just been lunching with him."

Mrs. Conyers was enchanted at this news.

"Then you can really tell us what he is like," she said. "We have heard some—of course I don't believe them—not exactly flattering accounts of him. Naturally you don't want to listen to everything you hear, but Mildred *is* my youngest sister, and she *does* do some rather reckless things sometimes. Do describe him to me."

At that moment tea was brought in by the maid, and, before Mrs. Conyers could further insist upon a reply, the General himself appeared. He was still limping slightly from his fall. He grasped my arm near the elbow for a second in a grip of steel, as if making a sudden arrest. Generals, as a collective rank, incline physically to be above, or below, average stature. Aylmer Conyers, notably tall, possessed in addition to his height, much natural distinction. In fact, his personality filled the room, although without active aggression. At the same time he was a man who gave the impression, rightly or wrongly, that he would stop at nothing. If he decided to kill you, he would kill you; if he thought it

73

sufficient to knock you down, he would knock you down: if a mere reprimand was all required, he would confine himself to a reprimand. In addition to this, he patently maintained a good-humoured, well-mannered awareness of the inherent failings of human nature: the ultimate futility of all human effort. He wore an unusually thick, dark hairy suit, the coat cut long, the trousers narrow, a high stiff collar, of which the stud was revealed by the tie, and beautifully polished boots of patent leather with grey cloth tops. He looked like an infinitely accomplished actor got up to play the part that was, in fact, his own. At the same time he managed to avoid that almost too perfect elegance of outward appearance to be found in some men of his sort, especially courtiers. The hairiness of the suit did that. It suggested that a touch of rough force had been retained as a reminder of his strenuous past, like ancient, rusty armour hanging among luxurious tapestries.

"Never get that last bit right," he said. "... *Nunc et in hora mortis nostrae* ... always a shade flat on that high note in *hora* ..."

He slowly shook his head, at the same time lowering himself into an arm-chair, while he straightened out his left leg with both hands as if modelling a piece of delicate sculpture. Evidently it was still rather painfully stiff. After achieving the best angle for comfort, he began to conduct through the air the strokes of an imaginary baton, at the same time allowing himself to hum under his breath:

> "*Tum, tumtitty, tum-te-tum*
> *Te-tum te-titty tum-tum-te-titty,* **tum-te-titty**
> *Amen, A-a-a-a-ame-e-e-en* ..."

Mrs. Conyers, throughout these movements and sounds, all of which she completely ignored, could scarcely wait for the maid carrying the tea-tray to leave the room.

"Too late to learn at my age, much too late," said the General. "But I go on trying. Never mind, I'm not getting on too badly with those arrangements of Saint-Saëns."

"Aylmer, you remember I told you Nicholas knows Mr. Widmerpool?"

"What, this Nicholas?"

"Yes."

"You know the fellow who is going to marry Mildred?"

"Yes."

If Mrs. Conyers had already told her husband of my acquaintance with Widmerpool, the General had entirely forgotten about that piece of information, for it now came to him as something absolutely new, and, for some reason, excruciatingly funny, causing him to fall into an absolute paroxysm of deep, throaty guffaws, like the inextinguishable laughter of the Homeric gods on high Olympus, to whose characteristic faults and merits General Conyers's own nature probably approximated closely enough. A twinge of pain in his leg brought this laughter to an end in a fit of coughing.

"What sort of a fellow is he?" he asked, speaking now more seriously. "We haven't heard too satisfactory an account of him, have we, Bertha? Is he a good fellow? He'll have his hands full with Mildred, you may be sure of that. Much younger than her, isn't he?"

"I was at school with him. He must be about——"

"Nonsense," said the General. "You can't have been at school with him. You must be thinking of someone else of that name—a younger brother, I expect."

"He is a year or two older than me——"

"But you couldn't have been *at school* with him. No, no, you couldn't have been at school with him."

Mrs. Conyers, too, now shook her head in support of her husband. This claim to have been at school with Widmerpool was something not to be credited. Like most people who have known someone as a child, they were unwilling to believe that I could possibly have arrived at an age to be reasonably regarded as an adult. To have ceased, very recently, to have been an undergraduate was probably about the furthest degree of maturity either of them would easily be inclined to concede. That Widmerpool's name could be put forward as a contemporary of myself was obviously the worst shock the General had yet sustained on the subject. His earlier attitude suggested the whole affair to be one of those ludicrous incidents inseparable from anything to do with his wife's family; but the news that he might be about to possess an additional brother-in-law more or less of an age with myself disturbed him more than a little. He began to frown angrily.

"I met a young fellow called Truscott last week," he said. "There was a question of his coming on to a board from which I retired the other day. He is connected with the by-products of coal and said to have a good brain. I asked him if by any chance he knew Widmerpool—without divulging the nature of my interest, of course—and he spoke with the greatest dislike of him. The greatest dislike. It turned out they had been in Donners-Brebner together at one time. Truscott said Widmerpool was a terrible fellow. Couldn't trust him an inch. Now that may be a pack of lies. I've never been in the habit of listening to gossip. Haven't got time for it. Naturally I didn't tell Truscott that, in case it made him dry up. Thought it my duty to hear whatever he had to get off his chest. I must say he produced a whole string of crimes to be laid at Widmerpool's door, not the least of which was to have got him—Truscott—sacked from Donners-Brebner. Now what I say is that a man who marries Mildred must be a man with a will of his own. No good marrying Mildred otherwise. Now a man with a will of his own is often a man to make enemies. I know that as well as anyone. Evidently Widmerpool had made an enemy of Truscott. That isn't necessarily anything against Widmerpool. He may be an excellent fellow in spite of that. Getting rid of Truscott may have been a piece of first-class policy. Who am I to judge? But what I do know is this. Bertha's sister, Mildred, has been used to a lot of her own way. Do you think that Mr. Widmerpool is going to be able to manage a woman some years older than himself and used to a lot of her own way?"

I had not thought of Truscott for years. At the university he had been billed for a great career: prime minister: lord chancellor: famous poet: it was never finally decided which rôle he would most suitably ornament; perhaps all three. Now I remembered being told by someone or other that Widmerpool, before himself leaving the firm, had contrived to have Truscott ejected from Donners-Brebner. The General had certainly brought a crisp, military appraisal to the situation. I was wondering what to answer—since I saw no way of giving a simple reply to a subject so complicated as Widmerpool's character—when the maid reappeared to announce another guest.

"Lady Frederica Budd."

The niece whose condition of unassailable rectitude had given such satisfaction to Alfred Tolland, and at the same time caused some unfriendly amusement to Molly Jeavons, was shown into the room. This crony of Mrs. Conyers, widow with several children and lady-in-waiting, was a handsome woman in her thirties. She was dressed in a manner to be described as impregnable, like a long, neat, up-to-date battle-cruiser. You felt that her clothes were certainly removed when she retired for the night, but that no intermediate adjustment, however minor, was ever required, or would, indeed, be practicable. This was the eldest of the Tolland sisters, formed physically in much the same mould as Blanche and Priscilla; though I could see no resemblance between her and her brothers as I remembered them. She kissed Mrs. Conyers. The General greeted her warmly, though with a touch of irony in his manner. I was introduced. Lady Frederica looked at me carefully, rather as if she were engaged upon an army inspection: a glance not unfriendly, but extensively searching. I could see at once that she and Molly Jeavons would not be a couple easily to agree. Then she turned towards the General.

"How are you feeling after your fall?" she asked.

"A bit stiff. A bit stiff. Took a fearful toss. Nearly broke my neck. And you, Frederica?"

"Oh, I've been rather well," she said. "Christmas was spoiled by two of the children developing measles. But they have recovered now. All very exhausting while it lasted."

"I spent Christmas Day cleaning out the kennels," said the General. "Went to Early Service. Then I got into my oldest clothes and had a thorough go at them. Had luncheon late and a good sleep after. Read a book all the evening. One of the best Christmas Days I've ever had."

Frederica Tolland did not seem greatly interested by this account of the General's Christmas activities. She turned from him to Mrs. Conyers, as if she hoped for something more congenial.

"What have you been doing, Bertha?" she asked.

"I went to the sales yesterday," said Mrs. Conyers, speaking as if that were a somewhat disagreeable duty that had been long on her mind.

"Were you nearly trampled to death?"

"I came away with a hat."

"I went earlier in the week," said Frederica. "Looking for a cheap black dress, as a matter of fact. So many royalties nearing their century, we're bound to be in mourning again soon."

"Have they been working you hard?" asked the General. I had the impression that he might be a little jealous of

Frederica, who, for her part, was evidently determined that he should not be allowed to take himself too seriously. There was just a touch of sharpness in their interchanges.

"Nothing really lethal since the British Industries Fair," she said. "I had to throw away my best pair of shoes after *that*. You are lucky not to have to turn out for that sort of thing. It will finish me off one of these days."

"You come and carry my axe at the next levée," said the General. "Thought I was going to drop with fatigue the last time I was on duty. Then that damned fellow Ponsonby trod on my gouty toe."

'We saw your Uncle Alfred the other night, Frederica," said Mrs. Conyers.

She spoke either with a view to including me in the conversation or because habit had taught her that passages of this kind between her husband and Frederica Budd might become a shade acrimonious: perhaps merely to steer our talk back to the subject of Widmerpool.

"He was looking well enough," she added.

"Oh no, really?" said Frederica, plainly surprised at this. "Where did you meet him? I thought he never went out except to things like regimental dinners. That is what he always says."

"At Molly Jeavons's. I had not been there before."

"Of course. He goes there still, doesn't he? What strange people he must meet at that house. What sort of a crowd did you find? I really must go and see Molly again myself some time. For some reason I never feel very anxious to go there. I think Rob was still alive when I last went to the Jeavonses'."

These remarks, although displaying no great affection, were moderate enough, considering the tone in which Molly Jeavons herself had spoken of Frederica.

"That was where I found Nicholas again," said Mrs. Conyers.

She proceeded to give some account of why they knew me. Frederica listened with attention, rather than interest, again recalling by her manner the checking of facts in the course of some official routine like going through the Customs or having one's passport examined. Then she turned to me as if to obtain some final piece of necessary information.

"Do you often go to the Jeavonses'?" she asked.

The inquiry seemed to prepare the way to cross-questioning one returned from the remote interior of some little-known country after making an intensive study of the savage life existing there.

"That was the first time. I was taken by Chips Lovell, whom I work with."

"Oh yes," she said vaguely. "He is some sort of a relation of Molly's, isn't he?"

She showed herself not at all positive about Lovell and his place in the world. This surprised me, as I had supposed she would know him, or at least know about him, pretty well. A moment later I wondered whether possibly she knew him, but pretended ignorance because she disapproved. Lovell was by no means universally liked. There were people who considered his behaviour far from impeccable. Frederica Budd might be one of these. A guarded attitude towards Lovell was only to be expected if Molly Jeavons was to be believed. At that moment the General spoke. He had been sitting in silence while we talked, quite happy silence, so it appeared, still pondering the matter of Widmerpool and his sister-in-law; or, more probably, his own rendering of Gounod and how it could be bettered. His sonorous, commanding voice, not loud, though pitched in a tone to carry across parade-ground or battle-field, echoed through the small room.

"I like Jeavons," he said. "I only met him once, but I took to him. Lady Molly I hardly know. Her first husband,

John Sleaford, was a pompous fellow. The present Sleaford —Geoffrey—I knew in South Africa. We see them from time to time. Bertha tells me Lady Molly was teasing your Uncle Alfred a lot the other night. People say she always does that. Is it true?"

The general laughed a deep ho-ho-ho laugh again, like the demon king in pantomime. He evidently enjoyed the idea of people teasing Alfred Tolland.

"I think she may rag Uncle Alfred a bit," said Frederica, without emotion. "If he doesn't like it, he shouldn't go there. I expect Erridge came up for discussion too, didn't he?"

I suspected this was said to forestall comment about Erridge on the part of the General himself. There was a distinct rivalry between them. Men of action have, in any case, a predisposition to be jealous of women, especially if the woman is young, good looking or placed in some relatively powerful position. Beauty, particularly, is a form of power of which, perhaps justly, men of action feel envious. Possibly there existed some more particular reason: the two of them conceivably representing rival factions in their connexion with the Court. I supposed from her tone and general demeanour that Frederica could hardly approve of her eldest brother's way of life, but, unlike her uncle, was not prepared to acquiesce in all criticism of Erridge.

"Do you know my brother, Erridge—Warminster, rather?" she asked me, suddenly.

She smiled like someone who wishes to encourage a child who possesses information more acute, or more interesting, than that available to grown-ups; but one who might be too shy or too intractable to impart such knowledge.

"I used to know him by sight."

"He has some rather odd ideas," she said. "But I expect you heard plenty about that at Molly Jeavons's. They have hardly anything else to talk about there. He is a real blessing to them."

81

"Oh, I think they have got plenty to talk about," said Mrs. Conyers. "Too much, in fact."

"I don't deny that Erridge has more than one bee in his bonnet," said the General, unexpectedly. "But I doubt if he is such a fool as some people seem to think him. He is just what they call nowadays introverted."

"Oh, Erry isn't a fool," said Frederica. "He is rather too clever in a way—and an awful nuisance as an eldest brother. There may be something to be said for his ideas. It is the way he sets about them."

"Is it true that he has been a tramp?" I asked.

"Not actually been one, I think," said Frederica. "Making a study of them, isn't it?"

"Is he going to write a book about it?" asked Mrs. Conyers. "There have been several books of that sort lately, haven't there? Have you read anything else interesting, Nicholas? I always expect people like you to tell me what to put down on my library list."

"I've been reading something called *Orlando*," said the General. "Virginia Woolf. Ever heard of it?"

"I read it when it first came out."

"What do you think of it?"

"Rather hard to say in a word."

"You think so?"

"Yes."

He turned to Frederica.

"Ever read *Orlando*?"

"No," she said. "But I've heard of it."

"Bertha didn't like it," he said.

"Couldn't get on with it," said Mrs. Conyers, emphatically. "I wish St. John Clarke would write a new one. He hasn't published a book for years. I wonder whether he is dead. I used to love his novels, especially *Fields of Amaranth*."

"Odd stuff, *Orlando*," said the General, who was not

easily shifted from his subject. "Starts about a young man in the fifteen-hundreds. Then, about eighteen-thirty, he turns into a woman. You say you've read it?"

"Yes."

"Did you like it? Yes or no?"

"Not greatly."

"You didn't?"

"No."

"The woman can write, you know."

"Yes, I can see that. I still didn't like it."

The General thought again for some seconds.

"Well, I shall read a bit more of it," he said, at last. "Don't want to waste too much time on that sort of thing, of course. Now, psychoanalysis. Ever read anything about that? Sure you have. That was what I was on over Christmas."

"I've dipped into it from time to time. I can't say I'm much of an expert."

"Been reading a lot about it lately," said the General. "Freud—Jung—haven't much use for Adler. Something in it, you know. Tells you why you do things. All the same, I didn't find it much help in understanding *Orlando*."

Once more he fell into a state of coma. It was astonishing to me that he should have been reading about psychoanalysis, although his mental equipment was certainly in no way inferior to that of many persons who talked of such things all day long. When he had used the word "introverted" I had thought that no more than repetition of a current popular term. I saw now that the subject had thoroughly engaged his attention. However, he wished to discuss it no further at that moment. Neither of the two ladies seemed to share his interest.

"Is it true that your sister, Mildred, is going to marry again?" asked Frederica. "Someone told me so the other day. They could not remember the name of the man. It hasn't been in the papers yet, has it?"

She spoke casually. Mrs. Conyers was well prepared for the question, because she answered without hesitation, allowing no suggestion to appear of the doubts she had revealed to me only a short time earlier.

"The engagement is supposed to be a secret," she said, "but, as everybody will hear about it quite soon, there is really no reason to deny the rumour."

"Then it is true?"

"It certainly looks as if Mildred is going to marry again."

No one, however determined to make a good story, could have derived much additional information on the subject from the manner in which Mrs. Conyers spoke, except in so far that she could not be said to show any obvious delight at the prospect of her sister taking a third husband. That was the farthest implication offered. There was not a hint of disapproval or regret; on the contrary, complete acceptance of the situation was manifest, even mild satisfaction not openly disavowed. It was impossible to withhold admiration from this façade, so effortlessly presented.

"And he——?"

"Nicholas, here, was at school with him," said Mrs. Conyers, tranquilly.

She spoke as if most people must, as a matter of course, be already aware of that circumstance; for it now seemed that, in spite of her husband's doubts, she had finally accepted the fact that I was within a few years of Widmerpool's age. The remark only stimulated Frederica's curiosity.

"Oh, do tell me what he is like," she said. "Mildred was just that amount older than me to make her rather a thrilling figure at the time when I first came 'out'. She was at the Huntercombes' once when I stayed there not long after the war. She was rather a dashing war widow and wore huge jade ear-rings, and smoked all the time and said the most hair-raising things. What is her new name to be, first of all?"

"Widmerpool," I said, since the question was addressed to me.

"Where do they come from?" asked Mrs. Conyers, anxious to profit herself from Frederica's interrogation.

"Nottinghamshire, I believe."

This reply was at worst innocuous, and might be taken, in general, to imply a worthy family background. İt was also—as I understood from Widmerpool himself—in no way a departure from the truth. Fearing that I might, if pressed, be compelled ultimately to admit some hard things about Widmerpool, I felt that the least I could do for an old acquaintance in these circumstances was to suggest, however indirectly, a soothing picture of generations of Widmerpools in a rural setting: an ancient, if delapidated, manor house: Widmerpool tombs in the churchyard: tankards of ale at The Widmerpool Arms.

"You haven't said what his Christian name is," said Frederica, apparently accepting, anyway at this stage, the regional superscription.

"Kenneth."

"Brothers or sisters?"

"No."

I admired the thoroughness with which Frederica set to work on an inquiry of this kind, as much as I had admired Mrs. Conyers's earlier refusal to give anything away.

"And he is in the City?"

"He is supposed to be rather good at making money," interpolated Mrs. Conyers.

She had begun to smile indulgently at Frederica's unconcealed curiosity. Now she employed a respectful yet at the same time deprecatory tone, as if this trait of Widmerpool's —his supposed facility of "making money"—was, extraordinary as this might appear, a propensity not wholly unpleasant when you become accustomed to it. At the same time she abandoned her former position of apparent neutrality, openly joining in the search. Indeed, she put the next question herself.

"His father is dead, isn't he?" she said. "Nottinghamshire, did you say?"

"Or Derbyshire. I don't remember for certain."

Widmerpool had once confided the fact that his grandfather, a business-man from the Scotch Lowlands, had on marriage changed his name from "Geddes"; but such an additional piece of information would sound at that moment too esoteric and genealogical : otiose in its exactitude. In a different manner, to repeat Eleanor Walpole-Wilson's remark made years before—"Uncle George used to get his liquid manure from Mr. Widmerpool's father"—might strike, though quite illogically, a disobliging, even objectionably facetious note. Eleanor's "Uncle George" was Lord Goring. It seemed best to omit all mention of liquid manure; simply to say that Widmerpool had known the Gorings and the Walpole-Wilsons.

"Oh, the Walpole-Wilsons," said Frederica sharply, as if reminded of something she would rather forget. "Do you know the Walpole-Wilsons? My sister, Norah, shares a flat with Eleanor Walpole-Wilson. Do you know them?"

"I haven't seen Eleanor for years. Nor her parents, for that matter."

The General now came to life again, after his long period of rumination.

"Walpole-Wilson was that fellow in the Diplomatic Service who made such a hash of things in South America," he said. "Got unstuck for it. I met him at a City dinner once, the Mercers—or was it the Fishmongers? Had an argument over Puccini."

"I don't know the Gorings," said Frederica, ignoring the General. "You mean the ones called 'Lord' Goring?"

"Yes. He is a great fruit farmer, isn't he? He talked about fruit on the only occasions when I met him."

"I remember," she said. "He is."

She had uttered the words "Lord Goring" with emphasis on the title, seeming by her tone almost to suggest that all members of that particular family, male and female, might for some unaccountable reason call themselves "Lord": at least implying that, even if she did not really suppose anything so absurd, she wished to indicate that I should have been wiser to have steered clear of the Gorings: in fact, that informed persons considered the Gorings themselves mistaken in burdening themselves with the rather ridiculous pretension of a peerage. When I came to know her better I realised that her words were intended to cast no particular slur on the Gorings; merely, since they were not personal friends of hers, to build up a safe defence in case they turned out, in her own eyes, undesirable.

"I think Widmerpool *père* was mixed up with the fruit-farming side of Goring life."

"But look here," said General Conyers, suddenly emerging with terrific violence from the almost mediumistic trance in which he had sunk after the mention of Puccini. "The question is simply this. Can this fellow Widmerpool handle Mildred? It all turns on that. What do you think, Nicholas? You say you were at school with him. You usually know a fellow pretty well when you have been boys together. What's your view? Give us an appreciation of the situation."

"But I don't know Mrs. Haycock. I was only nine or ten when I first met her. Last night I barely spoke to her."

There was some laughter at that, and the necessity passed for an immediate pronouncement on the subject of Widmerpool's potentialities.

"You must meet my sister again," said Mrs. Conyers, involuntarily smiling to herself, I suppose at the thought of

Widmerpool as Mildred's husband.

After that, conversation drifted. Mrs. Conyers began once more to talk of clothes and of how her daughter, Charlotte, had had a baby in Malta. The General relapsed once more into torpor, occasionally murmuring faint musical intonations that might still be ringing the changes on "... *nunc et in hora* ..." Frederica rose to go. I gave her time to get down the stairs, and then myself said good-bye. It was agreed that so long a period must not again elapse before I paid another visit. Mrs. Conyers was one of those persons who find it difficult to part company quickly, so that it was some minutes before I reached the hall of the block of flats. In front of the entrance Frederica Budd was still sitting in a small car, which was making the horrible flat sound that indicates an engine refusing to fire.

"This wretched car won't start," she shouted.

"Can I help?"

At that moment the engine came to life.

"Shall I give you a lift?" she said.

"Which way are you going?"

"Chelsea."

I, too, was on my way to Chelsea that evening. It was a period of my life when, in recollection, I seem often to have been standing in a cinema queue with a different girl. One such evening lay ahead of me.

"Thank you very much."

"Jump in," she said.

Now that she had invited me into her car, and we were driving along together, her manner, momentarily relaxed while she had been pressing the self-starter, became once more impersonal and remote; as if "a lift" was not considered an excuse for undue familiarity between us. When the car had refused to start she had seemed younger and less chilly: less part of the impeccable Conyers world. Now she returned to an absolutely friendly, but also utterly impregnable outpost of formality.

"You have known Bertha and the General for a long time?"

"Since I was a child."

"That was when you met Mildred?"

"Yes."

"You probably know all the stories about their father, Lord Vowchurch?"

"I've heard some of them."

"The remark he is said to have made to King Edward just after Bertha's engagement had been announced?"

"I don't know that one."

"It was on the Squadron Lawns at Cowes. The King is supposed to have said: 'Well, Vowchurch, I hear you are marrying your eldest daughter to one of my generals,' and Bertha's father is said to have replied: 'By Gad, I am, sir, and I trust he'll teach the girl to lead out trumps, for they'll have little enough to live on.' Edward VII was rather an erratic bridge-player, you know. Sir Thomas Lipton told me the story in broad Scotch, which made it sound funnier. Of course, the part that appealed to Sir Thomas Lipton was the fact that it took place on the Squadron Lawn."

"How did the King take it?"

"I think he was probably rather cross. Of course it may not be true. But Lord Vowchurch certainly was always getting into trouble with the King. Lord Vowchurch was supposed to be referring to some special game of bridge when he had been dummy and things had gone badly wrong with King Edward's play. You said you'd met my Uncle Alfred, didn't you?"

"A couple of times."

"And you know whom I mean by Brabazon?"

"The Victorian dandy—'Bwab'?"

"Yes, that one."

"Who said he couldn't remember what regiment he had

exchanged into—after leaving the Brigade of Guards because it was too expensive—but 'they wore green facings and you got to them by Waterloo Station'?"

"That's him. How clever of you to know about him. Well, when Uncle Alfred was a young man, he was dining at Pratt's, and Colonel Brabazon came in from the Marlborough Club, where he had been in the card-room when the game was being played. According to Uncle Alfred, Colonel Brabazon said: 'Vowchurch expwessed weal wesentment while his Woyal Highness played the wottenest wubber of wecent seasons—nothing but we-deals and we-vokes.'"

"I had no idea your uncle had a fund of stories of that kind."

"He hasn't. That is his only one. He is rather a shy man, you see, and nothing ever happens to him."

This was all very lively; although there was at the same time always something a shade aloof about the manner in which these anecdotes were retailed. However, they carried us down the King's Road in no time. There was, in addition, something reminiscent about the tone in which they were delivered, a faint reminder of Alfred Tolland's own reserve and fear of intimacy. Amusing in themselves, the stories were at the same time plainly intended to establish a specific approach to life. Beneath their fluency, it was possible to detect in Frederica Budd herself, at least so far as personal rather than social life was concerned, a need for armour against strangers. Almost schooled out of existence by severe self-discipline, a faint trace of her uncle's awkwardness still remained to be observed under the microscope. There could be no doubt that I had scored a point by knowing about "Bwab".

"I met your sister, Priscilla, at the Jeavonses the other night—only for a minute or two. Chips Lovell drove us both home."

She did not seem much interested by that, hardly answering. I remembered, then, that she probably did not care for Lovell. However, her next words were entirely unexpected.

"I am on my way to call on my sister, Norah, now," she said. "It seemed rather a long time since I had set eyes on her. I thought I would just look in to see that she is behaving herself. Why not come and meet her—and see Eleanor again."

"Just for a second. Then I shall have to move on."

At the sound of this last statement I was aware of a faint but distinct disapproval, as if my reply had informed her quite clearly—indeed, almost grossly—that I was up to no good; yet made her at the same time realise that in a locality where so much human behaviour commanded disapprobation, minor derelictions—anyway, in a man—must, in the interest of the general picture, be disregarded. However, together with that sense of constraint that she conveyed, I was by then also aware of a second feeling: a notion that some sort of temporary alliance had been hurriedly constructed between us. I could not explain this impression to myself though I was prepared to accept it.

By that time we had arrived before a dilapidated stucco façade in a side street, a house entered by way of a creaking, unlatched door, from which most of the paint had been removed. The hall, empty except for a couple of packing-cases, gave off that stubborn musty smell characteristic of staircases leading to Chelsea flats: damp: cigar smoke: face powder. We climbed the uncarpeted boards, ascending endlessly floor after floor, Frederica Budd taking the steps two at a time at a sharp pace. At last the attics were reached; and another battered door, upon which was fastened a brass knocker, formed in the image of the Lincoln Imp. Attached with four drawing-pins to the panel below this knocker was a piece of grubby cardboard inscribed with the names:

Frederica, ignoring the claims on the Lincoln Imp, clenched her fist and banged on the door with all her force, at the same time shouting in an unexpectedly raucous voice:

"Norah! Eleanor!"

There was a sound of someone stirring within. Then Eleanor Walpole-Wilson opened the door. She was wearing a very dirty pair of navy-blue flannel trousers and smoking a stub of a cigarette. Apart from her trousers and cigarette, and also a decided air of increased confidence in herself, she had changed very little from the days when, loathing every moment of it, she used to trail round the London ballrooms. She still wore her hair in a bun, a style which by then brought her appearance almost within measurable distance of "the mode"; or at least within hail of something that might, with a little good will, be supposed unconventionally chic. Square and broad-shouldered as ever, she was plainly on much better terms with herself, and with others, than formerly.

"I've brought an old friend to see you," said Frederica.

Eleanor showed no surprise at my arrival. There was even a slight suggestion of relief that Frederica Budd had not to be entertained singly; for towards Frederica Eleanor displayed a hint of her old aggressiveness, or at least gave indication that she was on the defensive. This sense of quiet but firm opposition became more positive when we moved into the sitting-room.

"How are you, Nicholas?" said Eleanor. "Fancy your turning up here. Why, you've got a grey hair. Just above your ear."

The place was horribly untidy, worse than the Jeavonses, and the furniture struck an awkward level between boudoir and studio: an ancient sofa, so big that one wondered how it could ever have been hoisted up the last flight of stairs, stood covered with chintz roses among two or three unsubstantial, faintly "Louis" chairs. The walls had been distempered yellow by some amateur hand. A girl was lying prone on the ground, her skirt rucked up to her thighs, showing a strip of skin above each stocking. This was Norah Tolland. She was pasting scraps on to the surface of a coal-scuttle.

"Hullo, Frederica," she said, without looking up. "I shan't be a moment. I must finish this before the paste runs out."

She continued her work for a few moments, then, wiping the paste from her hands with a red check duster, she rose from the ground, pulled her skirt down impatiently and gave her sister a peck on the cheek. Eleanor presented me, explaining that we had known each other "in the old days". Norah Tolland did not look very enthusiastic at this news, but she held out her hand. She was dark and very pale, with a narrow face like her sister's, her expression more truculent, though also, on the whole, less firm in character. The coltishness of her sister, Priscilla, had turned in Norah to a deliberate, rather absurd masculinity. Frederica glanced round the room without attempting to conceal her distaste, as if she felt there was much to criticise, not least the odour of turpentine and stale cake.

"I see you haven't managed to get the window mended yet," she said.

Her sister did not answer, only flicking back her hair from her forehead with a sharp, angry motion.

"Isobel is supposed to be coming in to see us some time today," she said, "with her new young man. I thought it was her when you arrived."

"Who is her new young man?"

"How should I know? Some chap."

93

"I saw her last night at Hyde Park Gardens."

"How were they all?" said Norah, indifferently. "Would you like a drink? I think there is some sherry left."

Frederica shook her head, as if the idea of alcohol in any form at that moment nauseated her.

"You?"

"No, thank you. I must really go in a moment."

The sherry did not sound very safe: wiser to forgo it.

"Don't leave yet," said Eleanor. "You've only just arrived. We must have a word about old times. I haven't seen the Gorings for ages. I always think of you, Nicholas, as a friend of Barbara's."

"How is Barbara?"

It seemed extraordinary that I had once, like Widmerpool, thought myself in love with Barbara. Now I could hardly remember what she looked like, except that she was small and dark.

"You know she married Johnny Pardoe?" said Eleanor.

"I haven't set eyes on either of them since the wedding."

"Things have been a bit difficult."

"What?"

"There was a baby that went wrong."

"Oh, dear."

"Then Johnny got awful odd and melancholy after he left the Grenadiers. You remember he used to be an absolutely typical guardee, pink in the face and shouting at the top of his voice all the time, and yelling with laughter. Now he has quite changed, and mopes for hours or reads books on religion and philosophy."

"Johnny Pardoe?"

"He sits in the library for weeks at a time just brooding. Never shoots now. You know how much he used to love shooting. Barbara has to run the place entirely. Poor Barbara, she has an awful time of it."

Life jogs along, apparently in the same old way, and then

suddenly your attention is drawn to some terrific change that has taken place. For example, I found myself brought up short at that moment, like a horse reined in on the brink of a precipice, at the thought of the astonishing reversal of circumstances by which Eleanor Walpole-Wilson was now in a position to feel sorry for Barbara Goring—or, as she had by then been for some years, Barbara Pardoe. The relationship between these two first cousins, like all other relationships when one is young, had seemed at that time utterly immutable; Barbara, pretty, lively, noisy, popular: Eleanor, plain, awkward, cantankerous, solitary. Barbara's patronage of Eleanor was something that could never change. "Eleanor is not a bad old thing when you get to know her," she used to say; certainly without the faintest suspicion that within a few years Eleanor might be in a position to say: "Poor Barbara, she does have a time of it."

While indulging in these rather banal reflections, I became aware that the two sisters had begun to quarrel. I had not heard the beginning of the conversation that had led to this discord, but it seemed to be concerned with their respective visits that summer to Thrubworth, their brother's house.

"As you know, Erry always makes these difficulties," Frederica was saying. "It is not that I myself particularly want to go there and live in ghastly discomfort for several weeks and feel frightfully depressed at seeing the place fall to pieces. I would much rather go to the seaside or abroad. But it is nice for the children to see the house, and they enjoy going down to talk to the people at the farm, and all that sort of thing. So if you are determined to go at just that moment——"

"All right, then," said Norah, smiling and showing her teeth like an angry little vixen, "I won't go. Nothing easier. I don't particularly want to go to the bloody place either, but it is my home, I suppose. Some people might think that ought to be taken into consideration. I was born there. I can't say I've had many happy moments there, it's true, but I like walking by myself in the woods—and I have plenty of other ways of amusing myself there without bothering either you or Erry or anyone else."

Eleanor caught my eye with a look to be interpreted as indicating that high words of this kind were not unexpected in the circumstances, but that we should try to quell them. However, before dissension could develop further, it was cut short abruptly by the door of the room opening. A small, gnarled, dumpy, middle-aged woman stood on the threshold. She wore horn-rimmed spectacles and her short legs were enclosed, like Eleanor's, in blue flannel trousers—somewhat shrunk, for her largely developed thighs seemed to strain their seams—into the pockets of which her hands were deeply plunged.

"Why, hullo, Hopkins," said Norah Tolland, her face suddenly clearing, and showing, for the first time since I had been in the room, some signs of pleasure. "What can we do for you?"

"Hullo, girls," said the woman at the door.

She made no attempt to reply to Norah's question, continuing to gaze round the room, grinning broadly, but advancing no farther beyond the threshold. She gave the impression of someone doing a turn on the stage.

"If you take to leaving your front door on the latch," she said at last, "you'll find a *man* will walk in one of these days, and then where will you be, I should like to know? By Jove, I see a man has walked in already. Well, well, well, never mind. There are a lot of them about, so I suppose you can't keep them out all the time. What I came up for, dear, was to borrow an egg, if you've got such a thing. Laid one lately, either of you?"

Norah Tolland laughed.

"This is my sister, Lady Frederica Budd," she said. "And Mr.——"

"Jenkins," said Eleanor, in reply to an appeal for my name.

Eleanor was, I thought, less pleased than Norah to see the woman they called Hopkins. In fact, she seemed somewhat put out by her arrival.

"Pleased to meet you, my dear," said Hopkins, holding out her hand to Frederica; "and you, my boy," she added, smirking in my direction.

"Miss Hopkins plays the piano most nights at the Merry Thought," said Eleanor.

This explanation seemed aimed principally at Frederica.

"You ought to look in one night," said Hopkins. "But come soon, because I've got an engagement next month to appear with Max Pilgrim at the Café de Madrid. I'll have to make sure that old queen, Max, doesn't hog every number. It would be just like him. He's as vain as a peacock. Can't trust a man not to try and steal the show anyway, even the normal ones, they're the worst of all. Now the other thing I wanted to remind you girls about is my album. You've still got it. Have you thought of something nice to write in it, either of you?"

It appeared that no good idea had occurred either to Eleanor or Norah for inscription in the album.

"I shall want it back soon," said Hopkins, "because another girl I know—such a little sweetie-pie with a little fragile face like a dear little dolly—is going to write some *lovely* lines in it. Shall I repeat to you what she is going to write? You will love it."

Frederica Budd, who had been listening to all this with a slight smile, imperceptibly inclined her head, as one might when a clown inquires from his audience whether they have understood up to that point the course of the trick he is about to perform. Eleanor looked as if she did not particularly wish to hear what was offered, but regarded any demur as waste of time. Hopkins spoke the words:

> *"Lips may be redder, and eyes more bright;*
> *The face may be fairer you see tonight;*
> *But never, love, while the stars shall shine,*
> *Will you find a heart that is truer than mine."*

There was a pause when Hopkins came to the end of her recitation, which she had delivered with ardour. She struck an attitude, her hand on her hip.

"Sweet, isn't it?" she said. "This friend of mine read it somewhere, and she memorised it—and so have I. I love it so much. That's the sort of thing I want. I'll leave the album a little longer then, girls, but remember—I shall expect something really nice when you do, both of you, think of a poem. Now what about that egg?"

Norah Tolland went into the kitchen of the flat. Hopkins stood grinning at us. No one spoke. Then Norah returned. On receiving the egg, Hopkins feigned to make it disappear up the sleeves of her shirt, the cuffs of which were joined by links of black and white enamel. Then, clenching her fist, she balanced the egg upon it at arm's length, and marched out of the room chanting at the top of her voice:

> *"Balls, Picnics and Parties,*
> *Picnics, Parties and Balls ..."*

We heard the sound of her heavy, low-heeled shoes pounding the boards of the uncarpeted stairs, until at length a door slammed on a floor below, and the voice was cut off with a jerk.

"She really plays the piano jolly well," said Norah.

It was a challenge, but the glove was not picked up.

"Rather an amusing person," said Frederica. "Do you

see much of her?"

"She lives a couple of floors below," said Eleanor. "She is rather too fond of looking in at all hours."

"Oh, I don't know," said Norah. "I like Heather."

"So you've made up your mind about Thrubworth?" said Frederica, as if the merits of Hopkins were scarcely worth discussing.

I explained that I must now leave them. Frederica, at the moment of saying good-bye, spoke almost warmly; as if her conjecture that I might be a support to her had been somehow justified. Norah Tolland was curt. It was agreed that I should ring up Eleanor one of these days and come to see them again. I had the impression that my departure would be the signal for a renewed outbreak of family feuds. Anxious to avoid even their preliminary barrage, I descended the rickety, foetid stairs, and proceeded on my way.

Later that evening, I found myself kicking my heels in one of those interminable cinema queues of which I have already spoken, paired off and stationary, as if life's co-educational school, out in a "crocodile", had come to a sudden standstill: that co-educational school of iron discipline, equally pitiless in pleasure and in pain. During the eternity of time that always precedes the termination of the "big picture", I had even begun to wonder whether we should spend the rest of our days on that particular stretch of London pavement, when, at long last, just as rain had begun to fall, the portals of the auditorium burst open to void the patrons of the earlier performance. First came those scattered single figures, who, as if distraught by what they have seen and seeking to escape at whatever the cost, hurry blindly from the building, they care not how, nor where; then the long serpentine of spectators to whom expulsion into the street means no more than a need to take another decision in life; who, accordingly, postpone in the foyer any such irksome effort of the will by banding themselves into small, irregular, restless groups, sometimes static, sometimes ineffectively mobile. As the queue of which we formed a link stumbled forward towards the booking office, I discerned through the mist of faces that must dissolve before we could gain our seats, the features of J. G. Quiggin. Our eyes met. He shook his head sharply from side to side, as if to express satisfaction that we should run into each other in so opportune a manner. A moment later he was near enough to make his small, grating tones heard above the murmur of other voices.

"I've been trying to get hold of you," he said.

"We must meet."

"There were some things I wanted to talk about."

Since we had been undergraduates together my friendship with Quiggin, moving up and down at different seasons, could have been plotted like a temperature chart. Sometimes we seemed on fairly good terms, sometimes on fairly bad terms; never with any very concrete reason for these improvements and deteriorations. However, if Quiggin thought it convenient to meet during a "bad" period, he would always take steps to do so, having no false pride in this or any other aspect of his dealings with the world. After such a meeting, a "good" period would set in; to be dissipated after a time by argument, disagreement or even by inanition. This periodicity of friendship and alienation had rotated, almost like the seasons of the year, until a year or two before: a time when Quiggin had "run away" with Peter Templer's wife, Mona. This act threatened to complicate more seriously any relationship that might exist between Quiggin and myself.

As things turned out, I had seen nothing either of Templer or Quiggin during the period immediately following the divorce. Templer had always been out or engaged when I had telephoned to him; and, as we had by then little left in common except having been friends at school, our intermittent meetings had entirely ceased. There was perhaps another reason why I felt unwilling to make more strenuous efforts to see him. He reminded me of Jean. That was an additional reason for allowing this course to prevail. I heard quite by chance that he had sold his Maidenhead house. It was said, whatever his inner feelings about losing Mona, that outwardly he was not taking things too hard: demonstrating a principle he had once expressed: "Women always think if they've knocked a man out, that they've knocked him out cold—on the contrary, he sometimes gets up again." However, no husband enjoys his wife leaving the house from one day to the next, especially with someone like Quiggin, in Templer's eyes unthinkable as a rival. Quiggin, indeed, belonged to a form of life entirely separate from Templer's, so that gossip on the subject of the divorce was exchanged within unconnected compartments: Templer's City acquaintances on the one hand: on the other, the literary and political associates of Quiggin.

"You are script-writing now, aren't you?" Quiggin asked, when we came within closer range of each other, and without any preliminary beating about the bush. "I want to have a talk with you about films."

My first thought was that he hoped to get a similar job. To be a script-writer was at that period the ambition of almost everyone who could hold a pen. There was no reason why Quiggin should prove an exception to the rule. So far as I knew, he had to yet make the experiment. I noticed that he had almost discarded his North Country accent, or perhaps thought it inappropriate for use at that moment. In his university days, one of his chief social assets had been what Sillery used to call "Brother Quiggin's Doric speech". He looked well fed, and his squat form was enclosed in a bright blue suit and double-breasted waistcoat. He was hatless, such hair as remained to him carefully brushed. I had never before seen him look so spruce.

"We've had a cottage lent us," he said. "I'd like you to come down for the week-end. Mona wants to see you again too."

My first instinct was to make some excuse about week-ends being difficult owing to the oppressive manner in which the film business was organised: in itself true enough. However, as it happened, an electricians' strike had just been called at the Studio, with the result that work was likely to be suspended for at least a week or two. I was unwilling to seem to condone too easily the appropriation of an old friend's wife; although it had to be admitted that Templer himself had never been over-squeamish about accepting, within his own circle, changes of partnership. Apart from such scruples, I knew enough of Quiggin to be sure that his cottage would be more than ordinarily uncomfortable. Nothing I had seen of Mona gave cause to reconsider this want of confidence in their combined domestic economy. It was generally supposed by then that they were married, although no one seemed to know for certain whether or not any ceremony had been performed.

"Whereabouts is your cottage?" I asked, playing for time.

The place turned out to be rather further afield than the destination of the usual week-end visit. While this conversation had been taking place, the queue had been moving forward, so that at that moment my own turn came at the booking office; simultaneously, the crowd behind Quiggin launched themselves on and outwards in a sudden violent movement that carried him bodily at their head, as if unwillingly leading a mob in a riot.

"I'll write the address to you," he bawled over his shoulder. "You must certainly come and stay."

I nodded my head, fumbling with tickets and money. Almost immediately Quiggin, driven ahead by his seemingly fanatical followers, was forced through the doors and lost in the night.

"Who was that?" asked the girl accompanying me.

"J. G. Quiggin."

"The critic?"

"Yes."

"I think he has gone off rather lately."

"I expect he goes up and down like the rest of us."

"Don't be so philosophical," she said. "I can't bear it."

We passed into the darkness and *Man of Aran*.

THREE

Curiosity, which makes the world go round, brought me in the end to accept Quiggin's invitation. There was, indeed, some slight mystery about its origin, for after our last meeting—late one evening in the days before he had gone off with Mona—there had been disagreement between us either about Milton as a poet, or (various writers had been discussed) Meredith as a novelist, as a result of which I thought myself finally in disgrace. Of recent years, so everyone agreed, Quiggin had become increasingly dogmatic on such subjects, unable to bear contradiction, and almost equally offended by verbal evasion that sought to conceal views differing from his own. Although publication of his long-promised work, *Unburnt Boats*, had been once more at the last moment postponed, Quiggin's occasional writings were at this time much in evidence. The subject matter of *Unburnt Boats*, thought to be largely autobiographical, remained, in spite of a good deal of speculation on the part of his friends, a closely guarded secret. His journalism was chiefly contributed to papers in which politics and literature attempted some fusion; and letters signed by him appeared with regularity in the "weeklies" on the subject of public liberties or unworthy conduct on the part of the police. In private, Quiggin considered that there was too much freedom in modern life; but he was a great champion of individual liberty in his letters to the Press.

Accustomed, like so many literary men of that decade, to describe himself as a communist, he may indeed have been a member of the Communist Party. Later, at different stages of his career, he disseminated such contradictory statements on the subject of his own political history that card-holding membership remains uncertain. Most of his acquaintances inclined to think that at one moment or another he had belonged to some not very distinguished grade of the Communist hierarchy. Certainly he pertained to the extreme Left and subscribed to several "anti-fascist" organisations. He himself tended to cloak his political activities in mystery in so far as they took practical form: occasionally hinting that these activities might be more important, even more sinister, than persons like myself supposed.

"The Lewis gun may be sounding at the barricades earlier than some of your Laodicean friends think," he had announced in a rasping undertone at the climax of our controversy about Milton—or Meredith.

"I can never remember what the Laodiceans did."

"They were 'neither hot nor cold'."

"Ah."

Such revolutionary sentiments, as I have said, were common enough then, especially in the verse of the period, on which Quiggin was an authority. However, he had seemed rather unusually annoyed that evening, so that in spite of his friendliness in the foyer of the cinema I was not at all sure what sort of a reception I should get when I arrived on his doorstep. I went by train, and found a taxi had been sent to meet me at the station. We drove a mile or two through pretty country and by the low stone wall of a large estate. Quiggin was living in a small, grey, comparatively modern house, hardly a cottage in the sense that comes immediately to the mind—the cottage in a forest inhabited by a peasant in a fairy story, or the gabled, half-timbered sort of the Christmas card by which a robin sits in the snow—but, although the building itself was bleak, the situation was pleasant enough, in fact enchanting: overlooking woods, fields and distant hills, not another house in sight.

Quiggin was in a mood to be agreeable. When he set out to please, he was rarely unable to keep the most unpromising people amused; or at least quiet. He would assume his North Country accent, together with an air of informed simplicity, that would charm all kind of unexpected persons, normally in hearty disagreement with his literary or political opinions. He was particularly accomplished at effecting a reversal of feeling in the case of those who, on introduction, had taken an immediate dislike to his face or his clothes. Probably with that end in view, he cultivated a certain irregularity of dress. For example, when he opened the door on my arrival he was wearing a dark-grey woollen garment with a zip-fastener down the front, which, in conjunction with rope-soled canvas shoes, made him look like an instructor in some unusual sport or physical exercise.

"Come in," he said, "Mona is blonding her hair. She will be along soon."

Mona's hair had been black in the days when I had first set eyes on her at Mr. Deacon's birthday party above the antique shop off Charlotte Street, but, even before she had married Templer—when her Cupid's bow mouth was still advertising toothpaste on the hoardings—it had already taken on a metallic honey colour. She looked distinctly sluttish when at length she appeared, far less trim than when married to Templer, a reversion to the Charlotte Street period when she had been an artists' model. However, she had not returned to the style of dress of her bohemian days, trousers and sandals or whatever was then the fashion. Instead, wearing an old black coat and skirt, an outfit not much suited to the country, she retained a kind of shabby smartness of appearance. I had not seen her for some time, and had forgotten the formal perfection of her face. Her skin was coarse, it was true, and her fixed smile recalled the days when her photograph was on the front of every London bus; yet, even admitting such defects, the detail of every feature insisted upon admiration. She was like a strapping statue of Venus, conceived at a period when more than a touch of vulgarity had found its way into classical sculpture.

I could not help thinking how odd it was that, having once married Templer, she should have deserted him for Quiggin. In the general way of gossip she had the reputation of a beautiful girl not particularly attractive to men. Naturally, with looks like hers, she had been accustomed to all the outward paraphernalia of male attack; certainly at what might be called the "picking-up" level. In a railway carriage, or on board ship, there had always been a man to approach her with greater or lesser delicacy; but Templer and Quiggin (my informant was Templer) were the only men to have taken her "seriously". It had even been suggested (by Quiggin's old friend and rival, Mark Members, probably without much truth) that in her early days Mona had had emotional leanings towards her own sex. Latterly, there had been no talk of that sort. Her manner usually suggested that she was interested in no one except herself; although the fact remained that she had abandoned a comfortable home, and relatively rich husband, to share Quiggin's far from destitute, though not particularly luxurious existence.

To Templer, accustomed to easy success with women, she had perhaps represented the one absolutely first-rate example of the goods he had been so long accustomed to handle—in the manner that a seasoned collector can afford to ignore every other point in any object he wishes to acquire provided it satisfies completely in those respects most difficult to attain. In some way, for Templer, Mona must have fulfilled that condition. Dozens of girls not very different from her were to be found in dress shops and art schools, but Templer, like a scholar who can immediately date a manuscript by the quality of the ink, of the texture of the parchment, had seen something there to crown his special collection: a perfect specimen of her kind. At least that seemed, on the face of it, the only reason why he should have married her.

To Quiggin, on the other hand, himself not particularly adept with girls, Mona must have appeared a wholly unexpected triumph, a "beauty" at whom passers-by turned to gaze in the street, who had positively thrown herself at his head—leaving her "boring" stockbroker husband to live with a writer and a revolutionary. Here was a situation few could fail to find flattering. It was clear from his demeanour that Quiggin still felt flattered, for, although sulky that afternoon, there seemed in general no reason to suppose that Mona regretted her past. Like Molly Jeavons, in such a different context, she appeared—so I had been told—to accept her completely changed circumstances. Her air of temporary dissatisfaction was no doubt merely the old one implying that insufficient attention was being paid to her whims. Perhaps for that reason she spoke of Templer almost at once.

"Have you been seeing anything of Peter?" she asked, without any self-consciousness.

"Not for some time, as it happens."

"I suppose he has found a new girl?"

"I shouldn't wonder."

She did not pursue the subject. It was just as if she had said: "Have you change for a pound?" and, on learning that I had no silver, immediately abandoned the matter. There was no question of emotion; only a faint curiosity. That, at least, was all she allowed to appear on the surface. Quiggin, on the other hand, looked a trifle put out at this early mention of Templer's name.

"By the way, ducks," he said, "I forgot to tell you I tried

to get the bath-lotion when I was last in London. The shop was out of it. I'll try again next time."

Mona compressed her lips in displeasure. Merely to have remembered to inquire for the bath-lotion she evidently considered insufficient on Quiggin's part. She began to hum to herself.

"You have a nice landscape here," I said. "Is there a house behind those trees? It looks as if there might be."

"Do you think it nice?" said Quiggin, his previous tone of harsh geniality somewhat impaired by Mona's mood. "You know these days I scarcely notice such things. Once I might have done—should have done, certainly, in my romantic period. I suppose by 'nice' you mean undeveloped. Give me something a bit more practical. You can keep your picturesque features so far as I am concerned. If English culture was organised on a rational—I do not even say a just—basis, I dare say there might be something to be said for the view from this window. As it is, I would much rather be looking at a well-designed power station. Perhaps, as being more rural, I should say a row of silos."

He smiled to show that he did not mean to be too severe. This was, after all, the kind of subject upon which we had often disagreed in the past. There was something about Quiggin that always reminded me of Widmerpool, but, whereas Widmerpool was devoid of all aesthetic or intellectual interests, as such, Quiggin controlled such instincts in himself according to his particular personal policy at any given moment. Widmerpool would genuinely possess no opinion as to whether the view from the cottage window was good or bad. The matter would not have the slightest interest for him. He would be concerned only with the matter of who owned the land. Perhaps that was not entirely true, for Widmerpool would have enjoyed boasting of a fine view owned by himself. Quiggin, on the other hand, was perfectly aware that there might be something to be admired in the contours of the country, but to admit admiration would be to surrender material about himself that might with more value be kept secret. His rôle, like Widmerpool's, was that of a man of the will, a rôle which adjudged that even here, in giving an opinion on the landscape, the will must be excercised.

"No," he said. "What I like in this place, as a matter of fact, is the excellent arrangement that the bath is in the scullery. Now that is realistic. Not a lot of bourgeois nonsense about false refinement. The owner had it put there quite recently."

"Does he live here himself?"

Quiggin smiled at this question as if it displayed an abyss of ignorance.

"No, he doesn't. He keeps it for lending to friends—usually people with views similar to my own—*our* own, I should say."

He slipped his arm round Mona's waist. She was not won over by this attention, disengaging his hand, and making no effort to assume the comportment of a woman gifted with keen political instincts. An extreme, uninhibited silliness had formerly been her principal characteristic. Now I had the impression she had become more aware of life, more formidable than in her Templer days.

"Your landlord is an active Leftist too, is he?"

"Of course."

"You speak as if all landlords belonged automatically to the Left."

"We are expected to do a bit of work for him in return for living here free," said Quiggin. "That's human nature. But everything he wants is connected with my own political life, so I did not mind that."

"Who is the owner?"

"You wouldn't know him," said Quiggin, smiling with a kind of fierce kindliness. "He is a serious person, as a matter of fact. You would not come across him at parties. Not the sort of parties you go to, at least."

"How do you know the sort of parties I go to?"

"Well, he wouldn't go to the sort of parties I used to see you at."

"Why? Does he go to parties only frequented by his own sex?"

Quiggin laughed heartily at that.

"No, no," he said. "Nothing of that kind. How like you to suggest something of the sort. He is just a politically conscious person who does not enjoy a lot of gallivanting about."

"I believe he is going to turn out to be Howard Craggs, after all this mystery you are making."

Quiggin laughed again.

"I still see a certain amount of Craggs," he admitted. "His firm may be launching a little scheme of mine in the near future—not a book. Craggs is politically sound, but I prefer a publishing house of more standing than Boggis & Stone for my books."

Since Quiggin's books remained purely hypothetical entities, it seemed reasonable enough that their publisher should exist hypothetically too. I was tempted to say as much, but thought it wiser to avoid risk of discord at this early stage. Quiggin was evidently enjoying his own efforts to stir up my curiosity regarding his landlord and benefactor.

"No, no," he said again. "My friend, the owner—well, as a good social revolutionary, I don't quite know how I should describe him. He is a man of what used to be regarded—by snobs—as of rather more distinction, in the old-fashioned sense, than poor Craggs."

"Poor Craggs, indeed. That just about describes him. He has the most loathsomely oily voice in the whole of Bloomsbury."

"What has been happening in London, talking of Bloomsbury?" asked Mona, bored by all this fencing on Quiggin's part. "Have there been any parties there, or anywhere else? I get a bit sick of being stuck down here all the time."

Her drawling, angry manner showed growing discontent, and Quiggin, clearly foreseeing trouble, immediately embarked upon a theme he had probably intended to develop later in the course of my visit.

"As a matter of fact there was something I wanted specially to ask you, Nick," he said hurriedly. "We may as well get on to the subject right away. Mona has been thinking for some time that she might make a career as a film star. I agree with her. She has got champion looks and champion talent too. She made more than one appearance on the screen in the past—small rôles, of course, but always jolly good. That gives the right experience. We thought you ought to be able to hand out some useful 'intros' now that you are in the business."

To emphasise his own enthusiasm for Mona's talent, Quiggin renewed in his voice all the force of his former rough honesty of tone. The inquiry revealed the cause of my invitation to the cottage. Its general application was not expected, though I had supposed Quiggin, rather than Mona, hoped to launch out into the fierce, chilling rapids of "the industry". However, since Mona was to be the subject of the discussion, we began to talk over possibilities of introductions to those who might be of use. Her previous employment in films seemed to have been of scarcely higher grade than superior crowd work, or the individual display on her part of some commodity to be advertised; although, at the same time, it could be said in her favour that when, in the past, she had belonged to the advertising world, she could have claimed some little fame as a well-known model.

Quiggin, whose grasp of practical matters was usually competent enough, must have known that I myself was unlikely to be any great help to an aspiring film star. As I had explained to Jeavons, I had little or no contact with the acting side of the business. But people of undoubted ability in their own line are often completely lost in understanding the nature of someone else's job. It was possible that he pictured nothing easier than introducing Mona to some famous director, who would immediately offer her a star part. Alternately, there was, of course, the possibility that Quiggin himself wished merely to allow the matter free ventilation in order to supply Mona with some subject upon which happily to brood. He might easily have no thought of practical result, beyond assuming that a prolonged discussion about herself, her beauty and her talents, held between the three of us over the course of the weekend, would have a beneficial effect on Mona's temper. This might even be a method of scotching the whole question of Mona's dramatic ambition, of which Quiggin might easily be jealous.

On the other hand, the film business, always unpredictable, might envisage Mona as a "discovery". Perhaps, after all, the change from the time when she had been married to Templer was not so great as physical and financial circumstances might make it appear. She was still bored: without enough to do. A woman who could "cook a bit" had been provided by the mysterious personage who had lent them the cottage. It was natural that Mona should want a job. Chips Lovell, always engaged in minor intrigue, would be able to offer useful advice. We were still discussing her prospects later that evening, sitting on kitchen chairs drinking gin, when a faint tapping came on the outside door. I thought it must be a child come with a message, or delivering something for the evening meal. Mona rose to see who was there. There was the noise of the latch; then she gave an exclamation of surprise, and, so it seemed to me, of pleasure. Quiggin, too, jumped up when he heard the voice, also looking surprised: more surprised than pleased.

The man who came into the room was, I suppose, in his early thirties. At first he seemed older on account of his straggling beard and air of utter down-at-heelness. His hair was long on the top of his head, but had been given a rough military crop round the sides. He wore a tweed coat, much the worse for wear and patched with leather at elbows and cuffs; but a coat that was well cut and had certainly seen better days. An infinitely filthy pair of corduroy trousers clothed his legs, and, like Quiggin, his large feet were enclosed in some form of canvas slipper or *espadrille*. It seemed at first surprising that such an unkempt figure should have announced himself by knocking so gently, but it now appeared that he was overcome with diffidence. At least this seemed to be his state, for he stood for a moment or two on the threshold of the room, clearly intending to enter, but unable to make the definitive movement required which would heave him into what must have appeared the closed community of Quiggin and myself. I forgot at the time that this inability to penetrate a room is a particular form of hesitation to be associated with persons in whom an extreme egotism is dominant: the acceptance of someone else's place or dwelling possibly implying some distasteful abnegation of the newcomer's rights or position.

At last, by taking hold of himself firmly, he managed to pass through the door, immediately turning his sunken eyes upon me with a look of deep uneasiness, as if he suspected —indeed, was almost certain—I was plotting some violently disagreeable move against himself. By exercising this disturbed, and essentially disturbing, stare, he made me feel remarkably uncomfortable; although, at the same time, there was something about him not at all unsympathetic: a presence of forcefulness and despair enclosed in an envelope of constraint. He did not speak. Quiggin went towards him, almost as if he were about to turn him from the room.

"I thought you were going to be in London all the week," he said, "with your committee to re-examine the terms of the Sedition Bill."

He sounded vexed by the bearded man's arrival at this moment, though at the same time exerting every effort to conceal his annoyance.

"Craggs couldn't be there, so I decided I might as well come back. I walked up from the station. I've got a lot of stuff to go through still, and I always hate being in London longer than I need. I thought I would drop in on the way home to show you what I had done."

The bearded man spoke in a deep, infinitely depressed voice, pointing at the same time with one hand to a small cardboard dispatch-case he carried in the other. This receptacle was evidently full of papers, for it bulged at top and bottom, and, since the lock was broken, was tied round several times with string.

"Wouldn't you rather deal with it another time?" Quiggin asked, hopefully.

He seemed desperately anxious to get rid of the stranger without revealing his identity. I strongly suspected this to be the landlord of the cottage, but still had no clue to Quiggin's secrecy on the subject of his name, if this suspicion proved to be true. The man with the beard looked fairly typical of one layer of Quiggin's friends: a layer which Quiggin kept, on the whole, in the background, because he regarded them for one reason or another—either politically or even for reasons that could only be called snobbish—to be bad for business. Quiggin possessed his own elaborately drawn scale of social values, no less severe in their way than the canons of the most ambitious society hostess; but it was not always easy for others to know where, and how, he drew his lines of demarcation. Possibly the man with the beard was regarded as not quite at a level to be allowed to drink with Quiggin when friends were present. However, he was not to be expelled so easily. He shook now his head resolutely.

"No," he said. "There are just one or two things."

He looked again in my direction after saying this, as if to make some apology either for intruding in this manner, or, as it were, on behalf of Quiggin for his evident wish that we should have nothing to do with each other.

"I haven't butted in, have I?" he said.

He spoke not so much to Quiggin as to the world at large, without much interest in a reply. The remark was the expression of a polite phrase that seemed required by the circumstances, rather than anything like real fear that his presence might be superfluous. My impression of him began to alter. I came to the conclusion that under this burden of shyness he did not care in the least whether he butted in on Quiggin, or on anyone else. What he wanted was his own way. Mona, who had gone through to the kitchen, now returned, bringing another glass.

"Have a drink, Alf," she said. "Nice to see you unexpectedly like this."

She had brightened up noticeably.

"Yes, of course, Alf, have a drink," said Quiggin, now resigning himself to the worst. "And sorry, by the way, for forgetting to explain who everybody is. My rough North Country manners again. This is Nick Jenkins—Alf Warminster."

This, then, was the famous Erridge. It was easy to see how the rumour had gone round among his relations that he had become a tramp, even if actual experience had stopped short of that status in its most exact sense. I should never have recognised him with his beard and heavily-lined face. Now that his name was revealed, the features of the preoccupied, sallow, bony schoolboy, with books tumbling from under his arm, could be traced like a footpath lost in the brambles and weeds of an untended garden: an overgrown crazy pavement. Examining him as a perceivable entity, I could even detect in his face a look of his sisters, especially Frederica. His clothes gave off a heavy, earthen smell as if he had lived out in them in all weathers for a long time.

"Alf owns this cottage," said Quiggin, reluctantly. "But he kindly allows us to live here until the whole place is turned into a collective farm with himself at the head of it."

He laughed harshly. Erridge (as I shall, for convenience, continue to call him) laughed uneasily too.

"Of course you know I'm frightfully glad to have you here," he said.

He spoke lamely and looked more than ever embarrassed at this tribute paid him, which was certainly intended by Quiggin to carry some sting in its tail: presumably the implication that, whatever his political views, whatever the social changes, Erridge would remain in a comfortable position. When Quiggin ingratiated himself with people—during his days as secretary to St. John Clarke, for example—he was far too shrewd to confine himself to mere flattery. A modicum of bullying was a pleasure both to himself and his patrons. All the same, I was not sure that Erridge, for all his outward appearance, might not turn out a tougher proposition than St. John Clarke.

"I don't know that farming is quite my line," Erridge went on, apologetically. "Though of course we have always done a bit of it here. Incidentally, is the water pumping satisfactory? You may find it rather hard work, I am afraid. I had the hand pump specially put in. I think it is a better model than the one in the keeper's cottage, and they seem to find that one works all right."

"Mona and I take our turn at it," said Quiggin; and,

117

grinning angrily in my direction, he added: "Guests are expected to do their stint at the pump as a rule. Pumping is a bit of a bore, as you say. You can't do it any better, or any quicker, or any way that makes the tank last longer. The pump movement is just short of the natural leverage of the arm from the elbow, which makes the work particularly laborious. But we get along all right. Pumping is a kind of image of life under the capitalist system."

Erridge laughed constrainedly, and took a gulp of gin, involuntarily making a grimace as he did so. This seemed to indicate that he belonged to the class of egotist who dislikes the taste of food and drink. He would probably have abstained from alcohol entirely had not his special approach to life made a duty of mixing on equal terms with people round him. He seemed now a little put out by Quiggin's lack of affection for the pump. Having installed the equipment himself, like most innovators or, indeed, most owners of property, he did not care for the disparagement of his organisation or possessions; at least on the part of persons other than himself.

"I met some of your sisters the other day," I said.

Erridge's face clouded at these words, while Quiggin gritted his teeth in irritation. This, as intended, was nothing short of a declaration that I knew more about Erridge and his background than Quiggin might think desirable, and also was not prepared to move solely upon lines laid down by Quiggin himself. Indeed, Quiggin may have hoped that the name "Warminster" inarticulately mumbled with the emphasis on the prefix "Alf", would in itself at the time convey little or nothing; later, he could please himself how much he revealed about his current patron. There was a moment's pause before Erridge answered.

"Oh, yes—yes——" he said. "Which—which ones——?"

"Priscilla and then Frederica, who took me to see Norah."

"Oh, yes," said Erridge. "Priscilla—Frederica—Norah."

He spoke as if he had now begun to remember them quite well. The manner in which he screwed up his face while making this effort of memory recalled his uncle, Alfred Tolland. Although, at first sight, it would have been difficult to think of two men whose outward appearance was superficially more different, something deeper remained in common. If Alfred Tolland had grown a beard, dressed in rags and slept out all night, or if Erridge had washed, shaved and assumed a stiff collar and dark suit, something more than a passing resemblance might have become evident. Indeed, Erridge's features had assumed some of that same expression of disappointment which marked his uncle's face when Molly Jeavons teased him; with the contrast that, in Erridge, one was reminded of a spoilt child, while Alfred Tolland's countenance was that of a child resigned from an early age to teasing by grown-ups. There could be no doubt that Erridge recoiled from the invocation of his immediate family. The world of his relations no doubt caused him chronic dissatisfaction. I saw no reason, for my own part, why he should be let off anything. If he lent Quiggin the cottage, he must put up with Quiggin's guests; especially those invited primarily to help Mona become a film star.

Silence fell. Erridge looked out towards the uncurtained window beyond which night had already fallen. Unlike his uncle, he had no wish to discuss his family. After all, it was perhaps hard that he should be forced to talk about them merely to plague Quiggin, though to try the experiment had been tempting. Quiggin himself had become increasingly restive during this interchange. Mona had spoken little, though undoubtedly cheered by the visit. Quiggin seemed to judge, perhaps correctly, that Erridge was displeased by all this chit-chat, and began to mention tentatively executed matters existing between them; although at the same time unquestionably anxious that Erridge should leave the cottage as soon as possible. However, Erridge, in spite of his own unwillingness to make conversation, showed equally no desire to move. He took an ancient leather tobacco-pouch from one of his pockets and began to roll himself a cigarette. When he had done this—not very successfully, for a good deal of tobacco protruded from each end of the twist of rice-paper—he licked the edge to seal it and lit the rather flimsy result of these labours. The cigarette seemed not to "draw" well, so after a minute or two he threw it into the grate. Sipping the drink Mona had given him, he again made a face, tipping back the kitchen chair upon which he sat until it cracked ominously. He sighed deeply.

"I was wondering whether it would be better for you to be secretary instead of Craggs," he said.

"What makes you think so?" asked Quiggin cautiously.

"Craggs always seems to have something else to do. The fact is, Craggs is so keen on running committees that he can never give any of them the right amount of attention. He is on to German refugees now. Quite right, of course, that something should be done. But last week I couldn't get hold of him because he was occupied with Sillery about the embargo on arms to Bolivia and Paraguay. Then there's the 'Smash Fascism' group he is always slipping off to. He would like us to pay more attention to Mosley. He wants to be doing the latest thing all the time, whether it's the independence of Catalonia or free meals for school-children."

"Anti-fascism comes first," said Quiggin. "Even before pacifism. In my opinion, the Sedition Bill can wait. After all, didn't Lenin say something about Liberty being a bourgeois illusion?"

Quiggin had added this last remark in not too serious a tone, but Erridge seemed to take it seriously, shifting about uncomfortably on his hard wooden seat as if he were a galley-slave during an interval of rest.

"Of course," he said. "I know he did."

"Well, then?"

"I don't always think like the rest of you about that."

He rose suddenly from his chair.

"I want to have a talk about the magazine some time," he said. "Not now, I think."

"Oh, that," said Quiggin.

He sounded as if he would have preferred "the magazine" not to have been so specifically named.

"What magazine?" asked Mona.

"Oh, it's nothing, ducks," said Quiggin. "Just an idea Alf and I were talking about."

"Are you going to start a magazine?"

Mona sounded quite excited.

"We might be," said Erridge, moving his feet about.

"It is all very vague still," said Quiggin, in a voice that closed the matter.

Mona was not to be so easily silenced. Whether her interest had been genuinely aroused or whether she saw this as a means expressing her own views or teasing Quiggin was not clear.

"But *how* thrilling," she said. "Do tell me all about it, Alf."

Erridge smiled in an embarrassed way, and pulled at his beard.

"It is all very vague, as J. G. has explained," he said. "Look here, why not come to dinner tomorrow night? We could talk about it then."

"Or perhaps later in the week," said Quiggin.

"I've got to go away again on Monday," Erridge said.

There was a pause. Quiggin glared at me.

"I expect you will have to go back to London on Sunday night, won't you, Nick?" he said.

"Oh, do come too," said Erridge, at once. "I'm so sorry. Of course I meant to ask you as well if you are staying until then."

He seemed distressed at having appeared in his own eyes bad mannered. I think he lived in a dream, so shut off from the world that he had not bothered for a moment to consider whether I was staying with Quiggin, or had just come in that night for a meal. Even if he realised that I was staying, he was probably scarcely aware that I might still be there twenty-four hours later. His reactions placed him more and more as a recognisable type, spending much of his time in boredom and loneliness, yet in some way inhibited from taking in anything relevant about other people: at home only with "causes".

"The trains are not too good in the morning," said Quiggin. "I don't know when you have to be at the Studio——"

"The Studio is closed all this week owing to the strike," I said. "So I had thought of going up on Monday morning in any case—if that is all right."

"Oh, are you on strike?" asked Erridge, brightening up at once, as if it were for him a rare, unexpected pleasure to find himself in such close contact with a real striker. "In that case you simply must come and have a meal with me."

"I'd love to, but it is not me on strike, I am afraid—the electricians."

"Oh, yes, the strike, of course, the strike," said Quiggin, as if he himself had organised the stoppage of work, but, in the light of his many similar responsibilities, had forgotten about its course. "In that case we would all like to come, Alf. It's an early supper, as I remember."

So far as Quiggin was concerned, it had been one of those great social defeats; and, in facing the fact squarely, he had done something to retrieve his position. Presumably he was making plans for Erridge to put up the money to install him as editor of some new, Left Wing magazine. It was perhaps reasonable that he should wish to keep their plans secret in case they should miscarry. However, now that the dinner had been decided upon, he accepted the matter philosophically. Erridge seemed to have no similar desire to discuss matters in private. He was, I think, quite unaware of Quiggin's unwillingness to allow others to know too much of their life together. I could see, too, that he was determined not to abandon the idea that I was myself a striker.

"But you support them by not going," he said. "Yes, come early. You might possibly like to look round the house—though there really is nothing to see there that is of the slightest interest, I'm afraid."

He moved once more towards the door, sunk again in deep despair, perhaps at the thought of the lack of distinction of his house and its contents. Shuffling his *espadrilles* against the stone floor, he caught his foot in the mat, swore gently and a trifle self-consciously, as if aspiring to act as roughly as he was dressed, and left with hardly a further word. Quiggin accompanied him to the door, and shouted a farewell. Then he returned to the room in which we sat. No one spoke for a minute or two. Quiggin slowly corked up the gin bottle, and put it away in a cupboard.

"Alf is *rather* sweet, isn't he?" said Mona.

"Alf is a good fellow," agreed Quiggin, a shade sourly.

"Where does he live?" I asked.

"Thrubworth Park. It is a big house beyond the trees you see from our windows."

Quiggin had been put out by this sudden appearance of Erridge. It had been a visit for which he was unprepared: a situation he had not bargained for. Now he seemed unable to decide what line he himself should take about his friend.

"How much do you know about him?" he asked at last.

"Hardly anything, except that he is said to have been a tramp. And, as I said just now, I met some of his sisters the other day."

"Oh, yes," said Quiggin, impatiently. "I am not at all interested in the rest of his family. He never sees anything of them, anyway. A lot of social butterflies, that's all they are. Just what you might expect. Alf is different. I don't know what you mean by being a tramp, though. Where did you get that story? I suppose you think everyone is a tramp who wears a beard."

"Aren't they? Some of his relations told me he had been experimenting in life as a tramp."

"Just the sort of thing they would put about," said Quiggin. "Isn't it like people of that class? It is true he has been making some study of local conditions. I don't think he stayed anywhere very luxurious, but he certainly didn't sleep in casual wards."

"His relations suppose he did. I think they rather admire him for it."

"Well, they suppose wrong," said Quiggin. "Alf is a very good fellow, but I don't know whether he is prepared to make himself as uncomfortable as that."

"What did he do then?"

"Useful work collecting information about unemployment," Quiggin conceded. "Distributed pamphlets at the same time. I don't want to belittle it in any way, but it is absurd to go round saying he was a tramp. All the same, the experience he had will be of political value to him."

"I think he is rather attractive," said Mona.

For some reason this did not seem to please Quiggin.

"Did you ever meet a girl called Gypsy Jones?" he said. "A Communist. Rather a grubby little piece. I'm not sure Alf may not be a bit keen on her. I saw them sitting together at a Popular Front meeting. All the same, he is not a man to waste time over women."

"What do you mean, 'waste time over women'?" said Mona. "Anyway, nobody could blame you for that. You think about yourself too much."

"I think about you too, ducks," said Quiggin mildly, no doubt judging it advisable to pacify her. "But Alf is an idealist. Rather too much of one sometimes, when it comes to getting things done. All the same, he has most of the right ideas. Shall I get that bottle out again? Supper doesn't seem to be nearly ready."

"Yes, get it out," said Mona. "I can't imagine why you put it away."

All this was reminiscent of the Templer household before Mona left her husband. During the twenty-four hours that followed, this recollection was more than once repeated. Quiggin, too, had begun to placate her with "treats", the impending dinner with Erridge certainly grading in that class. In fact Quiggin began to talk as if he himself had arranged the invitation as an essential aspect of the week-end. Although its potentialities had been reduced for him by my inclusion, there was, I think, nothing personal in that. He would equally have objected to any other friend or acquaintance joining the party. Dinner at Thrubworth was an occasion not to be wasted, for Mona had remarked: "We don't get invited every day of the week." I asked how long they had known Erridge.

"In the days when I was secretary to St. John Clarke," said Quiggin, smiling to show how distant, how incongruous, he now regarded that period of his life. "St. J. went one afternoon to a bookshop in Charing Cross Road, where he wanted to cast his eye over some of Lenin's speeches. As you know, St. J. was careful about money, and he had suggested I should hold the bookseller in conversation while he looked up just as much as he needed. This was at the beginning of St. J.'s conversion to Marxism. We found Alf pottering about the shop, trying to get through the afternoon. Old habits die hard, and, of course, up to the time I met him, St. J. had been a champion snob—and he wasn't altogether cured of his liking for a high-sounding name. He often said afterwards, when we knew each other well, that I'd saved him from snobbery. I only wish I could also have saved him from Trotskyism. But that is another story. It happened that St. J. had met Alf quite a time before at the home of one of Alf's relatives—is there a woman called Lady Molly Jeavons? There is—well, it was at her house. St. J. had a word or two with Alf in the bookshop, and, in spite of his changed view of life, forgot all about Lenin's speeches and asked him back to tea."

"And you have known him ever since?"

"Alf turned up trumps when St. J. behaved so foolishly about myself and Mona. Since then, I've done my best to canalise his enthusiasms."

"Has St. John Clarke still got his German boy as secretary?"

"Not he," said Quiggin. "Guggenbühl is a shrewd young man, Trotskyist though he be. He has moved on to something more paying. After all, he was smart enough to see Hitler coming and clear out of Germany. I hear he is very patronising to the German refugees arriving now."

"He is probably a Nazi agent."

"My God," said Quiggin. "I wouldn't wonder. I must talk to Mark about that when he comes back from America."

The possibility that Mark Members and himself had been succeeded in the dynasty of St. John Clarke's secretaries by one of Hitler's spies greatly cheered Quiggin. He was in a good mood for the rest of the day, until it was time to start for Thrubworth. Then, as the hour approached, he became once more nervous and agitated. I had supposed that, having secured Erridge for a patron some years before, Quiggin must be used by then to his ways. The contrary seemed true; and I remembered that in his undergraduate days he used to become irritable and perturbed before a party: master of himself only after arrival. He had changed into his suit of that cruel colour when at last we set off across the fields.

"What date is the house?"

"What house?"

"Where we are going."

"Oh, Thrubworth Park," said Quiggin, as if he had forgotten our destination. "Seventeenth century, I should say, much altered in the eighteenth. Alf will tell you about it. Though he doesn't really like the place, he likes talking about it for some reason. You will hear all you want about its history."

Passing into the wood to be seen from the windows of the cottage, we went through more fields and climbed a stile. Beyond was a deserted road, on the far side of which, set back some distance from the highway, stood an entrance —evidently not the main entrance—to a park, the walls of which I had already seen from another side on my way from the station the day before. A small, unoccupied lodge, now fallen into decay, lay beside two open, wrought-iron gates. We went through these gates, and made our way up a drive that disappeared among large trees. The park was fairly well kept, though there was an unfriended, melancholy air about the place, characteristic of large estates for which the owner feels no deep affection.

"I hope there will be something to drink tonight," said Mona.

"Is it a bit short as a rule?" I asked.

"Doesn't exactly flow."

"Why didn't you have a pint of gin before you came out then," asked Quiggin, gratingly, "if you can't ever get through an evening without wanting to feel tipsy at the end of it? There always seems enough to me. Not buckets but enough."

His nerves were still on edge.

"All right," said Mona. "Don't bite my head off. You grumbled yourself the last time you came here."

"Did I, ducks?"

He took her arm.

"We'll have a nice drink when we get back," he said, "if Alf should happen to be in one of his moods."

I felt apprehensive at the thought that Erridge might be "in one of his moods". Quiggin had not mentioned these "moods" before, although their nature was easy to imagine from what had been said. I wished we could continue to walk, as we were doing, through glades of oak and chestnut trees in the cool twilight, without ever reaching the house and the grim meal which now seemed to lie ahead of us. We had continued for about ten minutes when roofs came suddenly into view, a group of buildings of some dignity, though without much architectural distinction: a seven-teenth-century mansion such as Quiggin had described, brick at the back and fronted in the eighteenth century with stone. The façade faced away from us across a wide stretch of lawn, since we had arrived at the side of the house among a network of small paths and flowerbeds, rather fussily laid out and not too well kept. Quiggin led the way through these borders, making for a projection of outbuildings and stables. We passed under an arch into a cobbled yard. Quiggin made for a small door, studded with brass nails. By the side of this door hung an iron bell-pull. He stopped short and turned towards me, looking suddenly as if he had lost heart. Then he took hold of himself and gave the bell a good jerk.

"Does one always come in this way?"

"The front of the house is kept shut," he said.

"What happens inside?"

"The state rooms—if that is what you call them—are closed. Alf just lives in one corner of the place."

"In the servants' quarters?"

"More or less. That is probably what they used to be."

We waited for a long time. Quiggin appeared unwilling to ring again, but, under pressure from Mona, at last decided to repeat his wrench at the bell. There was another long pause. Then steps could be heard moving very slowly and carefully down the stairs. Inner fumbling with the door-knob took place, and the door was opened by a manservant. I recognised Smith, the butler temporarily employed by the Jeavonses on my first visit to their house.

"Lord Warminster?" muttered Quiggin interrogatively.

Smith made no answer. A kind of grimace had crossed his features when he saw Quiggin and Mona; naturally enough, he did not give me any sign of recognition. Apart from this brief, indeed scarcely perceptible contraction of nose and lips—perhaps a nervous twitch—he expressed no further welcome. However, he stood aside to allow us to enter. We trooped in, finding ourselves in a kind of back hall where several passages met. There was an impression of oak chests, shabby bookcases full of unreadable books, mahogany dressers and other huge pieces of furniture, expelled at one time or another from the central part of the house; the walls covered with large oil paintings of schools long fallen out of fashion. Smith, as if suffering from some painful disease in the lower half of his body, strode uncertainly before us towards a narrow flight of stairs. We followed in silence. Even Mona seemed overawed by the cavernous atmosphere of gloom. Passing through corridors, and still further corridors, all lined with discredited canvases and an occasional marble bust, Smith stopped before a door. Then he turned almost savagely upon us.

"Mr. and Mrs. Quiggin—and what other name?"

Fancy made him seem to emphasise the word "Mrs.", as

if he wished to cast doubt on the legal union of the two of them. Quiggin started, then mumbled my name grudgingly. Smith threw open the door, bawling out his announcement, and propelled us within.

Erridge was sitting at a desk, the upper part surmounted by a glass-fronted bookcase filled with volumes enclosed for the most part in yellow paper wrappers. He jumped up immediately we entered, removing his spectacles and stumbling forward confusedly, as if our arrival was totally unexpected. He had been writing, and the open flap of the desk was covered with letters and papers which now cascaded to the floor; where they lay in a heap for the rest of the time we were in the house. A dark wall-paper and heavy mahogany furniture, not very different in style to that exiled to the back parts of the house, made the room seem smaller than its real extent, which was in fact considerable. There were no pictures, though rectangular discoloured patches on the walls showed where frames had once hung. Over the fireplace hung a chart which I took to be the Tolland pedigree, but on closer examination proved to illustrate in descending scale some principle of economic distribution. Shelves holding more books—classics, Baedekers and a couple of bound copies of the *Boy's Own Paper*—covered the far wall. At the end of the room stood a table littered with current newspapers and magazines. Another smaller table had been laid with four places for a meal.

It was clear that Erridge lived and moved and had his being in this room. I wondered whether he also spent his nights there on the sofa. Such rough and ready accommodation might easily be in keeping with his tenets: except that the sofa looked rather too comfortable to assuage at night-time his guilt for being rich. Still embarrassed, so it seemed, by the unexpectedness of our arrival, he had now begun to walk quickly up and down the room, as if to give expression and relief to the nervous tension he felt. Quiggin, his own self-possession completely restored by contact with his host—like the warm glow that comes after a plunge in cold water—must have recognised these symptoms in Erridge as normal enough. He took Mona by the arm and drew her towards the window, where the two of them stood side by side, looking down at the gardens and the park beyond. They began to discuss together some feature of the landscape.

Left by myself in the middle of the room, I was at first uncertain whether to join Quiggin and Mona in their survey of the Thrubworth grounds, or, by interrupting his pacing with some conventional remarks, to follow up Erridge's vague but general greeting to the three of us on arrival. The latter course threatened to entail an attempt to march up and down the room beside him: like officers waiting for a parade to begin. On the other hand, to move away towards Quiggin and the window would seem ineffective and unfriendly. I decided to glance at the economic chart for a minute or two in the hope that the situation might assume a less enigmatic aspect; but when a moment later Erridge paused by his desk, and began laboriously to straighten some of the few papers that remained there, I saw that he and I, sooner or later, must establish some kind of host–guest relationship, however uneasy, if we were to spend an evening together. The quicker this were done the better, so far as my own peace of mind was concerned. I therefore tackled him without further delay.

"I saw your butler some months ago at the Jeavonses'."

Erridge started, at last coming to himself.

"Oh, did you, yes," he said, laughing uncomfortably, but at least putting down the pages of typescript which he was shuffling together. "Smith went there while I was—while I was away—doing this—this—sort of investigation. He has been with me for—oh, I don't know—several years. Our other butler died. He had something ghastly wrong with his inside. Something really horrible. It was quite sudden. Smith is rather a peculiar man. He doesn't have very good health either. You can never guess what he is going to say. You know Aunt Molly, do you?"

Erridge's face had begun to work painfully when he spoke of his earlier butler's unhappy state of health and subsequent death. It was easy to see that he found the afflictions of the human condition hard even to contemplate; indeed, took many of them as his own personal responsibility.

"I've been there once or twice."

"You seem to know a lot of my relations," said Erridge. He made this remark in a flat, despondent tone, as if interested, even faintly surprised that such a thing should happen, but that was all. He appeared to wish to carry the matter no further, uttering no warning, but certainly offering no encouragement. It would probably have been necessary to discover a fresh subject to discuss, had not Quiggin at that moment decided that the proper period of segregation from Erridge was at an end—or had been satisfactorily terminated by my own action—so that he now rejoined us.

"I was showing Mona the place where I advise you to have those trees down," he said. "I am sure it is the right thing to do. Get them out of the way."

"I'm still thinking it over," said Erridge, again using an absolutely flat tone.

He did not show any desire to hear Quiggin's advice about his estate, his manner on this subject contrasting with his respectful reception of Quiggin's political comments. Mona sat down on the sofa and gave a little sigh.

"Would you—any of you—like a drink?" asked Erridge.

He spoke inquiringly, as if drink at that hour were an unusual notion that had just occurred to him. It was agreed that a drink would be a good idea. However, Erridge seemed to have little or no plan for implementing his offer. All he did further was to say: "I expect Smith will be back in a minute or two."

Smith did, indeed, return a short time later. He added a large jug of barley water to the things on the table.

"Oh, Smith," said Erridge. "There is some sherry, isn't there?"

"Sherry, m'lord?"

It was impossible to tell from Smith's vacant, irascible stare whether he had never before been asked for sherry since his first employment at Thrubworth, or whether he had himself, quite simply, drunk all the sherry that remained.

"Yes, sherry," said Erridge, with unexpected firmness. "I am sure I remember some being left in the decanter after the doctor came here."

Erridge said the word "doctor" in a way that made me think he might add hypochondria to his other traits. There was something about the value he gave to the syllables that emphasised the importance to himself of a doctor's visit.

"I don't think so, m'lord."

"I know there was," said Erridge. "Please go and look."

A battle of wills was in progress. Clearly Erridge had little or no interest in sherry as such. Like Widmerpool, he did not care for eating and drinking: was probably actively opposed to such sensual enjoyments, which detracted from preferable conceptions of pure power. Quiggin, of course, liked power too; though perhaps less for its own sake than for the more practical consideration of making a career for himself of a kind that appealed at any given moment to his imagination. Quiggin could therefore afford to allow himself certain indulgences, provided these did not endanger the political or social front he chose to present to the world. In supposing that Erridge, like most people who employ eccentric servants, was under Smith's thumb, I now saw I had made an error of judgment. Erridge's will was a strong one. There could be no doubt of that. At his words Smith had bowed his head as one who, having received the order of the bowstring, makes for the Bosphorus. He turned in deep dejection from the room. Erridge's sallow cheeks had almost taken on a touch of colour. In this mood his beard made him look quite fierce.

"You would like some sherry, wouldn't you?" he repeated to Mona.

He was suffering a twinge of conscience that to the rest of us his demeanour to Smith might have sounded arrogant: out of keeping with his fundamental beliefs.

"Oh, *yes*," said Mona.

She adopted towards Erridge a decidedly flirtatious manner. Indeed, I wondered for a moment whether she might now be contemplating a new move that would make her Countess of Warminster. Almost immediately I dismissed such a speculation as absurd, since Erridge himself appeared totally unaware that he was being treated to Mona's most seductive glance. Turning from her, he began to discuss with Quiggin the economics of the magazine they hoped to found. The Quiggin plan was evidently based on the principle that Erridge should put up the money, and Quiggin act as editor; Erridge, on the other hand, favoured some form of joint editorship. I was surprised that Mona showed no sign of dissatisfaction at Erridge's indifference to her. I noted how much firmer, more ruthless, her personality had become since I had first met her as Templer's wife, when she had seemed a silly, empty-headed, rather bad-tempered beauty. Now she possessed a kind of hidden force, of which there could be no doubt that Quiggin was afraid.

Smith returned with sherry on a salver. There was just enough wine to give each of us a full glass. I remarked on the beauty of the decanter.

"Are you interested in glass?" said Erridge. "Some of it is rather good here. My grandfather used to collect it. I don't know, by the way, whether you would like to look round the house by any chance. There is nothing much to see, but some people like that sort of thing. Or perhaps you would rather do that after dinner."

"Oh, we are more comfortable here with our drinks, aren't we, Alf?" said Quiggin. "I don't expect you want to trudge round the house, do you, Nick? I am sure I don't."

I think Quiggin knew, even at this stage, that there was no real hope of sabotaging the project, because Erridge was already determined to go through with it; but he felt at the same time, in the interests of his own self-respect, that at least an effort should be made to prevent a tour of the house taking place. Erridge's face fell; looking more cheerful again at the assurance that, after we had dined, I should like to "see round". Smith appeared with some soup in a tureen, and we ranged ourselves about the table.

"Will you drink beer?" asked Erridge doubtfully. "Or does anyone prefer barley water?"

"Beer," said Quiggin, sharply.

He must have felt that the suggested tour of the house had strengthened his own moral position, in so much as the proposal was an admission of self-indulgence on the part of Erridge.

"Bring some beer, Smith."

"The pale ale, m'lord?"

"Yes, I think that is what it is. Whatever we usually drink on these occasions."

Smith shook his head pessimistically, and went off again. Erridge and Quiggin settled down to further talk about the paper, a conversation leading in due course to more general topics, among these the aggressive foreign policy of Japan.

"Of course I would dearly like to visit China and see for

135

myself," Quiggin said.

It was a wish I had heard him express before. Possibly he hoped that Erridge would take him there.

"It would be interesting," Erridge said. "I'd like to go myself."

Soup was followed by sausages and mash with fried onions. The cooking was excellent. The meal ended with cheese and fruit. We·left the table and moved back to the chairs round the fireplace at the other end of the room. Mona returned to the subject of her film career. We had begun to talk of some of the minor film stars of the period, when the sound of girls' voices and laughter came from the passage outside. Then the door burst open, and two young women came boisterously into the room. There could be no doubt that they were two more of Erridge's sisters. The elder, so it turned out, was Susan Tolland; the younger, Isobel. The atmosphere changed suddenly, violently. One became all at once aware of the delicious, sparkling proximity of young feminine beings. The room was transformed. They both began to speak at once, the elder one, Susan, finally making herself heard.

"Erry, we were passing the gates and really thought it would be too bad mannered not to drop in."

Erridge rose, and kissed his sisters automatically, although not without some shade of warmth. Otherwise, he showed no great pleasure at seeing them; rather the reverse. I had by then become familiar with the Tolland physical type, to which Susan Tolland completely conformed. She was about twenty-five or twenty-six, less farouche, I judged, than her sister, Norah; less statuesque than Frederica, though resembling both of them. Tall and thin, all of them possessed a touch of that angularity of feature most apparent in Erridge himself: a conformation that in him became a gauntness recalling Don Quixote. In the girls this inclination to severity of outline had been bred down, leaving only a liveliness of expression and underlying sense of melancholy: this last characteristic to some extent masked by a great pressure of high spirits, notably absent in Erridge. His eyes were brown, those of his sisters, deep blue.

Would it be too explicit, too exaggerated, to say that when I set eyes on Isobel Tolland, I knew at once that I should marry her? Something like that is the truth; certainly nearer the truth than merely to record those vague, inchoate sentiments of interest of which I was so immediately conscious. It was as if I had known her for many years already; enjoyed happiness with her and suffered sadness. I was conscious of that, as of another life, nostalgically remembered. Then, at that moment, to be compelled to go through all the paraphernalia of introduction, of "getting to know" one another by means of the normal formalities of social life, seemed hardly worth while. We knew one another already; the future was determinate. But what—it may reasonably be asked—what about the fact that only a short time before I had been desperately in love with Jean Duport; was still, indeed, not sure that I had been wholly cured? Were the delights and agonies of all that to be tied up with ribbon, so to speak, and thrown into a drawer to be forgotten? What about the girls with whom I seemed to stand nightly in cinema queues? What, indeed?

"Aren't we going to be told who everyone is?" said Susan, looking round the room and smiling.

Although her smile was friendly, charming, there could be no doubt that, like her sister, Norah, Susan was capable of making herself disagreeable if she chose.

"Oh, sorry," said Erridge. "What am I thinking of? I am not used to having so many people in this room."

He mumbled our names. Isobel seemed to take them in; Susan, less certainly. Both girls were excited about something, apparently about some piece of news they had to impart.

"Have you come from far?" asked Quiggin.

He spoke in an unexpectedly amiable tone, so much muting the harshness of his vowels that these sounded almost like the ingratiating speech of his associate, Howard Craggs, the publisher. Quiggin had previously named Erridge's family in such disparaging terms that I had almost supposed he would give some outward sign of the disapproval he felt for the kind of life they lived. He would have been capable of that; or at least withholding from them any mark of cordiality. Now, on the contrary, he had wrung the girls' hands heartily, grinning with pleasure, as if delighted by this opportunity of meeting them both. Mona, on the other hand, did not trouble to conceal traces of annoyance, or at least disappointment, at all this additional feminine competition put into the field against her so suddenly and without warning.

"Yes, we've come rather miles," said Susan Tolland, who was evidently very pleased about something. "The car made the most extraordinary sounds at one point. Isobel said it was like a woman wailing for her demon lover. I thought it sounded more like the demon himself."

"Anyway, here you are in 'sunny domes and caves of ice'," said Quiggin. "You know I get more and more interested in Coleridge for some reason."

"Do you—do you want anything to eat, either of you?" Erridge inquired, uneasily.

He pointed quite despairingly at the table, as if he hoped the food we had just consumed would, by some occult process, be restored there once more; as if we were indeed living in the realm of poetic enchantment adumbrated by Quiggin.

"We had a bite at The Tolland Arms," said Isobel, taking a banana from the dish and beginning to peel it. "And very disgusting the food was there, too. We didn't know you would be entertaining on a huge scale, Erry. In fact we were not even certain you were in residence. We thought you might be away on one of your jaunts."

She cast a glance at us from under her eyelashes to indicate that she was not laughing openly at her brother, but, at the same time, we must realise that the rest of the family considered his goings-on pretty strange. Quiggin caught her eye, and, with decided disloyalty to Erridge, smiled silently back at her: implying that he too shared to the fullest extent the marrow of that particular joke. Isobel threw herself haphazardly into an armchair, her long legs stretched out in front of her.

"Where have you come from?" asked Erridge.

He spoke formally, almost severely, as if forcing himself to take an interest in his sisters' behaviour, however extraordinary; behaviour which, owing to the fortunate dispensations of circumstances, could never affect him personally to the smallest degree. Indeed, he spoke as if utter remoteness from his own manner of life, for that very reason, made a subject otherwise unexciting, even distasteful, possess aspects impossible for him to disregard. It was as if his sisters, in themselves, represented customs so strange and incalculable that even the most detached person could not fail to allow his attention to be caught for a second or two by such startling oddness.

"We've been at the Alfords'," said Isobel, discarding the banana skin into the waste-paper basket. "Throw me an orange, Susy. Susan had an adventure there."

"Not an adventure exactly," said her sister. "And, anyway, it's my story, not yours, Isobel. Hardly an adventure. Unless you call getting married an adventure. I suppose some people might."

"Why, have you got married, Susan?" asked Erridge.

He showed no surprise whatever, and very little interest, at the presentation of this possibility: merely mild, on the whole benevolent, approval.

"I haven't yet," said Susan, suddenly blushing deeply. "But I am going to."

She was, I think, suddenly overwhelmed at the thought of marriage and all it implied. The announcement of her engagement, planned with great dash, had not been entirely carried off with the required air of indifference. I even wondered for a moment whether she was not going to cry. However, she mastered herself immediately. At the sight of her sister's face, Isobel began to blush violently too.

"To whom?" asked Erridge, still completely calm. "I am so glad to hear the news."

"Roddy Cutts."

The name clearly conveyed nothing whatever to her brother, who still smiled amiably, unable to think of anything to say.

"There was a Lady Augusta Cutts who used to give dances when I was a young man," he said, at last.

He spoke as if he were at least as old as General Conyers. No doubt the days when he had occasionally gone to dances seemed by then infinitely distant: indeed, much further off, and no less historic, than the General's cavalry charge.

"Lady Augusta is his mother."

"Oh, yes?"

"She is rather a terror."

There was a pause.

"What does he do?" asked Erridge, as if conscious that it might seem bad-mannered to drop the subject altogether, however much he himself hoped to move on to something more interesting.

"I can't tell you exactly," said Susan. "But he has something he does. I mean he doesn't absolutely beg his bread from door to door. He looks into the Conservative Central Office once in a way too."

Erridge's face fell at the mention of this last establishment. Quiggin, however, came to the rescue.

"Much as I hate the Tories," he said, "I've heard that Cutts is one of their few promising young men."

Everyone, including Susan Tolland herself, was surprised by this sudden avowal on the part of Quiggin, who was showing at least as much enthusiasm on the subject of the engagement as might have been expected from Erridge himself.

"I grant it may not be my place to say so," Quiggin went on, switching at the same time to a somewhat rougher delivery. "But you know, Alf, you really ought to celebrate rightly in a bottle of champagne. Now, don't you think there is some bubbly left in that cellar of yours?"

This speech astonished me, not because there was anything surprising in Quiggin's desire for champagne, but on account of a changed attitude towards his host. Erridge's essentially ascetic type of idealism, concerned with the mass rather than the individual, and reinforced by an aristocratic, quite legitimate desire to avoid vulgar displays, had no doubt moved imperceptibly into that particular sphere of parsimony defined by Lovell as "upper-class stinginess". To demand champagne was deliberately to inflame such responses in Erridge. Possibly Quiggin, seeing unequivocal signs of returning sulkiness in Mona, hoped to avert that mood by this daring manoeuvre: equally, as a sheer exercise of will, he may have decided at that moment to display his power over his patron. Neither motive would be out of keeping with his character. Finally, he might have hoped merely to ingratiate himself with Susan Tolland—certainly a pretty girl—whom he possibly cast for some at present unrevealed rôle in his future plans. Whatever his reason, he received a very encouraging smile from her after making this proposal.

"What a jolly good idea," she said. "As a matter of fact I was waiting for Erry to suggest it."

Erridge was undoubtedly taken aback, although not, I

think, on the ground that the suggestion came from Quiggin. Erridge did not traffic in individual psychology. It was an idea that was important to him, not its originator. The whole notion of drinking champagne because your sister was engaged was, in itself, obviously alien to him; alien both to his temperament and ideals. Champagne no doubt represented to his mind a world he had fled. Now the wine was presented as a form of rite or observance, almost, indeed, as a restorative or tonic after hearing dangerously exciting news, he seemed primarily concerned with the question whether or not any champagne remained in the house. The fact that Quiggin had put forward the proposal must at least have disposed of any fears as to whether in this manner a coarse display of his own riches might be symbolised. However, even faced with this utterly unforeseen problem, Erridge was by no means thrown off his guard. I could not help admiring the innate caution with which he seasoned his own eccentricity. Even in Erridge, some trace of that "realism" was observable of which Chips Lovell used to speak; among the rest of the Tollands, as I discovered later, a characteristic strongly developed.

"I really cannot reply to that question offhand," Erridge said—and one caught a faint murmur of ancestral voices answering for the Government some awkward question raised by the Opposition—"As you know I hardly ever drink anything myself, except an occasional glass of beer—certainly never champagne. To tell the truth, I hate the stuff. We'd better ask Smith."

Smith, as it happened, appeared at that moment with coffee. Already he showed signs of being nervously disturbed by the arrival of the girls, his hands shaking visibly as he held the tray; so much so that some of the liquid spilled from the pot.

"Smith, is there any champagne left in the cellar?"

Erridge's voice admitted the exceptional nature of the

inquiry. He asked almost apologetically. Even so, the shock was terrific. Smith started so violently that the coffee cups rattled on the tray. It was evident that we were now concerned with some far more serious matter than the earlier pursuit of sherry. Recovering himself with an effort, Smith directed a stare of hatred at Quiggin, at once revealed by some butler's instinct as the ultimate cause of this unprecedented demand. The colourless, unhealthy skin of his querulous face, stretched like a pale rubber mask over the bones of his features, twitched a little.

"Champagne, m'lord?"

"Have we got any? One bottle would do. Even a half-bottle."

Smith's face puckered, as if manfully attempting to force his mind to grapple with a mathematical or philosophical problem of extraordinary complexity. His bearing suggested that he had certainly before heard the word "champagne" used, if only in some distant, outlandish context; that devotion to his master alone gave him some apprehension of what this question—these ravings, almost—might mean. Nothing good could come of it. This was a disastrous way to talk. That was his unspoken message so far as champagne was concerned. After a long pause, he at last shook his head.

"I doubt if there is any champagne left, m'lord."   .

"Oh, I'm sure there is, Smith, if you go and look," said Susan. "You see it is to celebrate my engagement, Smith. I'm going to get married."

Another twitch passed quickly, almost like a flash of lightning, over Smith's face. I had by no means taken a fancy to him, either here or at the Jeavonses', but it was impossible not to feel some sympathy for his predicament: forced at short notice to adapt himself to the whims of his different employers; for it was unlikely that his Thrubworth routine was anything like that at the Jeavonses'.

"Very pleased to hear the news, m'lady," he said. "Wish you the best of luck. I expect it will be Lady Isobel's turn soon."

These felicitations were handsome on Smith's part, although Isobel, in spite of being several years younger than her sister, evidently had no wish for comparison between them to be drawn in a manner which made her, by representing, as it were, those girls not yet engaged, seem to come out second best. However, if Smith hoped by drawing attention to engagements in general to dispose of the question of champagne, he was disappointed.

"Anyway, Smith, do go and have a look," said Isobel. "My throat is absolutely parched."

Erridge might have no wish to drink champagne, even if available, but he had also clearly decided that things had gone too far for the idea to be abandoned without loss of face on his own part. Smith, too, must finally have realised that, for he now set down the coffee tray and abandoned the room in full retreat, moving like a man without either enthusiasm or hope.

"Smith doesn't seem to get any soberer," said Susan, when he had shut the door.

"As a matter of fact, Smith hasn't had one of his real bouts for a long time," said Erridge.

He spoke reprovingly.

"So drink is Smith's trouble, is it?" said Quiggin, with great geniality. "You never told me that. I often thought he might be one over the eight. That explains a lot."

"Smith sometimes takes a glass too much," said Erridge, shortly, perhaps beginning to notice, and resent, the change in Quiggin's manner since the arrival of the girls. "I usually pretend not to notice. It must be an awful job to be a butler anyway. I don't really approve of having indoor menservants, but it is hard to run a house this size without them, even when you live, like me, in only a small part of it.

I can't get rid of the place, because it is entailed—so there it is."

He sighed. There was rather an awkward pause. Erridge was perhaps getting cross. It was possible that the entail was not a popular subject in the family.

"What sort of luck will he have in the cellar?" asked Isobel. "I must say champagne is just what I need."

"I really don't know," said Erridge. "As I told you, I hardly drink anything myself."

"Do you keep it locked?" asked Susan.

Erridge coloured a little.

"No," he said. "I like trusting people, Susan."

Susan showed no disposition to accept this observation as a snub, although her brother was obviously displeased by her flippancy. It was natural that anyone should be annoyed whose evening had been so radically altered by force of circumstance. He had been looking forward to some hours of discussing plans for the magazine, discussion which my own presence would not have hindered. A third, and unconcerned, party might even have made Quiggin more tractable, for a certain amount of patron–protégé conflict clearly took place between them. Now, the arrival of his sisters had transformed the room into a place not far removed from one of those haunts of social life so abhorrent to him. Instead of printing charges, advertising rates, the price of paper, names of suitable contributors, their remuneration and other such matters which by their very nature, carried with them a suggestion of energy, power and the general good of mankind, he was now compelled to gossip about such trifles as Susan's engagement, a subject in which he could not feel the smallest interest. This indifference was not, I felt sure, due to dislike of Susan, but because the behaviour of individuals, consanguineous or not, held, as such, no charm whatever for him. His growing vexation was plain: not lessened by Quiggin's manifest betrayal of principles with the two girls.

"Do you like driving, Lady Susan?" asked Quiggin.

"Oh, all right," she said. "We rattled along somehow."

"Have you had your car long?"

When he asked that, she began to blush furiously again.

"It is a borrowed car," she said.

"It's Roddy's," said Isobel. "Just to show him what married life is going to be like. Sue took his car away from him, and made him go back by train."

"Oh, shut up," said her sister. "You know it was the most convenient arrangement."

This cross-fire continued until the return of Smith. He brought with him a bottle, which he banged down quite fiercely on the table. It was Mumm, 1906: a magnum. Nothing could have borne out more thoroughly Erridge's statement about his own lack of interest in wine. It was, indeed, a mystery that this relic of former high living should have survived. Some latent sense of its lofty descent must from time to time have dominated Smith's recurrent desire, and held him off. I could not help reflecting how different must have been the occasions when its fellows had been consumed; if, in truth, we were to consume this, which seemed not yet absolutely certain.

"Just the one left," said Smith.

He spoke in anguish, though not without resignation. Erridge hesitated. Almost as much as Smith, he seemed to dislike the idea of broaching the wine for the rest of us to drink. A moral struggle was raging within him.

"I don't know whether I really ought not to keep it," he said. "If there is only one. I mean, if someone or other turned up who——"

He found no individual worthy enough to name, because he stopped suddenly short.

"Oh, *do* let's, Alf," said Mona.

She had hardly spoken since the arrival of Susan and

Isobel Tolland. Her voice sounded high and strained, as if she were suffering strong nervous tension.

"Oh, yes," said Erridge. "You're right, Mona. We'll break its neck and celebrate your engagement, Sue."

He was undoubtedly proud of fetching from somewhere deeply embedded in memory this convivial phrase; also cheered by the immediate, and quite general, agreement that now was the moment to drink so mature—so patriarchal—a vintage. Smith disappeared again. After another long delay he returned with champagne glasses, which had received a perfunctory rub to dispel dust accumulated since at least the time of Erridge's succession. Then, with the peculiar deftness of the alcoholic, he opened the bottle. The explosion was scarcely audible. He poured the wine, a stream of deep dull gold, like wine in a fairy story, at the same time offering an almost inaudible, though certainly generous, appreciation of the occasion by muttering: "I'll be drinking your ladyship's health myself later this evening." Susan thanked him. Erridge, who had himself refused a glass, shifted his feet about uneasily. Traces of the Mumm's former excellence remained, like a few dimly remembered words of some noble poem sunk into oblivion, or a once famous statue of which only a chipped remnant still stands.

"Have you informed Hyde Park Gardens yet?" asked Erridge.

He spoke as if that were a new thought; one that worried him a little.

"I rang up," said Susan.

The champagne had perhaps helped her to recover casualness of tone.

"What was said?"

"Great delight."

I knew this reference must be to their stepmother, Katherine, Lady Warminster, of whom Lovell had given me some account, describing her as "frightfully amusing". Invalid and somewhat eccentric, she was, I suspected, a less easy-going figure than Lovell's words might lead one to suppose. There seemed indications that her stepchildren regarded her as formidable. She had always hated the country, so that her husband's death had provoked none of those embarrassments, not uncommon, in which an heir has to apply pressure to enjoy sole rights in his inheritance. On the contrary, the difficulty had been to persuade Erridge to take over Thrubworth when Lord Warminster, a traveller and big-game hunter of some celebrity, died abroad. That had been five or six years before, when Erridge's political views were still comparatively undeveloped. Lovell's picture of Erridge's early days depicted a vague, immature, unhappy young man, taking flats and leaving them, wandering about on the Continent, buying useless odds and ends, joining obscure societies, in general without friends or interests, drifting gradually into his present position.

"I'm glad the news was well received," said Erridge.

"So was I," said Susan. "Jolly glad."

This interchange on the subject of their stepmother was somehow of a much closer intimacy than anything said previously about the engagement. In relation to Lady Warminster, the Tollands presented a united front. Their sentiments towards her were not, one felt, at all unfriendly; on the contrary, rather well disposed. They were at the same time sentiments charged with that powerful family feeling with which no outward consideration, not even love or marriage, could compete, except upon very unequal terms.

"Have you been over the house?" asked Isobel, beside whom I was sitting on the sofa.

We had drunk the champagne, and the atmosphere had become more relaxed. Erridge heard the question, and spoke himself, before I could answer. Although he had had nothing to drink, he had not been able to withstand the increased warmth of relationship that the rest of us had drawn from the wine.

"Why, no, you haven't seen the house yet," he said. "Would you by any chance like to go round, Jenkins? There is really little or nothing of any interest to see, I must warn you, except a hat that is supposed to have belonged to the younger Pitt."

"I should like to go round very much."

"I expect you will prefer to stay where you are, J.G.," said Erridge, who may have decided to take this opportunity of making a tour of the house as a kind of counterblast to Quiggin's demand for champagne. "And I don't expect you will want to go round either, Mona, as you have seen it all several times. Jenkins and I will walk through the rooms very quickly."

However, both Quiggin and Mona insisted that they would like to take part in the tour, in spite of its repetitive character, so far as they themselves were concerned; and the Tolland girls agreed, rather loudly, that there was nothing they enjoyed more than their eldest brother's showmanship in this particular undertaking.

"Those anti-fascist pamphlets will have to wait for another night," Quiggin muttered to Erridge.

He spoke, as if to salve his conscience, as he rose from his chair.

"Oh, yes," said Erridge testily, as if he wished to be reminded of the pamphlets as little as Quiggin. "Anyway, I want to go through them carefully—not with a lot of people interrupting."

He strode firmly in front of us. We followed down several passages, emerging at last at the head of a broad staircase. Erridge descended. Half-way down, where the wall of the landing faced the hall, hung the full-length portrait, by Lawrence, of an officer wearing the slung jacket of a hussar. Erridge stopped in front of the picture.

"The 4th Lord Erridge and 1st Earl of Warminster," he said. "He was a very quarrelsome man and fought a number of duels. The Duke of Wellington is supposed to have said of him: 'By God, Erridge has shown himself a greater rake than Anglesey and more damn'd a fool than ever was Combermere. It is my firm belief that had he been present on the field of Waterloo we should never have carried the day.'"

"But that was only when the Duke was cross," said Isobel. "Because he also remarked: 'Erridge spoke out last night when Brougham extolled the virtues of Queen Caroline. I never saw a man so put out of countenance as was Brougham by his words.' I always wonder what he said. Of course, one knows in a general way, but it would be nice to know the actual phrases."

"I think he probably used to score off Wellington," said Susan. "And that was why the Duke was so sharp with him. Erridge was probably the more cunning of the two."

"Oh, rot," said Isobel. "I bet he wasn't. Dukes are much more cunning than earls."

"What makes you think so?" said her brother.

Not greatly pleased by this opinion, he did not wait for an answer, but moved on down the stairs. Denigration of ancestors was more agreeable to him than banter regarding the order of peerage to which he belonged. Not for the first time that evening one was conscious of the bones of an old world pomposity displayed beneath the skin of advanced political thought. However, he soon recovered from this momentary discomposure.

"Of course the Tollands were really nobody much at the beginning of the fourteenth century," he said. "That is when they first appear. Lesser gentry, I suppose you might call them. I think they probably made their money out of the Black Death."

As such a foundation of the family fortunes seemed of interest, I inquired further. Erridge was taken aback by the question.

"Oh, I don't know for certain," he said. "There was a big industrial and social upheaval then, as you probably know. The Tollands may have turned it to good account. I think they were a pretty awful lot."

He appeared a little disturbed by this perhaps over close attention on my own part to the detail of the history he provided. The girls giggled. Quiggin came to the rescue.

"When did these *kulaks* begin their career of wholesale exploitation?" he asked.

He sweetened the inquiry with some harsh laughter. Erridge laughed too, more at home with Quiggin in his political phraseology than in domestic raillery with his sisters.

"*Kulaks* is the word," he said. "I think they went up in the world when one of them was knighted by Edward IV. Then another was Esquire of the Body to Henry VIII, whatever that may have been, and lost his job under Bloody Mary. They've been an awfully undistinguished lot on the whole. They were Cavaliers in the Civil War and got a peerage under Queen Anne. John Toland, the deist, was no relation, so I've been told. I should rather like to have claimed him."

We entered a long room hung with portraits. The younger Pitt's hat stood within a glass case in one corner by the window. The furniture, as described by Lovell, was under dust-sheets.

"I never use any of these rooms," said Erridge.

He pulled away the dust-sheets without ceremony; leaving in the centre of the room a heap of linen on the floor. The furniture was on the whole mediocre; although, as at the Jeavonses', there was a good piece here and there. The pictures, too, apart from the Lawrence—the bravura of which gave it some charm—were wholly lacking in distinction. Erridge seemed aware of these deficiencies, referring more than once to the "rubbish" his forbears had accumulated. Yet, at the same time, in his own peculiar way, he seemed deeply to enjoy this opportunity of displaying the house: a guilty enjoyment, though for that reason no less keen.

"We really ought to have my Uncle Alfred here," said Erridge. "He regards himself as rather an authority on family history—and, I must say, is a very great bore on the subject. Nothing is worse than someone who takes that sort of thing up, and hasn't had enough education to carry it through."

I recalled Alfred Tolland's own remarks about his nephew's failure to erect a memorial window. Erridge, whose last words revealed a certain intellectual arrogance, until then dormant, probably found it convenient to diminish his own scrutiny of family matters where tedious negotiation was concerned. In any case, however much an oblique contemplation of his race might gratify him, there could be no doubt that he regarded any such weakness as morally wrong.

"It makes a very nice museum to live in," said Quiggin.

We had completed the tour and returned to the room where we had dined. No trace seemed to remain of Quiggin's earlier objections to the tour. His inconsistencies, more limited by circumstances than those of Erridge, were no less pronounced. Erridge himself, entirely at ease while displaying his possessions, now began once more to pace about the room nervously.

"How are you and Isobel getting back, Susy?" he asked.

He sounded apprehensive, as if he feared his sisters might have come with the idea of attempting to stay for several months: perhaps even hoping to take possession of the house entirely and entertain at his expense on a huge scale.

"Well, I've got Roddy's car," said Susan, blushing again at mention of her future husband. "We thought if you could put us up for the night, we'd start early for London tomorrow morning."

Erridge was not enthusiastic about this proposal. There was some discussion. However, he could not very well turn his sisters out of the house at that hour of the night, so that in the end he agreed, at the same time conveying a warning that the sheets might not be properly aired.

"All right," said Isobel. "We'll get rheumatic fever. We don't mind. I can't tell you how smart Roddy's car is, by the way. If we get up reasonably early, we shall reach London in no time."

"It is rather a grand car," said Susan. "I don't know whether anyone would like a lift in the morning."

This seemed an opportunity not to be missed. I asked if I might accept the offer.

"Yes, do come," said Isobel. "It will be too boring otherwise, driving all the way to London with Susy talking of nothing but arrangements for her wedding."

"We will pick you up when we come past the cottage, which we do, anyway," said Susan. "I warn you I am frightfully punctual."

Quiggin did not look too pleased at this, but, having enjoyed his evening, he was by that time in a mood to allow such an arrangement to pass. Erridge, already suppressing one or two yawns, seemed anxious now that we should go, and give him an opportunity to make for bed. Mona, too, had been silent for a long time, as if lost in thought. She looked tired. It was time to say good night.

"See you in the morning," said Isobel.

"I will be waiting at the gate."

Erridge came to the door and let us out. We passed once more through the dim glades of the melancholy park, now dramatised by moonlight. It was a warm night, damp, though without rain, and no wind stirred the trees. There was a smell of hay and wet timber in the air. The noise of owls came faintly as they called to each other under the stars.

"Alf is a champion lad," said Quiggin. "His sisters are grand girls too. You didn't take long to press your company on them, I must say."

"I've got to get back to London somehow."

"I didn't think the girls were up to much," said Mona. "They behaved as if they owned the place. I hate those tweed suits."

"You know, Alf is rather like Prince Myshkyn in *The Idiot*," said Quiggin. "A Myshkyn with political grasp. You wouldn't believe the money spent on good causes that he has got through, one way and another."

"What sort of thing?"

"He has helped a lot of individual cases that have been recommended to him from time to time. Howard Craggs got quite a bit out of him a year or two back, which I bet he never repaid. Then Alf has founded several societies and financed them. Refugees, too."

"Mind he doesn't meet Guggenbühl."

"I'll see to that," said Quiggin, laughing sourly.

"He ought to marry a nice girl who would teach him to look after his money instead of handing it out to all these wasters," said Mona.

One of her bad moods seemed on the way.

"All very good causes," said Quiggin, who seemed to enjoy contemplating this subject. "But sums that would make you gasp."

"Bloody fool," said Mona.

FOUR

In the Jeavonses' house everything was disposed about the rooms as if the owners had moved in only a week or two before, and were still picknicking in considerable disorder among their unsorted belongings. Whether the better pieces were Sleaford spoils, or derived from Molly's side of the family, Lovell was uncertain. Certainly Molly herself had not bought them; still less, Jeavons. Lovell said the only object the two of them were known to have acquired throughout their married life together was a cabinet made of some light, highly polished wood, designed—though never, I think, used—to enclose the wherewithal for mixing cocktails. In practice, bottles, glasses and ice were always brought into the drawing-room on a tray, the cabinet serving only as a plinth upon which to rest the cage enclosing two budgerigars. You could never tell who would carry in this drink tray; or, for that matter, who would open the front door. Regular servants were employed only spasmodically, their duties on the whole undertaken by such temporary figures as Erridge's Smith, or superannuated nurses and governesses of the Ardglass family, whose former dependants were legion. Even personal friends of Molly's, down on their luck for one reason or another, would from time to time lend a hand on the domestic side, while a succession of charwomen, gloomy or jocular, haunted the passages by day.

No one was ever, so to speak, turned away from the Jeavons table. The place was a hinterland where none of the ordinary rules seemed to apply and persons of every sort were to be encountered. Perhaps that description makes the company sound too diverting. Certainly Lovell was less complimentary. "Of course you hardly ever meet intelligent people there," he used to say, for some reason cherishing in his mind that category of person, without too closely defining means of recognition. "And you rarely see anyone whom *I* would call really smart." Then he was accustomed to relent a little, and add: "All the same, you may find absolutely anybody at Aunt Molly's."

In making this practical—even brutal—analysis, I think Lovell merely meant that individuals deeply ambitious of receiving a lot of grand invitations would never dream of wasting time among the rag, tag and bobtail normally to be found at the Jeavonses'; but he probably intended at the same time to imply that such over-eager people might sometimes be surprised—possibly even made envious—by the kind of visitor from Molly's past—or, for that matter, her uncomfortable present—who was the exception in the house rather than the rule. A powerful substratum of relations was usually to be found there, Ardglass and Sleaford connexions, as a rule: not, on the whole, the most eminent members of those families. Jeavons, certainly no snob in the popular and derogatory sense (although he had acquired for everyday purposes a modicum of lore peculiar to his wife's world) would from time to time produce a relation of his own—for example, a nephew who worked in Wolverhampton—but, even had he so desired, he could never have attempted to compete in point of number with the ramifications of Molly's family: the descendants of her grandfather's ninety-seven first cousins. It was at the Jeavonses' that I met the Tolland sisters again.

Lovell, probably unreliable, I thought, upon such a point, said that Jeavons used occasionally to kick over the traces of married life.

"He goes off by himself and gets tight and picks up a

woman," Lovell said. "Just once in a way, you know. One evening he brought an obvious tart to the house to have a drink."

"Were you there?"

"No. Someone told me. One of the Tollands, I think."

I questioned the truth of the story, not so much because I wholly disbelieved it, as on account of the implications of such behaviour, suggesting additionally mysterious avenues of Jeavons's life, which for some reason I felt unwilling, almost too squeamish, to face. However, Lovell himself agreed that whichever Tolland sister had produced the story was probably no very capable judge of the degrees of fallen womanhood, and might easily have used the term without professional connotation: admitting, too, had any such incident taken place, that the girl was unlikely to have been remarked as someone very unusual in such a social no man's land as the Jeavons drawing-room. He conceded finally that Molly would be more than equal to dealing with an intrusion of just that sort, even had she decided—something very unlikely—that the trespassing guest had unexpectedly passed beyond some invisible, though as it were platonically defined, limit as to who might, and who might not, be suitably received under the Jeavons' roof.

All the same, the story, even if untrue, impressed me as of interest in its bearing on a sense of strain suffered, perhaps continuously, by Jeavons himself. At worst, the supposed introduction of a "tart" into his house was a myth somehow come into existence, which represented in highly coloured terms a long since vanquished husband's vain efforts publicly to demonstrate his own independence from a wife's too evident domination. The legend itself was a kind of tribute to Molly's strength: a strength of which her first husband too, for all I knew, might in his time have been made equally aware; although Lord Sleaford, at least outwardly, was better equipped to control a wife of Molly's sort.

"I don't think she was unhappy when she was married to Uncle John," Lovell used to say. "Of course, he was rather a dull dog. Still, lots of women have to put up with dull dogs—not to say dirty dogs—without the advantage of lots of money and a stately home. Besides, Ted is a dull dog, too. I suppose Aunt Molly prefers husbands like that."

My own feeling was that Jeavons could not be described as "dull": even though he had appeared so, in that very phrase, to Widmerpool equally with Lovell. On the contrary, Jeavons seemed to me a person oddly interesting.

"Molly never really got on with her contemporaries," Lovell said. "The kind of people one associates with Lady Diana—and all that. She knew some of them, of course, very well, but she couldn't be called one of that, or any other, set. I dare say Uncle John was afraid of his wife being thought 'fast'. She was very shy, too, I believe, in those days. Quite different from what she is like now."

A picture of Molly Jeavons was beginning to emerge: separateness from her "young married" contemporaries: perhaps a certain recoil from their flamboyance in any case, nothing in common with the fleeting interest in the arts of that new fashionable world. She might have the acquisitive instinct to capture from her first marriage (if that was indeed their provenance) such spoils as the Wilson and the Greuze, while remaining wholly untouched by the intellectual emancipation, however skin-deep, of her generation: the Russian Ballet: the painters of the Paris School: novels and poetry of the period: not even such a mournful haunt of the third-rate as the Celtic Twilight had played a part in her life. She had occupied a position many women must have envied, jogging along there for a dozen years without apparent dissatisfaction or a breath of scandal; then contentedly taking on an existence of such a very different kind, hardly noticing the change. All that was interesting. The fact was, perhaps, that her easy-going, unambitious manner of life had passed unremarked in a vast house like Dogdene, organised in the last resort by the industrious Sleaford, who, according to Lovell, possessed rather a taste for interfering in domestic matters. While married to him, Molly remained a big, charming, noisy young woman, who had never entirely ceased to be a schoolgirl. When the Dogdene frame was removed, like the loosening of a corset of steel, the unconventional, the eccentric, even the sluttish side of her nature became suddenly revealed to the world.

So far as "getting on" with her second husband was concerned, the strongest protest she ever seemed to make was: "Oh, Teddy, dear, do you ever catch hold of the right end of the stick?" spoken kindly, and usually not without provocation; for Jeavons could be slow in grasping the point of a story. Some husbands might certainly take even that rebuke amiss, but Jeavons never seemed to question Molly's absolute sway over himself, the house and all those who came there. I heard her say these words on subsequent visits after Lovell had introduced me there. Neither Widmerpool nor Mrs. Haycock had turned up again since that first night, and I made some inquiry about them.

"Oh, you know Mr. Widmerpool?" said Molly, at once beginning to laugh. "How extraordinary that you should know him. But perhaps you said so before. He has got jaundice. What a thing to happen when you are going to get married."

"How disagreeable for him. But I am not altogether surprised. He always makes a great deal of fuss about his health. I think he has had jaundice before."

"You know him well then?"

"Fairly well—though I don't often see him."

"He is rather amusing, isn't he?" said Molly. "Quite a

wit in his way. But he must look awful now that he is bright yellow."

I agreed that the disease would give Widmerpool an unattractive appearance. It seemed to me extraordinary that she should have thought him "amusing". I sometimes found his company enjoyable, because we had experienced much in common; but I could never remember him making an entertaining remark. I wondered what he could have said to cause that judgment: learning in due course that she was quite reckless in the characteristics she attributed to individuals. A chance remark would have the effect of swaying her entirely in favour of one person, or of arousing the bitterest opposition to another. She was very critical of many of the people who came to see her, and hoarded an accumulation of largely unfounded inferences about their character. These inaccuracies seemed to cancel each other out in some manner, so that in the last resort Molly was no worse informed, indeed in point of acuteness often better placed, than what might be regarded as "the average".

"Do you think he is in love with Mildred?" she asked sharply.

"I really don't know. I suppose so. If he wants to marry her."

I was not at all prepared for the question.

"Oh, that doesn't necessarily follow at all," she said. "I feel rather sorry for him in some ways. Mildred is not an easy person. I've known her such a long time. She isn't a bit easy. But now you simply must come up to my bedroom and see the monkey. I bought him today from a man in Soho, where I went to get some pimentos."

A good deal of the life of the Jeavons' household was, in fact, lived in Molly's bedroom, either because a sick animal was established there (with the budgerigars, four principal dogs and at least as many cats inhabited the house), or simply because Molly herself had risen late, or retired early to rest, in either case holding a kind of reception from her bed, a Victorian fourposter that took up most of the room. On a chest of drawers beside the bed stood a photograph of Leavons in uniform breeches: puttees: at the back of his head a floppy service cap of the kind stigmatised by Mrs. Haycock in her youth as a "gorblimey". He held a knotted bamboo swagger cane under one arm, and, wearing on his tunic the ribbon of the M.C. (awarded after the action in which he had been so seriously wounded), he looked the complete subaltern of war-time musical comedy.

"Come along, all of you," said Molly. "You must all see the monkey. You too, Tuffy. You simply must see him."

I had already recognised the tall, dark, beaky-nosed woman to whom she spoke as Miss Weedon, former secretary of my old friend Charles Stringham's mother, Mrs. Foxe. Miss Weedon, now in her late forties, had been his sister Flavia's governess. After Flavia grew up, she had stayed on to help with Mrs. Foxe's social engagements and charities. I had been waiting an opportunity to have a word with her. I reintroduced myself as we climbed the stairs with the other people who wished—or were being compelled—to visit the monkey. Miss Weedon, wholly unchanged, still sombrely dressed, gave me a keen look.

"But of course I remember," she said. "Charles brought you to luncheon in the London house before he went to Kenya to stay with his father. They had forgotten to get a ticket for Charles in a theatre party that had been made up—the Russian Ballet, I think. I was put to all kind of trouble to produce the extra ticket. However, I got it for him in the end."

'I, too, remember the incident; and also the look of adoration Miss Weedon had given Stringham when she entered the room. I well recalled that passionate glance, although even then—that night at the Jeavonses'—I had not yet guessed the depths of her devotion. I wondered what she did with herself now. Stringham, when last we had seen something of each other, had told me: "Tuffy has come into a little money," and that she was no longer his mother's secretary. I found in due course that Miss Weedon was a close friend of Molly's; in fact that she re-enacted at the Jeavonses' many of her former duties when in the employment of Mrs. Foxe, although, of course, in a household organised on very different terms. It was impossible to know from her manner how unexpected, or the reverse, she found the fact that we had met again at this place. In her profound, though mysterious, dimness, she was typical of the background of Jeavons gatherings.

"I always regret that Charles ever made that journey to Kenya," she said.

She spoke severely, as if I had myself been in part to blame for allowing such a thing ever to have taken place; even though at the same time she freely forgave me for such former thoughtlessness.

"Why?"

"He was never the same afterwards."

I had to admit to myself there was some truth in that. Stringham had never been the same after Kenya. It had been a water-shed in his life.

"Perhaps it was just because he became a man," she said. "Of course, his upbringing was impossible—always, from the beginning. But he changed so much after that trip to Africa. He was a boy when he went—and such a charming boy—and he really came back a man."

"People do grow up. At least some do."

"I am afraid Charles was not one of them," she said gravely. "He became a man, but he did not grow up. He is not grown up now."

I hardly knew what to answer. It was one of those head-first dives into generalisation that usually precedes between two persons a greater conversational intimacy. However, Miss Weedon made no attempt to expand her statement; nor, so to speak, to draw closer in her approach to the problem of Stringham. She merely continued to look at me with a kind of chilly amiability; as if, by making an immediate confession that I was a former friend of his, I had, so far as she was concerned, just managed to save my bacon. When a boy, I had regarded her as decidedly formidable. I still found her a trifle alarming. She gave an impression of complete singleness of purpose: the impression of a person who could make herself very disagreeable if thwarted.

"Do you ever see Charles now?" I asked.

She did not answer at once, as if waiting a second or two in order to make up her mind how best to deal with that question; perhaps trying to decide the relative merits of plain statement and diplomatic evasion. Finally she came down on the side of bluntness.

"Yes, I do see him," she said. "Quite often. You probably know he drinks too much—really much too much. I am trying to help him about that."

She stared at me very composedly. Once more I hardly knew how to reply. I had not expected our conversation to take this unreservedly serious turn; especially as we had by then reached the bedroom, and were only delayed in our introduction to the ape by the concourse of people who surrounded him, offering homage and applauding Molly's particularisation of his many charms of character.

"Charles had certainly had rather too much the last time I saw him," I said, trying to pass off the matter of Stringham's drunkenness as if it were just a question of getting rather tight once in a way, which I knew to be far from the truth. "That was at a dinner he and I went to—two or three years ago at least."

"You have not seen him since then?"

"No."

"It still goes on. But I think I shall be able to help him."

I had no clear idea of how she would set about "helping" Stringham, but the way she spoke made me conscious of her undoubted strength of will. In fact, her voice chilled my blood a little, she sounded so firm. However, at that moment we found ourselves confronted by the monkey—named by his owners "Maisky", after the then Soviet Ambassador—and were introduced by Molly to shake hands with him. He was sitting thoughtfully among the cushions of a spacious basket, from time to time extending a small, dry paw in greeting to Molly's guests as they came into his immediate presence. A saucer of nuts stood beside him. There was something of Quiggin in his seriousness and self-absorption: also in the watchful manner in which he glanced from time to time at the nuts, sometimes choosing one specially tempting to crack.

"Have you known Lady Molly long?" asked Miss Weedon, after we had taken leave of Maisky, and were returning down the stairs.

"Only a short time."

"I thought I had never seen you here before."

"I was brought by Chips Lovell."

"Oh, yes. One of her nephews. Rather a pushing young man. She was very good to him when he was a boy and his parents did not take much trouble about him. She is a very kind-hearted woman. Quite exceptionally kind-hearted. The house is always full of people she is doing good turns to. Children stay here while their parents are fixing up a divorce. Penniless young men get asked to meals. Former servants are always being given help of one sort or another. There is an old cousin of her husband's ill in one of the upper bedrooms now. She has nowhere else to go, and will certainly never leave the house alive. I really cannot think how Lady Molly stands some of the people who come here.

Many are quite dreadful."

"They certainly seem a mixed bag."

"They are worse than that, some of them."

"Really?"

"At the same time, you may find yourself talking to someone like Charles's former father-in-law, Lord Bridgnorth—whom Charles detests and thinks the most conceited, pompous man in the world—who eats out of Lady Molly's hand. He even takes her advice about his horses. Lady Plynlimmon was here at tea the other day. She really seemed quite interested in what Mr. Jeavons was saying about Germany, although usually she won't speak to anyone who is not in the Cabinet. Not long ago Lord Amesbury looked in on his way to a court ball, wearing knee breeches and the Garter. Lady Molly was giving the vet a meal she had cooked herself, because everyone else was out for one reason or another and she had made him come in from miles away in the suburbs to see a cat that had fever. I happened to drop in, and found all three of them eating scrambled eggs together."

By that time we had once more reached the drawing-room. Miss Weedon ceased to enlarge upon these occasional—indeed, very occasional—glories of the Jeavons' salon; which were, as it happened, in marked contrast to the company gathered together that evening. I asked if she knew Mrs. Haycock.

"Certainly I do," said Miss Weedon. "Do you remember a boy called Widmerpool who was at school with Charles and yourself? I think you were all in the same house together, were you not? Charles used to give imitations of him. I am sure you must remember. Well, Mrs. Haycock is going to marry Mr. Widmerpool."

She nodded her head sharply, to emphasise what she had said. I was amazed that she should be familiar with Stringham's mimicry of Widmerpool. I could have found it within the bounds of possibility that she had heard of Widmerpool, but that Stringham should have shared with her such jokes as his brilliant, though essentially esoteric, Widmerpool imitations, I should never have guessed. This new light on Stringham's relationship with Miss Weedon suggested quite a different sort of intimacy to any I had previously surmised. I told her that I already knew of Widmerpool's engagement. That had been my reason for inquiry. Miss Weedon smiled her thin freezing smile.

"I think Mildred Haycock was quite glad to find someone to marry," she said. "Especially a man with such a good future in front of him. Of course he is a bit young for her. All the same, it is *easier* for a woman like Mrs. Haycock—who has two children, both quite old now—to be married. Then, also, although she is not badly off, she is very extravagant. Everyone says so."

"She has been living in the South of France?"

"Where she made herself rather notorious, I believe."

"Meanwhile, her fiancé is suffering from jaundice."

"Indeed," said Miss Weedon, smiling thinly again. "I expect she will find someone to console her. Commander Foxe, for example."

"Buster? How is he?"

"He might begin to take her out again. He retired from the navy some years ago. He has got rather fat. It worries him terribly. He does all kinds of things for it. Every sort of diet. Cures at Tring. It is really his sole interest now."

"And you thought Mrs. Haycock might take his mind off the weighing machine?"

Miss Weedon's mouth stiffened. I saw I had gone too far. She probably regretted her own indiscretion about Buster's past with Mrs. Haycock. I had not thought of Buster Foxe for years. Stringham had never cared for him. It sounded from Miss Weedon's tone as if Buster had been reduced—like Jeavons—to a purely subordinate position. There was a certain parallel in their situations. I wondered if they had ever met.

"And how is Mrs. Foxe herself?"

"Very well, I understand. As social as ever."

"What does Charles do about money now?"

"Money is rather a difficulty," said Miss Weedon, abandoning her air of cold malice, and now speaking as if we had returned to serious matters. "His father, with that French wife of his in Kenya, has not much to spare. Mrs. Foxe has the Warrington money, but it is only for her lifetime. She spends it like water."

At that moment Jeavons himself approached us, putting an end to any explanation Miss Weedon was about to offer on the subject of Stringham's financial resources.

"What do you make of Maisky?" asked Jeavons.

He spoke in a preoccupied, confidential tone, as if Miss Weedon's reply might make all the difference by its orientation to plans on foot for Maisky's education.

"I don't care for monkeys," said Miss Weedon.

"Oh, don't you?" said Jeavons.

He stood pondering this flat, forthright declaration of anti-simianism on Miss Weedon's part. The notion that some people might not like monkeys was evidently entirely new to him; surprising, perhaps a trifle displeasing, but at the same time one of those general ideas of which one can easily grasp the main import without being necessarily in agreement. It was a theory that startled by its stark simplicity.

"Molly has taken a great fancy to him," he said at last.

"I know."

"Oh, well," said Jeavons. "These fancies come and go."

Miss Weedon made no attempt to deny the truth of that observation. Nor did she elaborate her dislike of monkeys. She continued to smile her arctic smile. Jeavons slowly strolled off again, as if to think out the implications of what Miss Weedon had said. I was aware once more of my strong disagreement with those—among whom I suspected Miss Weedon might be numbered—who found Jeavons without interest. On the contrary, he seemed to me, in his own way, rather a remarkable person. An encounter with him away from his own home confirmed that there existed more sides to him than might be apparent in the Jeavons drawing-room.

This episode took place a month or two later, on an evening that had begun with having a drink with Feingold in the pub near the Studio. Feingold had plans to write a satirical novel about life in the film business. He wanted to tell me the plot in the hope that I might be able to suggest a suitable ending to the story. Returning to London later than usual as a result of Feingold's unwillingness to treat the subject in hand briefly (he himself lived in the neighbourhood of the Studio), I decided to dine off a sandwich and a glass of beer at some bar. The pubs in the neighbourhood of my own flat had not much to offer, so, quite fortuitously, I entered an establishment off the south side of Oxford Street, where an illuminated sign indicated an underground buffet. It was the kind of place my old, deceased friend, Mr. Deacon, used to call a "gin palace".

At the foot of the stairs was a large, low-ceilinged room filled with shiny black-topped tables and red wicker armchairs. The bar, built in the shape of an L, took up most of two sides of this saloon, of which the pillars and marbled wall decorations again recalled Mr. Deacon's name by their resemblance to the background characteristics of his pictures: *Pupils of Socrates*, for example, or *By the Will of Diocletian*. No doubt this bar had been designed by someone who had also brooded long and fruitlessly on classical themes, determined to express in whatever medium available some boyhood memory of *Quo Vadis?* or *The Last*

Days of Pompeii. The place was deserted except for the barman, and a person in a mackintosh who sat dejectedly before an empty pint tankard in the far corner of the room. In these oppressively Late Roman surroundings, after climbing on to a high stool at the counter, I ordered food.

I had nearly finished eating, when I became obscurely aware that the man in the corner had risen and was making preparations to leave. He walked across the room, but instead of mounting the stairs leading to the street, he came towards the bar where I was sitting. I heard him pause behind me. I thought that, unable at the last moment to tear himself away from the place, he was going to buy himself another drink. Instead, I suddenly felt his hand upon my shoulder.

"Didn't recognise you at first. I was just on my way out. Come and have one with me in the corner after you've finished your tuck-in."

It was Jeavons. As a rule he retained even in his civilian clothes a faded military air, comparable with—though quite different from—that of Uncle Giles: both of them in strong contrast with the obsolete splendours of General Conyers. A safety pin used to couple together the points of Jeavons's soft collar under the knot of what might be presumed to be the stripes of a regimental tie. That night, however, in a somewhat Tyrolese hat with the brim turned down all the way round, wearing a woollen scarf and a belted mackintosh, the *ensemble* gave him for some reason the appearance of a plain-clothes man. His face was paler than usual. Although perfectly steady on his feet, and speaking in his usual slow, deliberate drawl, I had the impression he had been drinking fairly heavily. We ordered some more beer, and carried it across the room to where he had been sitting.

"This your local?" he asked.

"Never been here before in my life. I dropped in quite by chance."

"Same here."

"It's a long way from your beat."

"I've been doing a pub crawl," he said. "Feel I have to have one—once in a way. Does you good."

There could be no doubt, after that, that Jeavons was practising one of those interludes of dissipation to which Lovell had referred, during which he purged himself, as it were, of too much domesticity.

"Think there is going to be a war?" he asked, very unexpectedly.

"Not specially. I suppose there might be—in a year or two."

"What do you think we ought to do about it?"

"I can't imagine."

"Shall I tell you?"

"Please do."

"Declare war on Germany right away," said Jeavons. "Knock this blighter Hitler out before he gives further trouble."

"Can we very well do that?"

"Why not?"

"No government would dream of taking it on. The country wouldn't stand for it."

"Of course they wouldn't," said Jeavons.

"Well?"

"Well, we'll just have to wait," said Jeavons.

"I suppose so."

"Wait and see," said Jeavons. "That was what Mr. Asquith used to say. Didn't do us much good in 1914. I expect you were too young to have been in the last show?"

I thought that inquiry rather unnecessary, not by then aware that, as one grows older, the physical appearance of those younger than oneself offers only a vague indication of their precise age. To me, "the Armistice" was a distant memory of my preparatory school: to Jeavons, the order to "cease fire" had happened only the other day. The possibility that I might have been "in the war" seemed perfectly conceivable to him.

"Some of it wasn't so bad," he said.

"No?"

"Most of it perfect hell, of course. Absolute bloody hell on earth. Bloody awful. Gives me the willies even to think of it sometimes."

"Where were you?"

"Joined up at Thirsk. Started off in the Green Howards. Got a commission after a bit in one of the newly-formed battalions of the Duke of Wellington's Regiment. I'd exchanged from the Duke's into the Machine-Gun Corps when I caught it in the tummy at Le Bassée."

"Pretty unpleasant?"

"Not so good. Couldn't digest anything for ages. Can't always now, to tell the truth. Some of those dinners Molly gives. Still, digestion is a funny thing. I once knew a chap who took a bet he could eat a cut-off-the-joint-and-two-veg at a dozen different pubs between twelve o'clock and three on the same day."

"Did he win his bet?"

"The first time," said Jeavons, screwing up his face painfully at the thought of his friend's ordeal, "someone else at the table lit a cigarette, and he was sick—I think he had got to about eight or nine by then. We all agreed he ought to have another chance. A day or two later he brought it off. Funny what people can do."

Conversation could be carried no further because at this point "closing time" was announced. Jeavons, rather to my surprise, made no effort to prolong our stay until the last possible moment. On the contrary, the barman had scarcely announced "Time, gentlemen, please," when Jeavons made for the stairs. I followed him. He seemed to have a course for himself clearly mapped out. When we reached the street, he turned once more to me.

"Going home?"

"I suppose so."

"Wouldn't like to prolong this night of giddy pleasure with me for a bit?"

"If you have any ideas."

"There is a place I thought of visiting tonight. A club of some sort—or a 'bottle party' as they seem to call it these days—that has just opened. Care to come?"

"All right."

"A fellow came to see Molly some weeks ago, and gave us a card to get in any time we wanted. You know, you buy a bottle and all that. Makes you a member. Chap used to know Molly years ago. Gone the pace a bit. Now he is rather hard up and managing this hide-out."

"I see."

"Ever heard of Dicky Umfraville?"

"Yes. In fact I met him once years ago."

"That's all right then. Umfraville is running the place. Molly would never dream of going near it, of course. Thought I might go and have a look-see myself."

"Is Dicky Umfraville still married to Anne Stepney?"

"Don't think he is married to anyone at the moment," said Jeavons. "That would make his third or fourth, wouldn't it?"

"His fourth. She was quite young."

"Come to think of it, Molly did say he'd had another divorce fairly recently," said Jeavons. "Anyway, he is more than usually on the rocks at the moment. He used to stay at Dogdene when Molly's first husband was alive. Gilded youth in those days. Not much left now. First-class rider, of course, Umfraville. Second in the National one year."

While we talked, Jeavons had been making his way in a south-easterly direction. We continued in silence for some time, threading a path through a tangle of mean streets, past the plate-glass windows of restaurants opaque with steam.

"I think we must be close now," said Jeavons, at last. "I know more or less where the place is, and Dicky has drawn a sort of map at the back of the card."

By that time we were in the neighbourhood of the Trouville Restaurant, a haunt of Uncle Giles, where one night, years before, I had joined him for a meal. The entrance to the club was concealed in an alleyway, by no means easy to find. We discovered the door at last. The name of the place was inscribed upon it on a minute brass plate, as if any kind of display was to be avoided. At the end of a narrow, dimly-lit passage a villainous-looking fellow with watery eyes and a nose covered with blue veins sat behind a rickety table. On the mention of Umfraville's name and production of the card, this Dickensian personage agreed that we might enter the precincts, after he had with his own hand laboriously inscribed our names in a book.

"The Captain's not in the club yet," he said, as he shut this volume, giving at the same time a dreadful leer like that of a very bad actor attempting to horrify a pantomime audience. "But I don't expect he'll be long now."

"Tell him to report to the Orderly Room when he comes," said Jeavons, causing the blue-nosed guardian of the door to reveal a few rotting teeth in appreciation of this military pleasantry.

The interior of the club was unimpressive. An orchestra of three, piano, drum and saxophone, were making a deafening noise in the corner of the next room. A few "hostesses" sat about in couples, gossiping angrily in undertones, or silently reclining in listless attitudes against the back of a chair. We seemed to be the first arrivals, not surprisingly, for it was still early in the evening for a place of this kind to show any sign of life. After a certain amount of palaver, a waiter brought us something to drink. Nothing about the club suggested that Umfraville's fortune would be made by managing it.

"Anyway, as I was saying," remarked Jeavons, who had, in fact, scarcely spoken for some considerable time, except for his negotiations with the doorkeeper and waiter. "As I was saying, you did have the odd spot of fun once in a while. Mostly on leave, of course. That stands to reason. Now I'll tell you a funny story, if you'll promise to keep it under your hat."

"Wild horses won't drag it from me."

"I suppose it's a story a real gent wouldn't tell," said Jeavons. "But then I'm not a real gent."

"You are whetting my appetite."

"I don't know why I should fix on you to hear the story," said Jeavons, speaking as if he had given much thought to the question of who should be his confidant in this particular matter, and at the same time taking a packet of Gold Flake from his trouser pocket and beginning to tear open the wrapping. "But I've got an idea it might amuse you. Did I see you talking to a fellow called Widmerpool at our house some little while ago—I believe it was the first night you ever came there?"

"You did."

I was interested to find that new arrivals at the Jeavonses' were so accurately registered in the mind of the host.

"Know him well?"

"Quite well."

"Then I expect you know he is going to marry someone called Mildred Haycock, who was also there that night."

"I do."

"Know her too?"

"Not really. I met her once when I was a small boy."

"Exactly. You were a small boy and she was already

174

grown up. In other words, she is quite a bit older than Widmerpool."

"I know. She was a nurse at Dogdene when your wife was there, wasn't she——?"

"Wait a moment—wait a moment," said Jeavons. "Not so fast. Don't rush ahead. That's all part of the story."

"Sorry."

"Well, as I was saying, you did occasionally have a spot of fun in those days. Especially on leave. That's the point. No good going too fast. Had to dodge the A.P.M., of course. Still, that's by the way. Now I happened to get ninety-six hours' leave at short notice when I hadn't time to make any arrangements. Found the easiest thing was to spend the time in London. Didn't know a soul there. Not a bloody cat. Well, after I'd had a bit of a lie-up in bed, I thought I'd go to a show. The M.O. had told me to look in on Daly's, if I got the chance. It was a jolly good piece of advice. *The Maid of the Mountains*. Top-hole show. José Collins. She married into the aristocracy like myself, but that's nothing to do with the story. I bought myself a stall thinking I might catch a packet in the next 'strafe' and never sit in a theatre again. Hadn't been there long before a large party came in and occupied the row in front of me. There was a couple of guardsmen in their grey great-coats and some ladies in evening dress. Among this lot was a nurse—a V.A.D.—who, as I thought—and it subsequently proved correct—began to give me the glad eye."

Jeavons paused to gulp his drink. He shook his head and sighed. There was a long silence. I feared this might be the termination of the story: a mere chronicle of nostalgic memory: a face seen on that one occasion, yet always remembered: a romantic dream that had remained with him all his life. I spurred him gently.

"What did you do about it?"

"About what?"

"The nurse who gave you the glad eye."

"Oh yes, that. In the interval we managed to have a word together in the bar or somewhere. Next thing I knew, I was spending my leave with her."

"And this was——"

"Mrs. Haycock—or, as she then was, the Honourable Mildred Blaides."

Jeavons's expression was so oracular, his tone so solemn, when he pronounced the name with the formal prefix attached, that I laughed. However, he himself remained totally serious in his demeanour. He sat there looking straight at me, as if the profound moral beauty of his own story delighted him rather than any purely anecdotal quality, romantic or banal, according to how you took it.

"And you never saw her again from that time until the other night?"

"Never set eyes on her. Of course, I've often heard Molly speak of Mildred Blaides and her goings-on, but I never knew it was the same girl. She and Molly used to meet sometimes. It so happened, for one reason or another, I was never there."

"Did she say anything about it the other night?"

"Not a word. Didn't recognise me. After all, I suppose I've got to take my place in what must be a pretty long list by now."

"You didn't say anything yourself?"

"Didn't want to seem to presume on a war-time commission, so I kept mum. Besides, it's just as well Molly shouldn't know. If you gas about that sort of thing too much, the story is bound to get around. Silly of me to tell you, I expect. You'll keep your trap shut, won't you?"

"Of course."

"Just thought it might interest you—especially as you know Widmerpool."

"It does—enormously."

"That's the sort of thing that happens in a war. Happens to some chaps in peacetime too, I suppose. Not chaps like me. Haven't the temperament. Things have changed a lot now anyway. I don't mean people don't sleep with each other any longer. Of course they do. More than ever, if what everyone says nowadays is true. But the whole point of view is different somehow. I expect you were too young to have seen *The Bing Boys*?"

"No, I wasn't too young. I saw the show as a schoolboy."

The band had momentarily ceased its hubbub. Jeavons leant forward. I thought he had something further to say which he wished to run no danger of being overheard. Instead, he suddenly began to sing, quite loud and in an unexpected deep and attractive voice:

> *"I could say such—wonderful things to you,*
> *There would be such—wonderful things to do ..."*

Taking this, perhaps not unnaturally, as a kind of summons, two of the girls at a neighbouring table rose and prepared to join us, a tall muscular blonde, not altogether unlike Mona, and a small, plump brunette, who reminded me of a girl I used to know called Rosie Manasch. (Peter Templer liked to say that you could recognise all the girls you had ever met in a chorus: like picking out your frinds from a flock of sheep.) Jeavons immediately checked this threatened incursion before it could take serious form by explaining that we were waiting for the "rest of the party". The girls withdrew. Jeavons continued the song as if there had been no interruption:

> *"If you were the only—girl in the world,*
> *And I was the only boy ..."*

He had only just time to finish before the band broke out again in a deafening volume of sound, playing some tune of very different tempo from that sung by Jeavons.

"People don't think the same way any longer," he bawled across the table. "The war blew the whole bloody thing up, like tossing a Mills bomb into a dug-out. Everything's changed about all that. Always feel rather sorry for your generation as a matter of fact, not but what we haven't all lost our—what do you call 'em—you know—somebody used the word in our house the other night—saying much what I'm saying now? Struck me very forcibly. You know—when you're soft enough to think things are going to be a damned sight better than they turn out to be. What's the word?"

"Illusions?"

"Illusions! That's the one. We've lost all our bloody illusions. Put 'em all in the League of Nations, or somewhere like that. Illusions, my God. I had a few of 'em when I started. You wouldn't believe it. Of course, I've been lucky. Lucky isn't the word, as a matter of fact. Still people always talk as if marriage was one long roll in the hay. You can take it from me, my boy, it isn't. You'll be surprised when you get tied up to a woman yourself. Suppose I shouldn't say such things. Molly and I are very fond of each other in our own way. Between you and me, she's not a great one for bed. A chap I knew in the Ordnance, who'd carried on quite a bit with the girls, told me those noisy ones seldom are. Don't do much in that line myself nowadays, to tell the truth. Feel too cooked most of the time. Never sure the army vets got quite all those separate pieces of a toffee-apple out of my ribs. Tickles a bit sometimes. Still, you have to step out once in a way. Go melancholy mad otherwise. Life's a rum business, however you look at it, and—as I was saying—not having been born to all this high life, and so on, I can't exactly complain."

It was clear to me now that, if Molly had had her day, so too in a sense had Jeavons, even though Jeavons's day had not been at all the same as his wife's: few days, indeed, could have been more different. He was one of those men, themselves not particularly aggressive in their relations with the opposite sex, who are at the same time peculiarly attractive to some women; and, accordingly, liable to be appropriated at short notice. The episode of Mildred Blaides illustrated this state of affairs, which was borne out by the story of his marriage. It was unlikely that these were the only two women in the course of his life who had decided to take charge of him. I was hoping for further reminiscences (though expecting none more extraordinary than that already retailed) when Dicky Umfraville himself arrived at our table.

Wearing a dinner jacket, Umfraville was otherwise unchanged from the night we had met at Foppa's. Trim, horsey, perfectly at ease with himself, and everyone around him, he managed at the same time to suggest the proximity of an abyss of scandal and bankruptcy threatening at any moment to engulf himself, and anyone else unfortunate enough to be within his immediate vicinity when the crash came. The charm he exercised over people was perhaps largely due to this ability to juggle with two contrasting, apparently contradictory tributes; the one, an underlying implication of sinister, disturbing undercurrents: the other, a soothing power to reassure and entertain. These incompatible elements were always to be felt warring with each other whenever he was present. He was like an actor who suddenly appears on the stage to the accompaniment of a roll of thunder, yet utterly captivates his audience a second later, while their nerves are still on edge, by crooning a sentimental song.

"Why," he said, "this is a surprise. I never thought we should persuade you to come along here, Ted. Why didn't you bring Molly with you? Are they treating you all right? I see they've brought you a bottle. Apply to me if there is any trouble. Would you like to meet any of the girls? They are not a bad crowd. I can't imagine that you want anything of the sort."

Jeavons did not answer. He barely acknowledged Umfraville's greeting. Once more he was lost in thought. He had undoubtedly had a fair amount to drink. Umfraville was not at all put out by this reception. He pulled a chair up to the table and glanced across at me.

"We've met before somewhere," he said.

"At Foppa's two or three years ago. You had just come back from Kenya. Hadn't you been racing with Foppa?"

"My God," said Umfraville, "I should think I do remember. Foppa and I had been to Caversham together. We are both interested in trotting races, which many people aren't in this country. You came in with a very charming young woman, while Foppa and I were playing piquet. Then your friend Barnby appeared with Lady Anne Stepney—and before you could say Jack Robinson, the next thing I knew was that the Lady Anne had become my fourth wife."

I laughed, wondering what he was going to say next. I knew that his marriage to Anne Stepney had lasted only a very short time.

"I expect you heard that Anne and I didn't manage to hit it off," he went on. "Charming child, but the fact was I was too old for her. She didn't like grown-up life—and who shall blame her?"

He sighed.

"I don't like it much myself," he said.

"Where is she now?"

I hardly knew whether the question was admissible. However, Umfraville had apparently achieved complete objectivity regarding his own life: certainly his matrimonial life.

"Living in Paris," he said. "Doing some painting, you

know. She was always tremendously keen on her painting. I fell rather short on that score too. Can't tell a Sargent from a 'Snaffles'. She shares a flat with a girl who also walked out on her husband the other day. Come on, Ted, you mustn't go to sleep. I agree this place is pretty boring, but I can't have it turned into a doss-house. Not for the first week or so, anyway."

Jeavons came too with a jerk. He began to beat time thoughtfully on the table.

"How are you doing here?" he asked.

He spoke severely, as if he had come to audit the accounts. Umfraville shrugged his shoulders.

"Depends how people rally round," he said. "I don't picture myself staying at this job long. Just enough to cover my most urgent needs—or rather my creditors' most urgent needs. These joints have a brief vogue, if they're lucky. We haven't been open long enough yet to see how things are going. I look upon your arrival, Ted, as a very good omen. Well, I suppose I must see everything about the place is going all right. Ought to have turned up earlier and done that already. I'll look in again. By the way, Max Pilgrim and Heather Hopkins are coming in later to do a turn."

He nodded to us, and moved away. People were now arriving in the club by twos and threes. The tables round us began to fill up. The girls lost some of their apathy. These newcomers offered little or no clue to the style of the place. They belonged to that anonymous, indistinct race of night-club frequenters, as undifferentiated and lacking in individuality as the congregation at a funeral. None of them was in evening dress.

"Rum bird, Umfraville," said Jeavons, thickly. "Don't like him much. Knows everybody. Wasn't a bit surprised when it turned out you'd met him before. Molly used to see quite a lot of him in the old days when he was a johnny about town."

"He married a girl much younger than himself as his fourth wife. They parted company, I hear."

"I know. The Bridgnorths' second daughter," said Jeavons. "She has been to the house. Badly brought up. Been taken down a peg or two, I hope. Bad luck on Eddie Bridgnorth to have a girl like that. Done nothing to deserve it."

Earlier in the evening, Jeavons had expressed only the vaguest knowledge of Umfraville's last marriage. Now, he seemed familiar with all its essential aspects. His awareness seemed quite unpredictable from one moment to another. The compassionate tone in which he had named Lord Bridgnorth clearly voiced regret for a member of a caste rather than an individual, revealing for a split second a side of Jeavons on the whole concealed, though far more developed than might be supposed on brief acquaintance; the side, that is to say, which had by then entirely assimilated his wife's social standpoint. Indeed, the words might have been uttered by Alfred Tolland, so conventional, yet at the same time so unaffected, was the reflection that Eddie Bridgnorth had done nothing to deserve a rackety daughter.

"I think I'll make a further inspection of these quarters," said Jeavons, rising. "Just as well to know your way about."

He made at first towards the band, but a waiter redirected him, and he disappeared through a small door. He was away a long time, during which two fresh elements were added to the composition of the room.

The first of these new components, a man and a woman, turned out to be Max Pilgrim and Heather Hopkins. They entered with the animation of professionals, almost as if their act had already begun, at once greeted by Umfraville who led them to a table near the band. I had never met Pilgrim, although I had more than once watched his performances at restaurants or cabarets, since that night, years before, when he had quarrelled so bitterly with poor Mr. Deacon at Mrs. Andriadis's party. Tall and stooping, smiling through large spectacles, there was something mild and parsonic about his manner, as if he were apologising for having to draw people's attention to their sins in so blatant a manner. He wore tails. Hopkins had cleaned herself up greatly since her application for the loan of an egg from Norah Tolland and Eleanor Walpole-Wilson. Her black coat and skirt, cut like a dinner jacket, had silk lapels above a stiff shirt, butterfly collar and black bow tie. Her silk stockings were black, too, and she wore a bracelet round her left ankle.

This couple had scarcely appeared when another, far less expected party came in, and were shown to a table evidently reserved for them. Mrs. Haycock led the way, followed by my old friend, Peter Templer; then Widmerpool, walking beside an unusually good-looking girl whose face I did not know. They were in evening dress. From the rather stiff way in which Templer carried himself, I guessed that he felt a shade self-conscious about the company he was keeping. By that time I was used to the idea that he no longer regarded Widmerpool with derision. After all, they did business together, and Widmerpool had helped Bob Duport to get a job. All the same, there remained something incongruous about finding Templer and Widmerpool embarked upon a *partie carée* at a night club. Night clubs were so much to be regarded as Templer's natural element, and so little Widmerpool's, that there seemed even a kind of injustice that Widmerpool should in this manner be forced to operate in a field so inappropriate to himself, and, on top of that, for Templer to be covertly ashamed of his company.

In addition to his air of being—almost literally—a fish out of water, Widmerpool looked far from well. Still yellow from his jaundice, he had grown thinner. His dinner jacket hung on him in folds. His hair was ruffled. His back was bent like that of an elderly man. Perhaps it was this flagging aspect of Widmerpool's that made Templer seem more elegant than ever. He, too, was thinner than when I had last seen him. His habitual tendency was to look just a little too well dressed, and that evening he gave the appearance of having walked straight out of his tailor's wearing an entirely new outfit. This glossy exterior, in juxtaposition with Widmerpool, could hardly have been more sharply emphasised. The unknown pretty girl was wearing an unadventurous frock, but Mrs. Haycock was dressed to kill. Enclosed within a bright emerald-green dress with huge leg-of-mutton sleeves, she was talking with great vivacity to Templer, whose arm from time to time she took and squeezed. She looked younger than when I had last seen her.

Before any sign of recognition could take place between the members of this party and myself, the band withdrew from their position at the end of the room, and settled down at one of the tables. A moment later Pilgrim and Hopkins mounted the dais, Hopkins appropriating the pianist's stool, while Pilgrim lounged against the drum. He glanced at his nails, like a nervous don about to lecture a rowdy audience of undergraduates. Hopkins struck a few bars on the piano with brutal violence. By that time Jeavons had returned.

"Found it all right," he said.

"Have you seen who has arrived?"

"Saw them on my way back. You know Mrs. H. doesn't look a bit different from what she looked in 1917."

This comment on Mrs. Haycock seemed to me an extraordinary proposition: either crudely untrue, or most uncomplimentary to her earlier appearance. In due course one learns, where individuals and emotions are concerned, that Time's slide-rule can make unlikely adjustments. Angular and flamboyant, Mrs. Haycock was certainly not without powers of attraction, but I doubted whether Jeavons saw in those severe terms. It was impossible to say. That side of her may, indeed, have constituted her charm for him both at that moment and in 1917. On the other hand, both then and in Umfraville's night club, she may have been equally no more than a romantic dream, a figure transcending any mere question of personal appearance. At that moment Pilgrim advanced a little way in front of the drum, and, in a shrill, hesitant voice, like that of an elderly governess, began to sing:

> *"Di, Di, in her collar and tie,*
> *Quizzes the girls with a monocled eye,*
> *Sipping her hock in a black satin stock,*
> *Or shooting her cuffs over* pernod *or* bock …"

"I've a damn good mind to ask her for a dance," said Jeavons. "Who are they with? Do you know them?"

"The man is called Peter Templer. I've known him for years."

"And the other girl?"

"I don't know."

"Who is Templer?"

"A stockbroker. He was divorced not so long ago from a very pretty model, who then married a writer called Quiggin. Templer is like your friend in the Ordnance, a great one with the girls."

"Looks it," said Jeavons.

When Pilgrim and Hopkins had left the table, Umfraville had moved to the party of which Templer seemed to be host. He was talking to Mrs. Haycock. Templer began to gaze round the room. He caught sight of me and waved. I signalled back to him. Meanwhile, Pilgrim was continuing his song, while Hopkins thumped away vigorously, with a great deal of facility, at the piano.

"Like a torpedo, in brogues or tuxedo,
She's tearing around at Cap Cod, or the Lido;
From Bournemouth to Biarritz, the fashion parades
Welcome debonaire Di in her chic tailor-mades ..."

"You see this sort of song, for instance," said Jeavons. "Who the hell wants to listen to something like that? God knows what it is all about, for one thing. Songs were quite different when I was younger."

The song came to an end and there was a little clapping. Templer came across the dance floor to our table. I introduced him, explaining that Jeavons had brought me; and also that Jeavons knew Widmerpool and Mrs. Haycock. I told him that at once, to forestall comments that might easily be embarrassing in the mood to which Jeavons had abandoned himself.

"So you already know that Widmerpool is getting married?" said Templer. "I was hoping to break the news to you. I am disappointed."

For someone in general so sure of himself, he was a shade self-conscious at being caught entertaining Widmerpool in a haunt of this kind, hardly a routine place to take a business acquaintance. He had probably hoped that the news of Widmerpool's engagement, by its broad humour, would distract attention from his own immediate circumstances.

"The old boy behaved rather well about my brother-in-law, Bob," he said, rather hurriedly. "And then Dicky kept on pestering me to come to this dive of his. Do you know Dicky?"

"Just met him once before."

"And then the girl I'm with loves to be taken to places she thinks 'amusing'. It seemed a chance of killing several birds with the same stone."

"Who is your girl?"

"She is called Betty. I can never remember her married

name. Taylor, is it? Porter? Something like that. We met at a dreadful bridge party the other day. Her husband is only interested in making money, she says. I can't imagine what she finds amiss in that. Rather a peach, isn't she?"

"Certainly."

"Why don't you both come over and join us?"

Templer addressed the question to me, but he turned in the direction of Jeavons as if to persuade him.

"As you know our friend Widmerpool already," said Templer. "I need not explain what he is like. I know he'll be glad to see both of you, even though he is a bit under the weather tonight."

Rather to my surprise, Jeavons at once agreed to join the Templer party. I was not nearly so certain as Templer that Widmerpool would be glad to see us. Jeavons bored him; while Templer and I were such old friends that he might suspect some sort of alliance against himself. He was easily disturbed by such apprehensions.

"What is wrong with Widmerpool?"

"Feeling low generally," said Templer. "Mildred had to drag him out tonight. But never mind that. It is extraordinary those two should be engaged. Women may show some discrimination about whom they sleep with, but they'll marry anybody."

Templer was already, so it appeared, on Christian name terms with Mrs. Haycock. We moved across, bearing our bottle with us. Widmerpool, as I could have foretold, did not look too well pleased to have us at the same table, but his state of health disposed him to show this no more than by offering a rather sour greeting. Mrs. Haycock, on the other hand, was delighted by this increase in numbers. Flushed in the face, she looked as hard as nails. She could hardly be called handsome, but there was a dash about her that Widmerpool could justly feel lacking in his own life as a bachelor. It was surprising to me not merely that he should be alarmed at the prospect of becoming her husband, but that he should ever have had the courage to propose; although, at the same time, plenty of reasons for his doing so presented themselves. Probably he was prepared—for he did most things rationally—to accept, even to welcome, attributes in a wife other men might have approached with caution. At the same time, the notion that he was entirely actuated by "rational" motives was also no doubt far from the truth. He was possibly not "in love", but at the same time impelled by feelings, if less definable than "love", no less powerful. It was perhaps his imagination which had been captured; which is, after all, something akin to love. Who can say? Mrs. Haycock turned a dazzling smile upon us.

"I'm Molly's husband," said Jeavons gruffly.

"But, of course."

She held out her hand, cordially, but without any suggestion that she knew him apart from her recent visit to the Jeavons house. It was certain, I had no doubt on that point, that she remembered nothing of having met him on the earlier occasion. I was curious to see how he would conduct himself. Mrs. Haycock faced me.

"I know you are an old friend of Kenneth's," she said. "As you can see, the poor boy is still as yellow as a guinea, isn't he? It was over-eating that did it."

"But he is always so careful about his food."

"Of course, he fusses all the time," she said. "Or used to. That is just it. I won't stand any nonsense of that sort. I like my food. Naturally, if you are banting, that is another matter. What I can't stand is people who pick at carrots and patent foods and never have a drink."

This description sounded a fairly exact definition of the meals Widmerpool enjoyed.

"I have been making him take me to some decent restaurants—such as there are in this country—and showed him how good food can be. I suppose some of it must have disagreed with him. He is back having his own way now, dining off a sardine and a glass of Malvern water."

Widmerpool himself smiled feebly at all this, as if making no attempt to deny the truth of the picture presented by her of his medical condition. All the time she was speaking, I could think of nothing but the story Jeavons had told me of his former adventure with her. Conversation became general, only Widmerpool continuing to sit in bleak silence. Templer's girl had large, liquid eyes, and a drawl reminiscent of Mona's. She was evidently very taken with Templer, gazing at him all the time, as if she could not believe her luck. I asked her what she thought of the Pilgrim–Hopkins turn.

"Oh, they were good, weren't they?" she said. "Didn't you think so, Peter?"

"A frightfully old-fashioned couple," said Templer. "The only reason they are still here is because their act was a flop at the Café de Madrid. Still, I'm glad you liked them, darling. It shows what a sweet nature you have. But I don't want you to wear clothes like Miss Hopkins. You won't do that, will you?"

She found this dissent from her own opinion delicious, darting excited, apprehensive glances at him from under her eyelashes. I saw that it was no good attempting, even conversationally, to compete. Mrs. Haycock would make easier going. I asked whether she and Widmerpool had decided where they were going to live after they were married.

"That's rather a big question," she said. "Kenneth's business keeps him most of the time in London. I like the idea of making our headquarters in Paris. We could have a small flat over there quite cheaply—in some dingy neighbourhood, if necessary. But I've lived too long in France to want to live anywhere else now. Anyway, for most of the year. Then there are the boys. That's another problem."

I thought for a second that she must refer to a personal obligation she owed to some male group living probably on the Riviera, to be generically thus classified. Seeing that she had not made herself clear, she added:

"My two sons, you know."

"Oh, yes."

"They are always cropping up."

"Are they at school?"

"Yes, of course they are," she said, as if that were a foolish question to ask. "That is, when they haven't been expelled."

She stared at me fixedly after saying this, still seeming to imply that I should already know about her sons, especially the fact that they were continually being expelled from school. Uncertain whether or not she intended to strike a jaunty or sombre note, I did not know whether to laugh or commiserate. In fact, so peculiar was her tone that I wondered now whether she were entirely sane. Although in most respects impossible to imagine anyone less like Mrs. Conyers, a change of expression, or tone of voice, would suddenly recall her sister. For example, when she spoke of her children, I was reminded of Mrs. Conyers invoking the General. There was, however, one marked difference between them. Mrs. Conyers bestowed about her a sense of absolute certainty that she belonged—could only belong—to the class from which she came, the world in which she lived. Mrs. Haycock, on the other hand, had by then largely jettisoned any crude certainties of origin. She may even have decided deliberately to rid herself of too embarrassing an inheritance of traditional thought and behaviour. If so, she had been on the whole successful. Only from time to time, and faintly, she offered a clue to correct speculation about herself: just as Jeavons would once in a way display the unmistakable action of his marriage on his point of view. On the whole, Mrs. Haycock's bluff manner suggested long association with people who were rich, but rich without much concern about other aspects of life.

"Of course I know they are dreadfully badly behaved," she said. "But what am I to do?"

She had that intense, voluble manner of speaking, often characteristic of those who are perhaps a little mad: a flow of words so violent as to give an impression of lack of balance.

"How old are they?"

"Fourteen and fifteen."

Widmerpool, who at that moment looked in no state to shoulder such responsibilities as a couple of adolescent stepsons habitually expelled from school, leant across the table to address Mrs. Haycock.

"I think I'll retire for a minute or two," he said, "and see what taking a couple of those pills will do."

"All right, my own, off you go."

Widmerpool scrambled out from where he sat in the corner next to the wall, and made for the door.

"Isn't he priceless?" said Mrs. Haycock, almost with pride. "Do you know his mother?"

"I've met her."

"Do you know that she suggested that she should live with us after we were married?"

Again she spoke in that strange, flat voice, looking hard at me, so that I did not know how to reply; whether to express horror or indulge in laughter. However, she herself seemed to expect no answer to her question. Whatever her feelings about Widmerpool's mother, they lay too deep for words. Instead of continuing to discuss her personal affairs, she pointed to Jeavons.

"Your friend seems to be going to sleep," she said. "You know I have always heard so much about him, and, although I've known Molly for years, I only met him for the first time the other night."

Her observation about Jeavons's state was true. Templer and his girl had risen to dance, and Jeavons had fallen into a coma similar to those in which General Conyers would sometimes sink. Jeavons seemed to have lost all his earlier enthusiasm to dance with Mrs. Haycock, a change of heart due probably to the amount of beer he had drunk earlier in the evening, before we met. I roused him, and he moved to the other side of the table, into the seat next to Mrs. Haycock.

"How is Molly?" she asked him.

"Molly is all right."

He did not sound too bright. However, he must have understood that something was expected of him, and made an effort.

"Where are you staying?" he asked.

"Jules's."

"In Jermyn Street?"

"I always have a suite there when I come over."

Jeavons suddenly straightened himself.

"Come and dance," he said.

This surprised me. I had supposed him to be speaking without much serious intention, even when he had first said he wanted to dance with her. After he had all but gone to sleep at the table, I thought he had probably found sufficient entertainment in his own reflections. On the contrary, he had now thrown off his drowsiness. Mrs. Haycock rose without the smallest hesitation, and they took the floor together. I was sure she had not recognised Jeavons; equally certain that she was aware, as women are, that some disturbing element was abroad, involving herself in some inexplicable manner. She danced well, steering him this way and that, while Jeavons jogged up and down like a marionette, clutching her to him as he attempted the syncopated steps of some long-forgotten measure. I remembered that he himself never danced when the carpet was rolled back and the gramophone played at the Jeavonses' house. I was still watching them circle the floor when Widmerpool returned from his absence in the inner recesses of the club. He looked worse than ever. There could be no doubt that he ought to go home to bed. He sat down beside me and groaned.

"I think I shall have to go home," he said.

"Didn't the pills work?"

"Quite useless. I am feeling most unwell. Why on earth have you come here with that fellow Jeavons?"

"I ran across him earlier in the evening, and he brought me along. I've met Umfraville before, who runs this place."

I felt, I did not know why, that it was reasonable for him to make this inquiry in an irritable tone; that some apology was indeed required for my appearance there at all. It was clear that the sooner Widmerpool left, the better for his state of health. He looked ghastly. I was going to suggest that he should make some sign to recall Mrs. Haycock to the table, so that they might leave immediately, when he began to speak in a lower voice, as if he had something on his mind.

"You know what we were talking about when we last met?"

"Yes—your engagement, you mean?"

"I—I haven't had an opportunity yet."

"You haven't?"

I felt unwilling to reopen all that matter now, especially in his present state.

"But we've been asked to stay at Dogdene."

"Yes?"

In spite of his malaise, Widmerpool could not keep from his voice a note of justifiable satisfaction.

"You know the house, of course."

"I've never stayed there."

"No, no," he said. "I mean you know about it. The Slea-fords' place."

"Yes, I know all that."

"Do you think it would be—would be the moment?"

"It might be a very good one."

"Of course it would make a splendid background. After all, if any house in the country has had a romantic history, it is Dogdene," he said.

The reflection seemed to give him strength. I thought of Pepys, and the "great black maid"; and immediately Widmerpool's resemblance to the existing portraits of the diarist became apparent. He had the same obdurate, put-upon, bad-tempered expression. Only a full-bottomed wig was required to complete the picture. True, Widmerpool shared none of Pepys's sensibility where the arts were concerned; in the aesthetic field he was a void. But they had a common preoccupation with money and professional advancement; also a kind of dogged honesty. Was it possible to imagine Widmerpool playing a similar rôle with the maid? There I felt doubtful. Was that, indeed, his inherent problem? Could it be that his love affairs had always fallen short of physical attack? How would he deal with Mrs. Haycock should that be so? I wondered whether their relationship was really so incongruous as it appeared from the exterior. So often one thinks that individuals and situations cannot be so extraordinary as they seem from outside, only to find that the truth is a thousand times odder.

While Widmerpool sat in silence, and I pondered these matters, there came suddenly a shrill burst of sound from the dance floor. I saw Mrs. Haycock break away violently from Jeavons. She clasped her hands together and gave peal after peal of laughter. Jeavons, too, was smiling, in his quiet, rather embarrassed manner. Mrs. Haycock caught his hand, and led him through the other dancing couples, back to the table. She was in a great state of excitement.

"Look here," she said. "We've just made the most marvellous discovery. Do you know that we both knew each other in the war—when I was a nurse?"

"What, when you were at Dogdene?" asked Widmerpool.

His mind, still full of the glories of that great house, remained unimpressed by this news. To him nothing could be more natural than the fact that Mrs. Haycock and Jeavons had met. She had been a V.A.D. at Dogdene: Jeavons had been a convalescent there. There was no reason why Widmerpool should ever speculate upon the possibility that their Dogdene interludes had not overlapped. He was, in any case, not at all interested in the lives of others.

"I never recognised him, which was quite mad of me, because he looks *just* the same."

"Oh, really?" said Widmerpool.

He could not see what the fuss was about.

"Isn't it absolutely marvellous to meet an old friend like that?"

"Why, yes, I suppose it is," said Widmerpool, without any great conviction.

"It's scrumptious."

Widmerpool smiled feebly. This was plainly a situation he found hard to envisage. In any case, he was at that moment too oppressed by his own state of health to attempt appreciation of Mrs. Haycock's former friendships.

"Look here, Mildred," he said, "I am still feeling far from well. I really think I will go home. What about you? Shall I take you back?"

Mrs. Haycock was appalled.

"Go back?" she said. "Why, of course not. I've only just arrived. And, anyway, there are millions of things I want to talk about after making this marvellous discovery. It is too priceless for words. To think that I never knew all these years. It is really *too* extraordinary that we should never have met. I believe Molly did it on purpose."

Widmerpool, to do him justice, did not seem at all surprised at this not very sympathetic attitude towards his own condition. There was something dignified, even a little touching, about the manner in which he absolutely accepted the fact that his state of health did not matter to Mrs. Haycock in the least. Perhaps by then already inured to indifference, he had made up his mind to expect no more from married life. More probably, this chance offered to slip away quietly by himself, going home without further trouble—even without delivering Mrs. Haycock to her hotel—was a relief to him. In any case, he seemed thankful, not only that no impediment had been put in his way of escape, but that Mrs. Haycock herself was in the best possible mood at the prospect of her own abandonment.

"Then I can safely leave you with Peter Templer and Mrs. Taylor—or is it Mrs. Porter?" he said. "You will also have Nicholas and Mr. Jeavons to look after you."

"My dear, of course, of course."

Widmerpool rose a little unsteadily. Probably the people round thought, quite mistakenly, that he had had too much to drink.

"I shall go then," he said. "I will ring you up tomorrow, Mildred. Make my apologies to Peter."

"Night, night," she said, not unkindly.

Widmerpool nodded to the rest of us, then turned, and picked his way through the dancers.

"But this is too, too amusing," said Mrs. Haycock, taking Jeavons by the arm. "To think we should meet again like this after all these years."

She poured out another drink for himself, and passed the bottle round the table, so delighted by the discovery of Jeavons that Widmerpool seemed now dismissed entirely from her mind. The sentiments of Jeavons himself at that moment were hard to estimate; even to know how drunk he was. He might have reminded Mrs. Haycock of their former encounter with some motive in his mind, or merely on impulse. The information could even have emerged quite fortuitously in the course of one of his long, rambling anecdotes. No one could predict where his next step would lead. Outwardly, he gave no impression of intoxication, except for those intermittent bouts of sleepiness, in which, for that matter, he probably often indulged himself at home when dead sober. Templer and his girl returned to the table.

"This is really rather a grim place," said Templer. "What do you say to moving on somewhere else—the Slip-in, or somewhere like that?"

"Oh, but darling Peter," said Mrs. Haycock, who had, so it appeared, met Templer for the first time that evening. "I've just begun to enjoy myself so much. Kenneth decided he wasn't feeling well enough to stay, so he has gone home—with many apologies—and now I have just found one of my oldest, my very oldest, friends here."

She pointed to Jeavons.

"Oh, yes," said Templer.

He looked a bit surprised; but there was, after all, no reason why Jeavons should not be one of her oldest friends, even if, in Templer's eyes, he was rather an oddity. If Templer's first predisposition had been embarrassment at being caught in a party with Widmerpool, his mood had later changed to one of amusement at the insoluble problem of why I myself was visiting a night club with Jeavons. Jeavons was not an easy man to explain. Templer had none of Chips Lovell's appreciation of the subtleties of such matters. The Jeavons house, irretrievably tinged, in however unconventional a manner, with a kind of life against which he had rigidly set his face, would have bored Templer to death. Mrs. Haycock was, for some reason, another matter; he could tolerate her. Patently rackety, and habituated to association with what Uncle Giles called "all sorts"—different, for some reason, from Molly Jeavons's "all sorts"—she presented no impediment to Templer. He sat down beside her and began to discuss other places that might be more amusing than Umfraville's club. Umfraville himself now returned, bringing with him Max Pilgrim and Heather Hopkins.

"May we join you for a moment?" he said. "You know, Mildred, I don't believe we have met since that terrible night at Cannes in—what was it?—about 1923, when Milly Andriadis gave that great party, and we walked round the port together and watched the sunrise."

We made room for them. Hopkins and Pilgrim were on their best behaviour. Templer's girl seemed for the moment almost to have forgotten him in the excitement of sitting with such celebrities. I found myself next to Templer and we had a moment to talk.

"How are you, Nick," he said. "I haven't seen you for centuries."

"No worse—and you?"

"Not too bad," said Templer. "Family worries of various kinds, though there is a lot to be said for no longer being married. The usual trouble is raging with Bob and that sister of mine. No sooner does Bob get a good job than he goes off with some girl. All men are brothers, but, thank God, they aren't all brothers-in-law. I believe Jean has left him again, and gone to stay in Rome with Baby Wentworth—or whatever Baby Wentworth is now called after marrying that Italian."

It was quite a good test, and I came out of it with flying colours; that is to say, without any immediate desire to buy an air ticket to Rome.

"You did know my sister, Jean, didn't you?" he said. "I mean I haven't been telling you a long story about someone you've never met?"

"Of course I knew her. And your other sister, too. I met her ages ago."

"Baby Wentworth is a cousin of mine," said Mrs. Haycock, suddenly breaking off an argument with Hopkins regarding the private life of the barman at the Carlton Hotel at Cannes. "What a pretty girl she is. When my father died, he hadn't managed to produce a son, so Baby's father succeeded. Her brother, Jack Vowchurch, is rather hell, I believe. I've never met him. They were quite distant cousins, and we never saw anything of them. Then one day at Antibes someone pointed out Baby to me. Didn't Sir Magnus Donners have rather a fancy for her? She was with him then."

"Wasn't your father the chap who rode his horse upstairs after dinner?" asked Jeavons, wholly unexpectedly.

"Yes, of course he was," said Mrs. Haycock. "His favourite hunter. That was before I was born. I think he was supposed to be celebrating something. 'Peace with Honour', would it have been? That kind of thing. I believe that was the story. We had a hunting-box at Melton Mowbray that season. They had to demolish the side wall of the house to retrieve the animal. It cost the hell of a lot of money, I know."

Once again, when she spoke of her father, I was reminded of Mrs. Conyers, even though the phraseology of the narrative was so different from any her sister would have employed.

"And then there was some other story," insisted Jeavons. "Setting fire to a fellow's newspaper in a train. Something like that."

This interest in Lord Vowchurch on the part of Jeavons I found astonishing.

"There are absolutely hundreds, darling," said Mrs. Haycock. "Do you know about when he squirted mauve ink over an archbishop at a wedding?"

"I met such a sweet archbishop at the Theatrical Garden Party last year," said Pilgrim. "Perhaps he wasn't an archbishop, but just a bishop. He wore a hat just like one of Heather's."

"I might get a clerical hat," said Hopkins. "That's not a bad idea. There is a place off Oxford Street where they sell black boaters. I've always wanted one."

I asked if she had been seeing much of Norah Tolland and Eleanor Walpole-Wilson.

"Oh, those two girls," she said. "I thought I'd met you before somewhere. No, I haven't been seeing them. I found out Eleanor had said a very unkind thing about me. I thought she was a friend, but I see I made a mistake."

"Look here," said Jeavons, who had cast off inertia and was now in his most lively mood. "Do you remember how that song used to go:

> 'He ran a pin
> In Gwendolyn,
> In Lower Grosvenor Place ...'

I can't remember the exact words."

By this time I was becoming tired of Umfraville's night club. Like Widmerpool, I wished to go home. Jeavons's companionship demanded an almost infinite capacity for adaptation to changed moods and circumstances. In many ways sympathetic, he lacked any of that familiar pattern of behaviour to be found, say, in Quiggin, so that in the last resort his company was exhausting rather than stimulating. Umfraville went off to attend to the club's administration. Discussion began once more as to whether the party should move elsewhere.

"I'll tell you what," said Mrs. Haycock. "If you all want to go to the Slip-in, why not leave me here with Ted. He and I will talk about old times for a bit. Then he can see me home."

That was agreed. There was still a lot of talk. I left before the final plan was put into execution. Out in the passage, Umfraville was instructing the villainous, blue-nosed custodian as to who could, and who could not, wisely be admitted to the club.

"Not going?" he said. "It's early yet."

"I've got to get up early tomorrow and write film-scripts."

"Good God," he said. "But, look here, just before you go, what's happened to Mildred Haycock these days? I hadn't seen her in an age. She seems to be holding up pretty well. I know Peter Templer, but who was the other chap who left the party early on?"

"He is called Widmerpool. She is engaged to him."

"Is she, indeed? What does he do?"

"A bill-broker."

Umfraville nodded his head sagely.

"Come again," he said. "Now that you know the way."

I passed through empty streets, thinking that I, too, should be married soon, a change that presented itself in terms of action rather than reflection, the mood in which even the most prudent often marry: a crisis of delight and anxiety, excitement and oppression.

FIVE

A background of other events largely obscured the steps leading up to my engagement to Isobel Tolland. Of this crisis in my life, I remember chiefly a sense of tremendous inevitability, a feeling that fate was settling its own problems, and too much reflection would be out of place. Marriage, as I have said, is a form of action, of violence almost: an assertion of the will. Its orbit is not to be charted with precision, if misrepresentation and contrivance are to be avoided. Its facts can perhaps only be known by implication. It is a state from which all objectivity has been removed. I shall say something, however, of the incident which at this juncture chiefly distracted attention from my own affairs.

Although that evening when we had dined at Thrubworth had been by no means the sole occasion when Quiggin had announced that he wanted to "see China and judge for himself", no one among his acquaintances supposed him at all likely to set sail at once for the Far East. The words were generally—and, as it turned out, correctly—assumed to be in the main rhetorical: merely buttressing opinions already propagated by him about the ominous situation in Asia. There was, for example, the matter of fare. High as his reputation stood as a critic, it was doubtful whether any publisher would be prepared to advance enough on a projected travel book, with a political bias, to transport Quiggin so far; while Erridge, sympathetic to the wish, had at the same time shown no impulse to foot the bill. Doubts had been maliciously expressed by Mark Members, just returned from his lecture tour in America, as to whether, when it came to the point, Quiggin would be impatient to enter an area in which the Japanese army was at that time engaged in active operations. Members may have been unjust. He was certainly applying to Quiggin the heartless criticism of an old friend. All the same, I should have been surprised to hear that Quiggin had set out upon that journey.

On the other hand, when Erridge for the same reason—"to see for himself"—turned out to be on his way to China, there was less to wonder at. Erridge had already shown himself prepared to undergo uncomfortable forms of travel; he was undoubtedly in a restless state of mind; he was interested in the political implications of the situation: finally, he could afford to buy a ticket. The enterprise might be the result of Quiggin's advocacy, or his own gnawing sense of moral obligation. The motive was almost immaterial. There was another far more absorbing aspect of his departure when it came about. He did not go alone. He took Mona with him.

Naturally this affair was discussed at great length at houses such as the Jeavonses', where no details were available, beyond the fact that Erridge and Mona were together on a P. & O. liner bound for the East; while Quiggin had been left in England. Their precise destination was unknown. The immediate Tolland family were, naturally, in a ferment of interest. Even so, the story made on the whole less stir than might be thought, for Erridge had by then so firmly established a reputation for eccentricity that those who knew him personally were prepared for anything. Since he inhabited no particular social milieu, his doings affected few individuals directly. Such persons were chiefly a small group of hangers-on, like Quiggin or Howard Craggs, the Left Wing publisher, and the members of some of Erridge's committees. For the rest of the world, those to whom his name alone was familiar, his behaviour as usual took on the unsubstantial shape of a minor paragraph in the newspaper, momentarily catching the attention, without at the same time giving a conviction of its subject's existence in "real life". Uncle Giles, with his very different circumstances, was in much the same case, in that no one knew, or, for that matter, greatly cared what he would do next, provided he made no disastrous marriage and kept out of prison. In Erridge's position, the question of marriage now loomed steeply for his relations, a matter of keen speculation, particularly since this was the first occasion when he was known to have been closely associated with any woman.

All this had considerable bearing on my own life at the time, because my engagement was made public in the same week that the Erridge–Mona story broke, and was naturally overshadowed—especially upon my first meeting with Katherine, Lady Warminster—by this far more striking family convulsion. Some people considered Mona's abandonment of Quiggin less remarkable than the fact that she should have stayed with him for several years. Others took the opportunity to recall that, after crossing the Rubicon of leaving Templer, further changes of partner were inevitable. That was all very well, but I had to admit to myself that, when I had seen them together at Thrubworth, I had never guessed they were about to run away together. Erridge had shown no sign whatever of having any so desperate a plan in view, while Mona's interest in him had appeared to be no more than the natural product of her own boredom at the cottage. Possibly at that time neither had contemplated any such development. All at once the urgency of action had swept irresistibly down upon them : a sudden movement that altered the value of every piece on the board. This would deal a serious blow to Quiggin. Even if he had never gone through the ceremony of marriage with Mona (which now seemed probable), his close relations with Erridge would scarcely survive such conduct; or would, at best, take some little time to repair on Erridge's return from China.

This escapade of Erridge's—at present it was spoken of merely as an escapade, because any question of marriage must in the first instance depend upon whether or not Mona was already Quiggin's wife—very considerably magnetised the atmosphere when for the first time I came to see his stepmother. No one yet knew how much Lady Warminster, on the whole alarmingly well informed on all topics connected with her relations, had up to that time been able to discover about Erridge and Mona. She was suspected, as usual, of possessing more information than she was prepared to admit. Like a foreign statesman, who, during important international negotiations, insists upon the medium of an interpreter in spite of his own familiarity with the language in which discussion is being conducted, she preferred every approach to be devious, and translated into her own idiom.

Although, by then, I had often visited the house in Hyde Park Gardens, she and I had not met on those earlier occasions, chiefly because Lady Warminster's health kept her for weeks at a time confined to her room. Views differed as to the extent to which hypochondria governed her life, some alleging that no one enjoyed better health, others taking her side in insisting that, delicate since childhood, she bore her ailments courageously. Smaller, older, quieter in manner and more handsome than Molly Jeavons, she was also much more awe-inspiring. Something of the witch haunted her delicate, aquiline features and transparent ivory skin: a calm, autumnal beauty that did not at all mask the amused, malicious, almost insane light that glinted all the time in her infinitely pale eyes. When young, she must have been very good-looking indeed.

Unlike her sister, who was entirely detached from intellectual interests of any sort, Lady Warminster lived largely in a world of the imagination. Her house, a complete contrast to the Jeavonses', reflected the more ordered side of her nature, surprising by the conventionality of its taste and air of stylised repose; at least until the rooms given over to her stepchildren were reached. These quiet, rich, rather too heavy decorations and furniture were deceptive. Little about the house could be thought quiet, or conventional, when closely examined. Perhaps, after all, when closely examined, no sort of individual life can truly be so labelled. However, against this formal background, when her health allowed, Lady Warminster wrote her books, historical studies of the dominating women of the past: Catherine the Great: Christina of Sweden: Sarah, Duchess of Marlborough: volumes rarely mentioned in the Press, though usually kindly treated by such critics as noticed them, on account of their engaging impetuosity of style and complete lack of pretension to any serious scholarship.

This literary preoccupation with feminine authority had come to Katherine Warminster, so it appeared, only after her second widowhood. Like her sister, Molly, she had no child by either husband, the first of whom had been one of those "well-born" City men for whom Peter Templer used to express such aversion. He had been a fairly successful stockbroker, fond of hunting and shooting, a man, so far as could be judged, with no salient characteristic. His wife had spent most of her days with friends who belonged to a world quite other than his own; latterly submitting to him in their marriage only to the extent of living in the country, where she was bored to death. She can have seen little more of Lord Warminster, when married to him, much of whose time was spent abroad unaccompanied by his wife, fishing in Iceland or pig-sticking in Bengal. This status of having twice married, without, so it might seem, great attachment to either husband, perhaps gave Lady

Warminster the mysterious, witch-like quality she dispensed so pervasively about her.

The second marriage was said—quite unexpectedly—to have improved, on the whole, Erridge's relations with his father, with whom, without any open quarrel, he had never been on good terms. Lord Warminster had accepted his son's idiosyncrasies stoically, together with anything else of which he disapproved in his children, attributing everything to their mother's Alford blood. The rest of the Tolland brothers and sisters had lived—Norah was an exception—amicably with their stepmother: the younger ones entirely brought up by her. Lady Warminster, eccentric herself, showed a decent respect for eccentricity. She had no wish to interfere with other people, her stepchildren or anyone else, provided her own convenience was not threatened, so that the Tollands were left largely to their own devices. Life at Hyde Park Gardens might be ruthless, but it was played out on a reasonably practical basis, in which every man was for himself and no quarter was given; while at the same time a curtain of relatively good humour was usually allowed to cloak an inexorable recognition of life's inevitable severities.

I was fortunate enough already to have established myself to some small extent in Lady Warminster's good graces by a book written a year or two before which she happened to have enjoyed, so that my own reception might have been a worse one. Even so, with a person of her sort that was not a matter upon which to presume. For a time we discussed affairs personal to Isobel and myself, and then, as soon as these could be politely, and quite kindly, dismissed, Lady Warminster gave a smile that showed plainly we should turn to more intriguing topics.

"I think you are one of the few people, either in or out of the family, who have met Erridge lately," she said. "So that you must now tell me what you think about this trip of his to China."

I assured her that I knew little or nothing of Erridge and his movements, but that the journey seemed a reasonable one for him to make in the light of his interests and way of life. I admitted that I had heard him discuss a visit to China.

"I agree with you," she said. "Erridge is much too much by himself. He will not be alone on the voyage, I think, will he?"

That was not easy to answer. I did not wish, at this early stage in our relationship, to be detected telling, or, indeed, implying, a deliberate lie. I hoped equally to avoid revealing all that was known about Erridge and Mona, scanty as that might be. I said that I knew no details about the arrangements made by Erridge for his journey.

"There are always plenty of people to talk to on boats," I suggested, with a sense of descending into banality of the most painful kind.

"Of course," she said, as if that notion had never before been so well presented to her. "Do you like the sea?"

"Not at all."

"Nor me," she said. "There is nothing I detest more than a sea voyage. But surely he is taking a secretary, or someone of that sort. I think he will. It will be so lonely otherwise. Especially as he is used to living by himself. You are never so lonely as when among a lot of people you do not know."

It was impossible to tell whether the reference to "a secretary" designated Mona, or some new figure in Erridge's life; or was merely a random shot to draw information.

"I don't think I know about a secretary."

"Perhaps I am mistaken. Someone may have said something of the sort. What did you think of Thrubworth? Erridge does not take much interest in the house, I am afraid. Still less in the grounds."

I commented on Thrubworth and its surroundings, again

208

aware that banality had not been avoided. Lady Warminster sighed. She moved her thin, pale hands, covered with a network of faint blue veins, lightly over the surface of a cushion.

"You were staying in the neighbourhood, I think."

"Yes."

"Not, by any chance, with the writer, J. G. Quiggin?"

"Yes—with J. G. Quiggin. I have known him a long time. Do you read his articles?"

"I was so interested when I heard Erridge had him living in that cottage. I enjoy Mr. Quiggin's reviews so much, even when I do not agree with them. They have not been appearing lately."

"No. I haven't seen any of them lately."

"Is there a Mrs. Quiggin?"

"Yes, she——"

"But I do not know why I am asking you this, because Susan and Isobel told me how they met you and the Quiggins, both of them; at Thrubworth. She is a great beauty, is she not?"

"I think she might certainly be called a great beauty."

"An actress?"

"No, a model. But she thinks of going on the films."

"Does she? And what does Mr. Quiggin think about that?"

"He seemed quite to like the idea."

"Did he?" she said. "Did he? How strange."

She paused for a moment.

"I like his articles so much," she went on, after a few seconds. "He is such—such a broad-minded man. So few critics are broad-minded. You know I want to talk to you about the new book I am writing myself. Will you give me your advice about it?"

For the time being the subject of Erridge was abandoned. I was glad of that. Lady Warminster had either learnt enough, or decided that for the moment, whatever her available knowledge, she would pursue the matter no further. Instead she talked for a time about Frederica, explaining that she had been so named on account of a Tolland great-uncle, a secretary of legation in Prussia, who, sharing an interest in painting, had been on friendly terms with the Empress Frederick. That was how the name had come into the family; that explained why Alfred Tolland had wanted to hear Mrs. Conyers's anecdote about the Empress, the night we had met at the Jeavonses'. Lady Warminster represented to a high degree that characteristic of her own generation that everything may be said, though nothing indecorous discussed openly. Layer upon layer of wrapping, box after box revealing in the Chinese manner yet another box, must conceal all doubtful secrets; only the discipline of infinite obliquity made it lawful to examine the seamy side of life. If these mysteries were observed everything might be contemplated: however unsavoury: however unspeakable. Afterwards, thinking over the interview when I had left the house, I knew something of what Alfred Tolland could feel after one of Molly Jeavons's interrogations. Lady Warminster might be outwardly quieter than her sister: her capacity for teasing was no less highly developed. A long time later, when the subject of Erridge and Mona had become a matter of common talk at the Jeavonses'—gossip which she must have known from her sister, even though they met rather rarely—Lady Warminster continued to refer to the association under enigmatic pseudonyms.

This mannered obscurity of handling the delicate problems of family life had nothing in common with the method of Chips Lovell, who, as I have indicated, spent a good deal of his time at the Studio telling the other script-writers about his relations. It would be easy to imagine a community in which this habit might have given offence, since many people feel disquisitions of that kind in some manner to derogate their own importance, few being interested in how others live. Lovell's material was presented with little or no editing, so it was for the listener to decide for himself whether the assumption in him of a working knowledge of the circles in which Lovell moved, or liked to think he moved, was complimentary of the reverse. Feingold, I think, considered the whole of these Lovell annals a fabrication from start to finish, a dream life legitimate in one exercising the calling of script-writer. He treated Lovell's stories of duchesses and grand parties like brilliantly improvised accounts of a brush with gangsters or Red Indians, narrated as if such florid adventures had not been in the least imaginary. Hegarty, on the other hand, on the rare occasions when he listened to anything anyone else said, would immediately cap all Lovell's anecdotes with stories of his own, sometimes sharp enough in their own way, but at the same time petrified into that strange, lifeless, formalised convention to illustrate human experience, particularly current among persons long associated with films. For my own part, I always enjoy hearing the details of other people's lives, whether imaginary or not, so that I found this side of Lovell agreeable.

When someone repeatedly tells you stories about their relations, pictures begin at last to form in the mind, tinged always in colours used by the narrator; so that after listening day after day to Lovell's recitals, I had become not only well versed in the rôle of each performer, but also involuntarily preoccupied with their individual behaviour. This concern for Lovell's relations had grown into something like a furtive interest in the comic strip of a daily paper, a habit not admitted to oneself. Lovell covered a good deal of ground. He was as ready to contemplate the doings of some distant cousins of his, whose only claim to fame seemed to be that they had emigrated to Vancouver and returned to live at Esher, as to recount the more splendid aspects of ancestral archives, for example, the epic of his mother's elopement with his father at a moment when her parents supposed her all but engaged to his more eligible cousin.

In these sagas, Lovell's "second Sleaford uncle" (to give him his nephew's initial label) played a surprisingly small part. That was altogether unexpected. Lovell liked talking about Dogdene, but not about his uncle. The fact was that Lord Sleaford lived a very secluded life there, undertaking in the neighbourhood a bare minimum of such duties as were expected of a landowner of his magnitude. He would give a small shooting party from time to time ("shepherd's pie for luncheon," Lovell said, "and not enough sprouts"), existing on the whole outside, or at best on the edge of any given world of recognisable social activity; especially that of a kind to be treated at any degree of sensationalism in print. In quite a different way, he sounded almost as much a recluse as Erridge.

Lovell himself was in a manner proud of this honourable, uncorrupted twilight in which Lord Sleaford had his being, infinitely removed from the gossip-column renown so dear to his own heart; but he also felt, perhaps reasonably enough, that the historical and architectural magnificence of Dogdene was all the time being wasted as a setting for great events.

"I know there is a lot to be said for a peer being quiet and well behaved," he used to say. "But really Uncle Geoffrey goes too far. When you think of the house parties they used to have at Dogdene, it is a bit depressing. You know, when George IV came to stay, they painted the place white and gold from top to bottom, including the Chinese Chippendale commodes. Even Aunt Molly, who never showed the slightest desire to cut a dash, quite often used to entertain royalty there. Then there was the occasional literary lion too. I believe Henry James was at Dogdene once. St. John Clarke was there just before the war. It wasn't the complete morgue it is now. The fact is, Uncle Geoffrey is a very dull man. Aunt Alice, though she does her best, isn't much better. If Uncle John hadn't died, I don't believe either of them would have married anybody— Uncle Geoffrey wouldn't have been able to afford a wife, anyway. As it is, they just patter about and read the newspapers and listen to the wireless—and that is the extent of it."

The general impression of Lord Sleaford that emerged from these fragments of information was certainly that of a person rather unusually lacking in any quality of liveliness of distinction. Dispiriting years as a younger son had destroyed in him any enterprise or geniality he might once have possessed. That was Lovell's theory. Like Alfred Tolland, he had consistently failed to make a career for himself, while at the same time lacking the philosophic detachment which gave Alfred Tolland a certain moral dignity: even a kind of saintliness. Inheritance of Dogdene had come too late to alter his routine, set, no doubt congenitally, in an unimaginative mould. Such was the portrait painted by Lovell, in which Lord Sleaford lived in my imagination with a certain rugged reality of his own; although I sometimes wondered whether, in this individual case, the uncompromising monochrome of Lovell's pigment might be tinged by the possibility that Lord Sleaford himself did not greatly care for his nephew: perhaps openly disapproved of him. That was a contingency to be borne in mind.

Lady Sleaford, as depicted by Lovell, possessed for me, on the other hand, none of her husband's clarity of outline. She was given no highlights, except the crumb of praise that she "did her best". Lovell had contrived to afford her no separate existence. She was simply the wife of Lord Sleaford. I pictured her as embodying all the unreality of a dowager on the stage: grey-haired: grotesquely dressed: speaking in a stiff, affected manner; possibly gazing through a lorgnette: a figure belonging to Edwardian drawing-room comedy. Armed with this vision of the Sleafords, I could not help wondering how Widmerpool had been asked to their house, according to Lovell, so rarely visited.

"Easy to explain," said Lovell. "Aunt Alice, the most conventional woman alive, is also one of those tremendously respectable people who long to know someone they regard as disreputable. To have Mildred Haycock as a friend has been the great adventure of Aunt Alice's life."

"And she includes Mrs. Haycock's husbands?"

"Not necessarily," said Lovell. "You've got something when you ask that. I very much doubt whether Haycock ever reached Dogdene. However, as the Widmerpool engagement took place over here—and Mildred, in any case, coming to England so rarely—I suppose an invitation to both of them was hard to refuse. You see, Mildred almost certainly invited herself. She probably took the opportunity of asking if her young man could come too."

This was a credible explanation.

"It is just like the Sleafords," said Lovell, "that Aunt Alice should disapprove of Molly Jeavons, who is really so frightfully well behaved, in spite of the ramshackle way in which she lives, and take to her bosom someone like Mildred, who has slept with every old-timer between Cannes and St. Tropez."

"What will the Sleafords think about Widmerpool?"

"He sounds just the sort of chap Uncle Geoffrey will like. Probably talk stocks and shares all day long, and go to bed every night at half-past ten sharp, after one glass of port. The port is quite good at Dogdene, I must admit. Only because no one has ever bothered to drink it. All the same, I am a bit surprised myself by their both getting an invitation. It is not so easy to penetrate Dogdene these days.

I know. I've tried."

I was, naturally, much occupied at this period with my own affairs, so that was all I heard about Widmerpool going to Dogdene before learning from Lovell—quite by chance one day at the Studio—that Mrs. Haycock's engagement had been broken off. Lovell hardly knew Widmerpool. He would have had no particular concern with the engagement had not Dogdene provided the background for this event. He had no details. I learnt more of the story as a result of Molly Jeavons announcing: "I shall have a few people in next week, Nicholas, a sort of party for yourself and Isobel. Something quite small."

When I had next been to the Jeavonses' house after the visit to Umfraville's night club, Jeavons himself had made no reference whatever to that excursion. Indeed, he hardly talked at all during the course of the evening, striding aimlessly about the room as if lost in thought. It was possible that his wound was giving him trouble. However, Molly spoke of the matter, pretending to be cross with me.

"You are a very dissipated young man," she said. "What do you mean by keeping poor Teddy up till all hours in the way you did? I never heard such a thing. Do you know he had to spend a whole week in bed after going out with you?"

I tried to make some apology, although at the same time feeling not greatly to blame for the way Jeavons behaved when he went out on his own. As a matter of fact, I had not been at all well myself the following day, and was inclined to blame Jeavons for having caused me to sit up so late.

"Just as well he found Mildred Blaides to look after him," said Molly. "I always thought they had known each other for ages, but it turned out they had only met once, a long time ago. You know she was a nurse at Dogdene during the war. Luckily she didn't turn up when Teddy was there, or she would have scalded him to death with hot-water bottles, or something of that sort. She was the worst nurse they ever had there—or in the whole of the V.A.D., for that matter."

Molly spoke with more than a touch of acrimony, but at the same time it was impossible to guess how much she knew, or suspected, of Jeavons's night out; impossible, if it came to that, to know with any certainty how that night had ended, even though the nostalgic mood of Jeavons's and Mrs. Haycock's impetuous nature might, in unison, give a strong hint.

"If Mildred is not careful," said Molly, "she will polish off Mr. Widmerpool before she has time to marry him. I hear he had to go home, he was feeling so ill."

I thought the sooner the subject of that night was abandoned, the better. While we had been talking, Jeavons had listened in silence, as if he had never before heard of any of the persons under discussion, including himself. I admired his detachment. I wondered, too, whether at that very moment his head was seething with forgotten melodies, for ever stirring him to indiscretion by provoking memories of an enchanted past.

"I can't have all the Tollands at this party," Molly had said. "So I had better have none of them. Bound to be jealousy otherwise. Just like Erridge to go to China when one of his sisters gets engaged."

Smith was again on duty with the Jeavonses on the day of the party. He looked haggard and more out of sorts than ever.

"You're late," he said, taking my hat. "It has all started upstairs. Quite a crowd of them arrived already. Hope her ladyship hasn't invited every blessed soul she knows."

The guests seemed, in fact, to have been chosen even more at random than usual. Certainly there had been no question either of asking people because they were already friends of Isobel or myself; still less, because Molly wanted either of us specifically to meet them. All that was most nondescript in the Jeavons entourage predominated, together with a few exceptional and reckless examples of individual oddity. I noticed that Alfred Tolland had not been included in the general prohibition against the Tolland family of my own generation. He was standing in the corner of the room, wedged behind a table, talking to—of all people—Mark Members, whom I had never before seen at the Jeavonses', and might be supposed, in principle, beyond Molly's normal perimeter, wide as that might stretch; or at least essentially alien to most of what it enclosed. To describe the two of them as standing looking at one another, rather than talking, would have been nearer the truth, as each apparently found equal difficulty in contributing anything to a mutual conversation. At the same time, the table cut them off from contact with other guests.

"I know you are interested in books, Nicholas," said Molly. "So I asked a rather nice young man I met the other day. He also writes or something. You will like him. A Mr. Members."

"I know him of old."

"Go and talk to him then. I don't think he is getting on very well with Alfred Tolland. It is a great compliment to Isobel that Alfred has come. As you know, he never goes out. At least that is what he says. I always tell him I believe he leads a double life of great wickedness. He tried to get out of coming tonight, but I told him he would never be asked to the house again if he did not turn up. Then he didn't dare refuse. Isobel, dear, there is someone I want you to meet."

Both Alfred Tolland and Mark Members showed relief at the arrival of a third party to break up their *tête-à-tête*. They had by then reached a conversational standstill. This was the first I had seen of Alfred Tolland since the announcement of my own engagement. I was aware that he could no longer be regarded as the embarrassed, conscience-stricken figure, vaguely familiar in the past. Now he fell automatically into place in the profusion of new relationships that follow an organic change of condition. He began at once to mutter incoherent congratulations. Members watched him with something like hatred in his beady eyes.

"Expect you've heard that Erridge has gone East," said Alfred Tolland. "Just heard it myself. Not—a—bad—idea. They are in a mess there. Perhaps the best thing. Might do him a lot of good. Get experience. Good thing to get experience. Ever been East?"

"Never."

"Got as far as Singapore once," he said.

It seemed incredible. However, there appeared to be no reason why he should invent such a thing. I said a word to Members, who stood there looking far from pleased.

"I shall have to be going now," said Alfred Tolland, snatching this offer of release. "I expect I shall see you at the dinner next . . ."

"I'm not sure yet. Don't know what our circumstances will be."

"Of course, of course. You can't say. I quite understand. Pity you weren't at the last one. Nice to feel that we . . ."

Exact expression of what it was nice for both of us to feel either evaded him, or was too precarious a sentiment to express in words. He merely nodded his head several times. Then he made for the door. Members sighed. He was in a bad humour.

"What on earth is this party?" he said in a low voice. "Did that man say something about your being engaged?"

"Yes. I am engaged."

"To whom?"

"Isobel Tolland—over there."

"Congratulations," said Members, without any exaggerated effusiveness, as if he disapproved of any such step in principle. "Many congratulations. I was stuck with that appalling bore for about twenty minutes. It was impossible to get away. Is he absolutely right in the head? What a strange house this is. I met Lady Molly Jeavons quite a long time ago at the Manaschs'. She asked me to come and see her. I called once or twice, but no one answered the bell, though I rang half a dozen times—and knocked too. Then she suddenly telephoned this invitation to me yesterday. She never mentioned your name. I did not think it would be quite like this."

"It is often different. You never know what it is going to be."

"Have you met her husband?" said Members, quite plaintively. "I talked to him for a while when I first arrived. He asked me if I ever played snooker. Then he introduced me to the man you found me with."

By then Members had several jobs of a literary kind which, since he was still a bachelor, must bring him in a respectable income. His American trip was said to have been a success. He no longer wrote verse with Freudian undertones, and he had abandoned anything so extreme as Quiggin's professional "communism", in the wake of which he had for a while half-heartedly trailed. Now he tended to be associated with German literature. Kleist; Grillparzer: Stifter: those were names to be caught on the echoes of his conversation. Latterly, he was believed to be more taken up with Kierkegaard, then a writer not widely read in this country. Members, no fool, was always a little ahead of the fashion. He was a lively talker when not oppressed, as at that moment, by a party he did not enjoy. His distinguished appearance and terse manner made him a popular spare man at intellectual dinners. "But one really does not want to eat amateur *paella* and drink Chelsea

Médoc for ever," he used to say: a world into which he felt himself somewhat rudely thrust immediately after losing his job as secretary to St. John Clarke. For a time now Members had been reappearing, so it was said, in the rather more elegant of the circles frequented by the famous novelist before his conversion to Marxism. In the light of this effort to maintain and expand his social life, Members found the Jeavons house a disappointment. He had expected something more grandiose. I tried to explain the household, but was glad when he brushed this aside, because I wanted to ask if he knew further details about Erridge and Mona. Members turned almost with relief to this subject.

"Of course I knew J.G. had got hold of Lord Warminster," he said impatiently. "Surely everyone has known that for a long time. We had dinner together before I went to America. J.G. told me about the magazine he hoped to persuade Warminster to start. I saw at once that nothing would come of it."

"Why not?"

"Warminster is too much of a crank."

"Do you know him?"

"No, but I know of him."

"How did the Mona situation arise?"

All at once Members was on his guard.

"But there is every prospect of Warminster becoming your brother-in-law, isn't there?"

"Most certainly there is."

Members laughed, not in his most friendly manner, and remained silent.

"Come on—out with it," I said.

We had by then known each other for a long time. It was not an occasion to stand on ceremony, as Members was well aware. He thought for a second or two, pondering whether it would be preferable to circulate a good piece of gossip, or to tease more effectively by withholding any information he might himself possess. In the end he decided that communication of the news would be more pleasurable.

"You know what Mona is," he said.

He smiled maliciously; for although, so far as I knew, there had never "been much" between them, he had known Mona years before her association with Quiggin; in fact I had first set eyes on Mona in the company of Members at Mr. Deacon's birthday party.

"She was altogether too much for Erridge, was she?" I asked. "When she struck."

"Erridge?"

"For Warminster, I mean—his family call him Erridge."

"Yes, Mona was too much for him. I don't think things got very far. Some sort of an assignation. J.G. found out about it. The next thing was the two of them had gone off together."

"How has J.G. taken it?"

"He was full of *gêne* at first. You know she had a stranglehold on him, I am sure. Now that he has cooled down, he is really rather flattered, as well as being furious."

"Were they married?"

"No."

"Is that certain?"

"Absolutely."

I should have liked to hear more, but at that moment Jeavons came up to us. He took an unfamiliar object from his coat pocket, and held it towards me.

"A present?"

"No," he said. "That reminds me we'll have to get you one, I suppose. Anyway, that's Molly's job. This is just for you to see. You might even want to buy one for yourself."

"What is it?"

"Guess."

"I don't like to say the word in company."

Jeavons extended his clasped fist towards Members, who shook his head angrily and turned away.

"For your car," urged Jeavons.

"I haven't got a car," said Members.

He was thoroughly cross.

"What do you really do with it?" I asked.

"Fix it on to the carburettor—then you use less petrol."

"What's the point?"

"Save money, of course. Are you a bloody millionaire, or what?"

Molly drew near our group as she crossed the room to refill one of the jugs of drink. She saw what Jeavons was doing and laid a hand on his arm.

"You'll never sell Nicholas one of those things," she said. "Nor Mr. Members, either, I'm sure. I don't myself think you will sell it to anyone, darling."

She moved on.

"It is called an atomiser," said Jeavons, slowly, as if he were about to lecture troops upon some mechanical device. "It saves thirty-three and a third consumption per mile. I don't expect it really saves you that for a moment, as a matter of fact. Why should it? Everybody would have one otherwise. It stands to reason. Still, you never know. It might do some good. Worth trying, I suppose."

He spoke without great conviction, gazing for a time at the object in his open palm. Then he returned it to his coat pocket, fumbling about for some time, and at last bringing out a tattered packet of Gold Flake. He nicked up one of the cigarettes with his thumb, and offered it to each of us in turn.

"Well," he said to me, "so you are going to get married."

Members watched him with absolute horror. Jeavons, I was sure, was wholly unaware of the poor impression he was making. Members could stand it no longer.

"I think I must go now," he said. "I have another party I

have to look in on. It was kind of Lady Molly and yourself to ask me."

"Not at all," said Jeavons. "Glad to see you. Come again."

He watched Members leave the room, as if he had never before seen anyone like him. His cigarette remained unlighted in his mouth.

"Odd bloke," he said. "I feel shocking this afternoon. Had too much lunch. Red in the face. Distended stomach. Self-inflicted wounds, of course."

We talked together for a minute or two. Then Jeavons wandered off among the guests. By then General and Mrs. Conyers had arrived. I went across the room to speak to them. They had come up from the country the day before. After making the conventional remarks about my engagement, Mrs. Conyers was removed by Molly to be introduced to some new acquaintance of hers. I was left with the General. He seemed in excellent form, although at the same time giving the impression that he was restless about something: had a problem on his mind. All at once he took me by the arm. "I want a word with you, Nicholas," he said, in his deep, though always unexpectedly mild, voice. "Can't we get out of this damned, milling crowd of people for a minute or two?"

The Jeavonses' guests habitually flowed into every room in the house, so that to retire to talk, for example in Molly's bedroom, or Jeavons's dressing-room, would be considered not at all unusual. We moved, in fact, a short way up the stairs into a kind of boudoir of Molly's, constricted in space and likely to attract only people who wanted to enjoy a heart-to-heart talk together: a place chiefly given over to cats, two or three of which sat in an ill-humoured group at angles to one another, stirring with disapproval at this invasion of their privacy. I had no idea what the General could wish to say, even speculating for an instant as to whether he was about to offer some piece of advice—too confidential and esoteric to risk being overheard—regarding the conduct of married life. The period of engagement is one when you are at the mercy of all who wish to proffer counsel, and experience already prepared me for the worst. The truth turned out to be more surprising.

As soon as we were alone together, the General sat down on a chair in front of the writing-table, straightening out his leg painfully. It still seemed to be giving trouble. Alone with him, I became aware of that terrible separateness which difference of age imposes between individuals. Perhaps feeling something of this burden himself, he began at first to speak of his own advancing years.

"I'm beginning to find all this standing about at Buck House a bit of a strain," he said. "Not so young as I was. Dropped my eyeglass not so long ago in one of the ante-rooms at St. James's and had to get a fellow who was standing beside me to pick it up for me. Secretary from the Soviet Embassy. Perfectly civil. Just couldn't get down that far myself. Afraid I'd drop my axe too, if I tried. Still, although I'm getting on in life, I've had a good run for my money. Seen some odd things at one time or another."

He moved his leg again, and groaned a bit. I always had the impression that he liked talking about his appearances at Court.

"I'm a great believer in people knowing the truth," he said. "Always have been."

Without seeing at all clearly where this maxim would lead us, I agreed that truth was best.

"Something happened the other day," said the General, "that struck me as interesting. Damned interesting. Got on my mind a bit, especially as I had beeen reading about that kind of thing. Odd coincidence, I mean. The fact is, you are the only fellow I can tell."

By that time I began to feel even a little uneasy, having

no idea at all what might be coming next.

"When you came to tea with us not so long ago, I told you I had been reading about this business of psycho-analysis. Don't tie myself down to Freud. Jung has got some interesting stuff too. No point in an amateur like myself being dogmatic about something he knows little or nothing about. Just make a fool of yourself. Don't you agree?"

"Absolutely."

"Well, a rather interesting illustration of some of the points I'd been reading about happened to come my way the other day. Care to hear about it?"

"I should like to very much indeed."

"In connexion with this fellow you say you were at school with—this fellow Widmerpool—who wanted to marry my sister-in-law, Mildred."

"I hear the engagement is off."

"You knew that already?"

"I was told so the other day."

"Common knowledge, is it?"

"Yes."

"Know why it's off?"

"No. But I wasn't altogether surprised."

"Nor was I, but it is an odd story. Not to be repeated, of course. Happened during their stay at Dogdene. Perhaps you've heard about that too?"

"I knew they were going to Dogdene."

"Ever stopped there yourself?"

"No. I've never met either of the Sleafords."

"I was once able to do Geoffrey Sleaford a good turn in South Africa," said the General. "He was A.D.C. to the Divisional Commander, and a more bone-headed fellow I never came across. Sleaford—or Fines, as he was then—had landed in a mess over some mislaid papers. I got him out of it. He is a stupid fellow, but always grateful. Made a point of trying out our poodle dogs at his shoots. Then Bertha knew Alice Sleaford as a girl. Went to the same dancing class. Bertha never cared much for her. Still, they get on all right now. Long and the short of it is that we stop at Dogdene from time to time. Uncomfortable place nowadays. Those parterres are very fine, of course. Alice Sleaford takes an interest in the garden. Wonderful fruit in the hot-houses. Then there is the Veronese. Geoffrey Sleaford has been advised to have it cleaned, but won't hear of it. Young fellow called Smethyck told him. Smethyck saw our Van Troost and said it was certainly genuine. Nice things at Dogdene, some of them, but I could name half a dozen houses in England I'd rather stop at."

None of this seemed to be getting us much further so far as Widmerpool was concerned. I waited for development. General Conyers did not intend to be hurried. I suspected that he might regard this narrative he was unfolding in so leisurely a manner as the last good story of his life; one that he did not propose to squander in the telling. That was reasonable enough.

"I was not best pleased," he said, "when Bertha told me we had been asked to Dogdene at the same time as Mildred and her young man. I know the Sleafords don't have many people to stop. All the same it would have been quite easy to have invited some of their veterans. Even had us there by ourselves. Just like Alice Sleaford to arrange something like that. Hasn't much tact. All the same, I thought it would be a chance to get to know something about Widmerpool. After all, he was going to be my brother-in-law. Got to put up with your relations. Far better know the form from the beginning."

"I've been seeing Widmerpool on and off for ages," I said, hoping to encourage the General's flow of comment. "I really know him quite well."

"You do?"

"Yes.'

"Now, look here," he said. "Have you ever noticed at all how Widmerpool gets on with women?"

"He never seemed to find them at all easy to deal with. I was surprised that he should be prepared to take on someone like Mrs. Haycock."

We had plunged into an intimacy of discussion that I had never supposed possible with an older man of the General's sort.

"You were?"

"Yes."

"So was I," he said. "So was I. Very surprised. And I did not take long to see that they were getting on each other's nerves when they arrived at Dogdene. She was being very crisp with him. Very crisp. Nothing much in that, of course. Engaged couples bound to have their differences. Now I know Mildred pretty well by this time, and, although I did not much take to Widmerpool when I first met him, I thought she might do worse at her age. What?"

"So I should imagine."

"Not every man would want to take her on. Couple of stepchildren into the bargain."

"No."

"All the same Widmerpool seemed to me rather a trying fellow. Half the time he was being obsequious, behaving as if he was applying for the job as footman, the other half, he was telling Geoffrey Sleaford and myself how to run our own affairs. It was then I began to mark down his psychological type. I had brought the book with me."

"How did he get on with Lord Sleaford?"

"Pretty well," said the General. "Pretty well. Better than you might think. You know, Widmerpool talks sense about business matters. No doubt of it. Made some suggestions about developing the home farm at Dogdene which were quite shrewd. It was with Mildred there was some awkwardness. Mildred is not a woman to hang about with. If he wanted to marry her, he ought to have got down to matters and have done it. No good delaying in things of that sort."

"He has been having jaundice."

"I knew he'd been ill. He made several references to the fact. Seemed rather too fond of talking about his health. Another sign of his type. Anyway, his illness was beside the point. The fact was, Mildred did not think he was paying her enough attention. That was plain as a pikestaff. Mildred is a woman who expects a good deal of fuss to be made over her. I could see he was in for trouble."

"What form did it take?"

"First of all, as I told you, she was a bit short with him. Then she fairly told him off to his face. That was on Saturday afternoon. Thought there was going to be a real row between them. Alice Sleaford never noticed a thing. In the evening they seemed to have made it up. In fact, after dinner, they were more like an engaged couple than I'd ever seen 'em. Now, look here, where would you put his type? Psychologically, I mean."

"Rather hard to say in a word—I know him so well——"

"It seems to me," said the General, "that he is a typical intuitive extrovert—classical case, almost. Cold-blooded. Keen on a thing for a moment, but never satisfied. Wants to get on to something else. Don't really know about these things, but Widmerpool seems to fit into the classification. That's the category in which I'd place him, just as if a recruit turns up with a good knowledge of carpentry and you draft him into the Sappers. You are going to say you are a hard-bitten Freudian, and won't hear of Jung and his ideas. Very well, I'll open another field of fire."

"But——"

"You haven't heard the rest of the story yet. I came down to breakfast early on Sunday morning. I thought I'd have a

228

stroll in the garden, and have another look at those hot-houses. What do you think I found? Widmerpool in the hall, making preparations to leave the house. Some story about a telephone call, and being summoned back to London. Fellow looked like death. Shaking like a jelly and the colour of wax. Told me he'd slept very badly. Hardly closed his eyes. I'm quite prepared to believe that. Alice Sleaford won't use the best bedrooms for some reason. Never know where you are going to be put."

"And did he go back to London?"

"Drove off, there and then, under my eyes. Whole house had been turned upside down to get him away at that hour on Sunday morning. Left a message for the host and hostess to say how sorry he was, neither of them having come down yet. Never saw a man more disgruntled than the Sleafords' chauffeur."

"But what had happened? Had there really been a telephone call? I don't understand."

"There had been some telephoning that morning, but the butler said it had been Widmerpool putting the call through. Only heard the true story that afternoon from Mildred when we were walking together in the Dutch garden. She didn't make any bones about it. Widmerpool had been in her room the night before. Things hadn't gone at all well. Made up her mind he wasn't going to be any use as a husband. Mildred can be pretty outspoken when she is cross."

The General said these things in a manner entirely free from any of those implied comments which might be thought inseparable from such a chronicle of events. That is to say he was neither shocked, facetious, nor caustic. It was evident that the situation interested, rather than surprised him. He was complete master of himself in allowing no trace of ribaldry or ill nature to colour his narrative. For my own part, I felt a twinge of compassion for Widmerpool in his disaster, even though I was unable to rise to the General's heights of scientific detachment. I had known Widmerpool too long.

"Mildred told me in so many words. Doesn't care what she says, Mildred. That's what young people are like nowadays. Of course, I don't expect Mildred appears young to you, but I always think of her as a young woman."

I did not know what comment to make. However, General Conyers did not require comment. He wished to elaborate his own conception of what had happened.

"Widmerpool's trouble is not as uncommon as you might think," he said. "I've known several cases. Last fellows in the world you'd suppose. I don't expect the name Peploe-Gordon means anything to you?"

"No."

"Dead now. Had a heart attack in the Lebanon. I remember it happened in the same week Queen Draga was murdered in Belgrade. At Sandhurst with me. Splendid rider. First-class shot. Led an expedition into Tibet. Married one of the prettiest girls I've ever seen. Used to see her out with the Quorn. He had the same trouble. Marriage annulled. Wife married again and had a string of children. This is the point I want to make. I saw Peploe-Gordon about eighteen months later at the yearling sales at Newmarket with another damned pretty girl on his arm. Do you know, he looked as pleased as Punch. Didn't give a damn. Still, you don't know what neuroses weren't at work under the surface. That is what you have got to remember. Looking back in the light of what I have been reading, I can see the fellow had a touch of exaggerated narcissism. Is that Widmerpool's trouble?"

"It wouldn't surprise me. As I said before, I've only dipped into these things."

"I don't set up as an expert myself. Last thing in the world I'd pretend to do. But look here, something I want to ask—do you know anything of Widmerpool's mother?"

"I've met her."

"What is she like?"

I felt as usual some difficulty in answering directly the General's inquiry, put in his most pragmatical manner.

"Rather a trying woman, I thought."

"Domineering?"

"In her way."

"Father?"

"Dead."

"What did he do?"

"Manufactured artificial manure, I believe."

"Did he . . ." said the General. "Did he . . ."

There was a pause while he thought over this information. It was undeniable that he had been setting the pace. I felt that I must look to my psycho-analytical laurels, if I was not to be left far behind.

"Do you think it was fear of castration?" I asked.

The General shook his head slowly.

"Possibly, possibly," he said. "Got to be cautious about that. You see this is how I should approach the business, with the greatest humility—with the *greatest* humility. Widmerpool strikes me as giving himself away all the time by his—well, to quote the text-book—purely objective orientation. If you are familiar with tactics, you know you can be up against just that sort of fellow in a battle. Always trying to get a move on, and bring off something definite. Quite right too, in a battle. But in ordinary life a fellow like that may be doing himself no good so far as his own subjective emotions are concerned. No good at all. Quite the reverse. Always leads to trouble. No use denying subjective emotions. Just as well to face the fact. All of us got a lot of egoism and infantilism to work off. I'd be the last to deny it. I can see now that was some of Peploe-Gordon's trouble, when I look back."

"I'm sure Widmerpool thought a lot about this particular matter. Indeed, I know he did. He spoke to me about it quite soon after he became engaged to Mrs. Haycock."

"Probably thought about it a great deal too much. Doesn't do to think about anything like that too much. Need a bit of relaxation from time to time. Everlastingly talks about his work too. Hasn't he any hobbies?"

"He used to knock golf balls into a net at Barnes. But he told me he had given that up."

"Pity, pity. Not surprised, though," said the General. "Nothing disturbs feeling so much as thinking. I'm only repeating what the book says, but I didn't spend thirty odd years in the army without discovering that for myself. Got to have a plan, of course, but no use knotting yourself up in it too tight. Must have an instinct abbut the man on the other side—and the people on your own side too. What was it Foch said? War not an exact science, but a terrible and passionate drama? Something like that. Fact is, marriage is rather like that too."

"But surely that was what Widmerpool was trying to make it? To some extent he seems to have succeeded. What happened sounded terrible and dramatic enough in its own way."

"I'll have to think about that," said the General. "I see what you mean. I'll have to think about that."

All the same, although I had raised this objection, I agreed with what he said. Marriage was a subject upon which it was hard to obtain accurate information. Its secrets, naturally, are those most jealously guarded; never more deeply concealed than when apparently most profusely exhibited in public. However true that might be, one could still be sure that even those marriages which seem outwardly dull enough are, at one time or another, full of the characteristics of which he spoke. Was it possible to guess, for example, what lay behind the curtain of his own experience? As I had never before conceived of exchanging such a conversation with General Conyers, I thought this an opportunity to inquire about a matter that had always played some part in my imagination since mentioned years earlier by Uncle Giles. The moment particularly recommended itself, because the General rarely spoke either of the practice or theory of war. The transient reference he had just made to Foch now caused the question I wanted to ask to sound less inept.

"Talking of the army," I said. "What did it feel like when you were in the charge?"

"In where?"

"The charge—after French's cavalry brigades crossed the Modder River."

The General looked perplexed for a moment. Then his expression altered. He grasped the substance of my inquiry.

"Ah, yes," he said. "When the whole cavalry division charged. Unusual operation. Doubted the wisdom of it at the time. However, it came off all right. Extraordinary that you should have known about it. That was the occasion you mean? Of course, of course. What was it like? Just have to think for a moment. Long time ago, you know. Have to collect my thoughts. Well, I think I can tell you exactly. The fact was there had been some difficulty in mounting me, as I wasn't officially attached to the formation. Can't remember why not at this length of time. Some technicality. Ride rather heavy, you know. As far as I can remember, I had the greatest difficulty in getting my pony out of a trot. I'm sure that was what happened. Later on in the day, I shot a Boer in the shin. But why do you ask?"

"I don't know. I've always wanted to ask, for some reason. Infantilism, perhaps. A primordial image."

The General agreed, cordially.

"You are an introvert, of course," he said.

"I think undoubtedly."

233

"Introverted intuitive type, do you think? I shouldn't wonder."

"Possibly."

"Anyway," said the General, "keep an eye on not over-compensating. I've been glad to tell that story about Widmerpool to someone who can appreciate the circumstances. Haven't made up my own mind about it yet. I've got a slow reactive rapidity. No doubt about that. Just as well to recognise your limitations. Can't help wondering about the inhibiting action of the incest barrier though—among other things."

He moved his leg once more, at the same time shifting the weight of his body, as he pondered this riddle. The angle of his knee and ankle emphasised the beauty of his patent leather boots.

"Well, I mustn't keep you up here away from the others any longer," he said. "Lots of people you ought to be meeting. You are going to be a very lucky young man, I am sure. What do you want for a wedding present?"

The change in his voice announced that our fantasy life together was over. We had returned to the world of everyday things. Perhaps it would be truer to say that our real life together was over, and we returned to the world of fantasy. Who can say? We went down the stairs once more, the General leading. Chips Lovell was talking to Miss Weedon, perhaps tiring of her company, because he slipped away at once when I came up to them, making for the drink-tray. Miss Weedon gave her glacial smile and congratulated me. We began to talk. Before we had progressed very far, Molly Jeavons, whose absence from the room I had not previously noticed, came hurriedly towards us.

"Oh, Tuffy, dear," she said. "Do go down and see what is happening in the basement. A policeman has just arrived to interview Smith about a postal-order. I don't think he can have come to arrest him, but it would be saintly of you if you could clear it all up."

Miss Weedon did not look very anxious to investigate this intrusion, but she went off obediently.

"Smith really is a dreadful nuisance," said Molly. "I don't mind him drinking more than he should, because he carries it pretty well, but I don't like some of the people who come to see him. I hope he hasn't got into trouble with one of them."

Jeavons joined us.

"What's the matter now?" he asked.

"A policeman has come to see Smith."

"Is Smith off to the Scrubs?"

"Don't be silly," she said; and to me: "What on earth were you talking to General Conyers about? I thought you were going to spend the rest of the evening together in my little room. I suppose you have heard your friend Mr. Widmerpool's engagement is off. Just as well, I should think. Mildred really goes too far. I've asked him tonight. I thought it might cheer him up."

"You have?"

"You speak as if you didn't want to meet him. Have you both had a row? Here he is, in any case."

After so recently hearing an account of his departure from Dogdene, I almost expected Widmerpool to display, morally, if not physically, the dishevelled state described by the General. On the contrary, as he pushed his way through the people in the room, I thought I had never seen him look more pleased with himself. His spectacles glistened. Wearing a short black coat and striped trousers, his manner suggested that he was unaware that such a thing as failure could exist: certainly not for himself. He came up to me at once.

"The door was open and I walked in," he said. "I think that is what Lady Molly likes. Various people were talking to a policeman in the hall. I hope nothing has gone wrong."

"Selling tickets for the police sports, I expect."

"I expect so," he said. "Curious how our situations have been reversed. You are getting married, while Mildred and I decided in the end it would be better not. We talked things over quietly, and came to the same conclusion. I think it was all for the best. She has returned to France. She prefers to live there. That was one of the bones of contention. Then, of course, there was also the disparity in age. Between you and me, I was not anxious to take on those two sons of hers. They sounded an unsatisfactory couple."

Miss Weedon now returned from her scrutiny of Smith and the policeman. With her accustomed efficiency, she appeared to have mastered the essential points of this entanglement. She spoke severely, as if she were once more a governess reporting unsatisfactory behaviour on the part of her charges.

"Smith had his name given as a reference," she said. "Some man he knows has been arrested. A small embezzlement. Smith is very upset about it. In tears, as a matter of fact."

"Oh, bless the man," said Molly. "Why did I ever say I would take him on again, when Erridge left England? I swore he should never again enter the house after he broke the Dresden coffee-pot. Do go and see, Teddy."

"The bloke must have been hard up for a reference, if he had to give Smith's name," said Jeavons, thoughtfully.

He moved off without undue haste, accompanied by Miss Weedon, whose demeanour was grave. Jeavons's face implied no hope of setting right any moral mishap of Smith's.

"My mother agrees that my decision is for the best," said Widmerpool.

"She does?"

"She liked Mildred. Thoroughly approved of her from the family point of view, for example," said Widmerpool.

"At the same time there are sides of Mildred she felt doubtful about. My mother never attempted to hide that from me. You know, Nicholas, it is wise to take good advice about such a thing as marriage. I hope you have done so yourself. I have thought about the subject a good deal, and you are always welcome to my views."

Russian Novels

The First Circle Alexander Solzhenitsyn   £3.95

The unforgettable novel of Stalin's post-war Terror.

'An unqualified masterpiece – this immense epic of the dark side of Soviet life.' *Observer*

'At once classic and contemporary . . . future generations will read it with wonder and awe.' *New York Times*

The White Guard Mikhail Bulgakov   £2.95

'A powerful reverie . . . the city is so vivid to the eye that it is the real hero of the book.' V. S. Pritchett, *New Statesman*

'Set in Kiev in 1918 . . . the tumultuous atmosphere of the Ukrainian capital in revolution and civil war is brilliantly evoked.' *Daily Telegraph*

FLAMINGO

FLAMINGO

Flamingo is a new, quality imprint publishing both fiction and non-fiction. Below are some recent titles.

Fiction

☐ A Chain of Voices *André Brink* £2.95
☐ An Instant in the Wind *André Brink* £2.50
☐ New Worlds: an Anthology *Michael Moorcock* (ed.) £3.50
☐ A Question of Upbringing *Anthony Powell* £2.50
☐ The Acceptance World *Anthony Powell* £2.50
☐ A Buyer's Market *Anthony Powell* £2.95
☐ The White Guard *Mikhail Bulgakov* £2.95

Non-fiction

☐ Old Glory *Jonathan Raban* £2.95
☐ The Turning Point *Fritjof Capra* £3.50
☐ Keywords (new edition) *Raymond Williams* £2.95
☐ Arabia Through the Looking Glass *Jonathan Raban* £2.95
☐ The Tao of Physics (new edition) *Fritjof Capra* £2.95
☐ The First Three Minutes (new edition) *Steven Weinberg* £2.50
☐ The Letters of Vincent van Gogh *Mark Roskill* (ed.) £3.50

You can buy Flamingo paperbacks at your local bookshop or newsagent. Or you can order them from Fontana Paperbacks, Cash Sales Department, Box 29, Douglas, Isle of Man. Please send a cheque, postal or money order (not currency) worth the purchase price plus 10p per book (or plus 12p per book if outside the UK).

NAME (Block letters) _____

ADDRESS _____

_____

_____